About the Author

Barry R Boughen was born in the early 1950s into a magical and wonderful world where freedom was a great resource. There was freedom to wander and roam, freedom to explore, freedom to learn in a simple world and freedom to think and come to personal conclusions. Barry could never look at anything without analysing and questioning it. What was it and how and why was it there? How did it come about and how did it work?

Sixty years of thought and analysing those thoughts have led him to writing this and other books. Please read and enjoy.

God, Religion and the Bible
One Man's Unbelief

Barry R Boughen

God, Religion and the Bible
One Man's Unbelief

Olympia Publishers
London

www.olympiapublishers.com
OLYMPIA PAPERBACK EDITION

A CIP catalogue record for this title is
available from the British Library.

ISBN: 978-1-84897-932-1

First Published in 2018

Olympia Publishers
60 Cannon Street
London
EC4N 6NP
Printed in Great Britain

Dedication

To my grandson Oscar
(A lad who thinks)

Acknowledgments

Rightly or wrongly I have spent much time recently debating religion and associated subjects in various Facebook groups. I have talked and debated with a vast array of people, some who agreed with me and some who were totally and utterly against my views. Some have debated calmly while some have become quite angry. It was never my intention to induce or promote anger and when this has happened I have just backed out of the argument. I love debating but I can never like or condone any amount of anger just because one side disagrees with the other. Personal views often turn to Ad Hominem arguments, which do nothing whatsoever to further the debate. All they do is prove the lack of knowledge, thought or compassion in the person using them.

By doing this debating I have learned much from many lovely people including atheists, theists, agnostics, scientists and even the angry folk and would like to thank them all sincerely for their contributions to my knowledge.

As humans, we are the only animals on the earth with the capability and need to understand and question everything. Other animals are not as stupid as man tries to make out, but I believe we are the only ones who can or need to think about where we came from and where we are going. I think it would be correct to say that we are the only animals who actually question, in any way at all, who we are, why we exist and what will happen tomorrow. Dolphins and chimps and a few others have quite advanced brains but we have been given the ability to analyse everything and learn from it. I certainly need, and have always needed, to question everything and so should we all. Aren't we privileged?

Preface

I dedicated my last book, *Wonderment* to my granddaughter Lucy, but this book I dedicate to my grandson Oscar and also anyone and everyone else who has the mind to think for themselves as he does. Oscar is only just approaching his teenage years but, like his granddad, he does think deeply about everything and does not accept anything until his mind is satisfied. The book is dedicated to all those who, like Oscar, reason through what is before them and then come to sensible conclusions using common sense, logic, reasoning and rationality along the way. These conclusions will then be their own conclusions and will be based totally upon thought, rather than being formed upon what is drilled into their head by others, often at an early and impressionable age.

Oscar told me that whilst in his junior school he was taught Christianity as fact, because the school he attended was a church school. Although he was only eight or nine years old he sensed that what was being drilled into him did not somehow make sense. To most children of that age all this, because it was being taught by adults who were also teachers, would just sink in with little thought. Oscar, however, has a mind that will not allow this. His mind is like mine and it questions everything and those questions demand answers. To most, just accepting what was told them by these adults in authority would have been fine. They would not think too much about it either way and, in their minds, none of it would really matter either way anyway.

To an enquiring mind though, this is nowhere near enough. Many youngsters would accept that the moon was made from cheese if that is what they are told, but if anyone was to tell Oscar that he would have to, somehow, prove the fact either way. Here I say, 'either way' because Oscar has an open mind and would not simply accept or refute the suggestion until proof had been found.

Despite these adults who held authority over him telling Oscar all about God, religion and the Bible, he could not just accept it. There were doubts in his mind so, in his spare time, he explored the Interweb and did his own research and then came to his own conclusions.

I will add here that these conclusions were arrived at totally without intervention from me. He knew my views but never asked me about them as he wanted to find out fully for himself. The first I knew was when he talked about his thoughts and conclusions to his mother, my daughter. It was very pleasing that Oscar totally agreed with me but it was far more pleasing that he came to all this totally with only his own thoughts and rationality to lean on. Oscar is my grandson, and my mate, and he is also my first point of call when I need advice on computers. I love him dearly but not only because of this. I really love his ability to look, listen, think, and draw his own conclusions and I praise him highly for it. It seems not everyone has this ability.

I know listening comes hard to many people today but I do truly dedicate this book to anyone who does listen, does learn and who does own up to and learn from their mistakes. Oscar's thinking will, hopefully, hold him in good stead for his future in what is rapidly becoming an all-too-uncertain world. Oscar is not yet a teenager but he does think for himself and does dissect the world he lives in. As I say, he is also always there for me when I have computer problems and he is my grandson and my mate and I love him dearly. Thanks mate, for letting me include you in this book.

Wonderment tackled the thorny issue of religion and religious dogma but it also tackled life in general, the wonderful world around us and the quirks of human nature such as the love and lust of war and harming each other. In this book, I am paying attention mostly to the arguments for and against religion which, in its time, held a great power and seemed correct to most. In these times of enlightened science and discoveries and great thinking minds, though, I feel it is time to get real. I feel it is time to move with science and the times and relegate religion to history and think about reality. As I said more than a couple of times in *Wonderment,* in the end reality is all we have and we can only harm our lives and the lives of others around us in trying to search for anything else. If we do not have reality, we have nothing.

No educated person could ever say we should just forget about religion as it holds a huge part in our world's history. Our world has been moulded by it for many centuries. We must teach it forevermore as it shows us what people thought; it shows a way of life that people thought they should adopt and follow; it shows how various religions and even religious hatred have moulded our world and it gives us what I think are totally untrue but at the same time totally beautiful, naive stories which hold a great place in our literature.

I have thought long and hard about religion and science and have looked at both in detail, and with a totally open mind, and at a whole host of evidence. It seems there is plenty to be found on the side of the science/Darwinian theory but I have yet to find a mere morsel of empirical evidence to substantiate the common vision of God, Jesus, creationism and religion. That is, of course, apart from the fact that 'it is written' in a little black book. I'm sorry but as with the story of Miss Elizabeth Bennett and Mr. Darcy, it is charming but in no way can it be held as a true historical account but as I always say and will say again, 'Please do prove me wrong.'

No one can totally disprove the God theory though and it remains, and always will remain, a mystery. We have Darwin's theory of evolution which has been scientifically proven but no one has yet proven the existence or non-existence of any god. The empirical evidence for any god is non-existent but then again, if I said I had a three-centimetre-tall fairy living in my jacket pocket no one could disprove that either. Very few would actually believe me if I claimed it to be true but no one could prove I was lying.

In my search for creationism evidence I have seen things such as a man pricking a balloon which, to him, represented the Big Bang. The needle entered the balloon, it went pop and he then said it proved the existence of God because when the balloon exploded, stars and planets did not burst forth. I somehow don't think his theory holds too much significance. In fact, this man's argument was so fundamentally wrong and ludicrous that, if he believed his argument as fact, in no way would he ever learn anything from anyone. In another article

I've read, it said that, if scientists understand evolution, then they must be able to turn a dog into a rat and vice versa. This is an argument which is so ludicrous that it is not even worthy of an argument against. Sometimes I will look at the Interweb and see articles which say, 'This is the ultimate proof that God exists'.

Even I am excited at the prospect. Yes, I would love to see proof as it would give me another whole spectrum to think about but no, these articles end up holding no surety of God's existence at all. They only give what the author has used to prove it in his or her own mind, a mind which is obviously easily corrupted and manipulated even by its owner. The end conclusion has to be that there is no evidence for God or religion or anything else that comes with it. Reality is all we have. It is all we have and luckily it is all we need.

A true religious believer told me that God is so great that he doesn't need to prove himself. The statement may be untrue but with him being so fundamentally religious in his mind, he had come up with something that could not be argued with. He didn't have to prove anything because his god didn't need to show proof. In his mind he could not lose either way.

I was walking through a local city today and came across three men who were preaching God on the streets. Two were handing out leaflets and one was doing the talking. He said, "Look around you at all the churches! If God didn't exist then he wouldn't have made the churches!" Good evidence or not? I'll leave it to you to decide.

Please read this book with an open mind and think about what I have to say. In places, I shall be giving my personal opinions but mostly what I am putting across is, hopefully, hard and irrefutable fact. I write the book to try and enlighten people and teach them to live more free and fulfilled lives, with morality being their only restraint but I do understand that some will be offended by its content. It certainly is not my intention to upset anyone even in any slight way but if my own personal views do offend, then that has to be a problem for the person who feels the offence. I shall set out my stall and put forward my views but in no way have I set out to offend. These are simply my views.

Some of my views are strong but all views are backed up with fact, thought and logic. We all have views and thoughts and are all perfectly entitled to them. My views are mine and your views are yours. We can all think but it is also so easy to be deluded. If, at the end of the book, you still feel I am the one who is deluded then that's fine with me. I love to argue and debate but in no way will I ever take offence whilst doing so. My books are written in a light and humorous way and this is because that is how I see the world and my life in it. Life is too short and I have no time to spend it being miserable. I believe this is my only life and I want to lead it in a light-hearted and yet kind, caring and fulfilled way. Life can be tough sometimes, without making it worse for yourself as well along the way. Life can knock you about sometimes but it is no good joining in and giving yourself a good kicking while you are down.

Providing I live my life according to natural morality I can live it, as can you, in a totally free way. I am the only person who ever tells me what to wear, what to eat, what to drink, what to do on Sundays and what parts of my body must be chopped off. My life is totally above all religious restraints and superstitions, and I am me. I live in a fantastic world and it is mine to enjoy to the full.

A little thought. Let's say I was to compile a book of simple sums for children in first schools and, in the book, I gave examples of sums and their answers, e.g. 3+3=7, 3x2=9 and 4-3=8. The consequences of this would be:

1. No publishing company would print the book for me because it was wrong.

2. No teachers would use the book because it was wrong.

3. Hopefully even some of the children in those schools would be bright enough to realise the sums were wrong.

4. The book would be teaching the wrong facts entirely, with no proof whatsoever that the answers I gave could possibly be correct in any way. 'Ah,' I would reply. 'But my book is not meant to be taken literally. It is supposed to be more allegorical than real.' 'Well,' everyone would immediately say, 'If it is not to be meant to be taken literally then what is the point of the book in the first place? You can't go around teaching young, impressionable and vulnerable children what is obviously wrong, can you? How can you even think about filling these naive and precious little minds with such nonsense and falseness?'

Does this story ring any bells at all?

Let me start the book and please, read it with an open mind. Let's analyse everything and see what conclusions we can come to. I know the conclusions here are mine and as I say, my conclusions may be different from yours but that doesn't matter. I have learned much in writing the book and I hope you can learn a little something from it too. Please enjoy.

The simplest of minds think they have all the answers but even the most brilliant scientist will always admit they have much to learn.

This was a thought of mine after watching the film *The Theory of Everything*, an amazing film about a truly amazing man, Stephen Hawking.

We all live on the same planet but it sometimes seems that we live in totally different worlds.

Heaven and Hell

Heaven

Heaven may not be in the back seat of my Cadillac but why not? Isn't it as good a place as any?

In *Wonderment*, I went into the stories of Creation, Adam and Eve and Noah's Ark in great detail and do not wish to bore you by going over them all again. What I want to do in this book is pick items at random and discuss them. I will touch again on the above stories as I do have a few things to add to them but for now, let me concentrate on two of the things which are central to religious beliefs: heaven and hell.

As a child of Christian parents and grandparents I was always told of heaven and hell but I never really thought too much or too deeply about them. I remember my old Nan saying to me once that if I swore I would go to hell. That statement confused me. It seemed I should have been totally frightened out of my skin at the prospect and consequences but I couldn't see the need to worry about her statement at all. That is, until I realised she had said hell and not Hull. I had heard that Hull was not too bad.

My parents never were great thinkers but it seemed my grandparents had little thought at all. My grandfather died when I was quite young but I know my Nan lived by superstitions and to a great extent, her life was ruled by them. Her funniest one was to hide all her silver when a thunderstorm threatened because she truly believed lightening was attracted to it. She would also open windows at the front and back of her bungalow so that a thunderbolt had a way out should it enter.

I am not an old, old man but in my sixty years or so, science and thinking have changed the world to a huge extent. How many people would follow my nan's examples today? People are getting better at thinking but so many still think little of life around them and so many, like my forebears, still accept the god and religion thing without any analysis. My parents were baptised and they had me baptised but they never really thought just what it meant and what kind of life they should lead after it. It was and still is 'what you do'. I do feel their thoughts were held back to a great extent by having to devote their time, thoughts and energies to greater worries such as putting food on the table and coins in the gas meter. Even today I know people do have stressful lives doing much the same as my parents did, but I do urge them to try and think fully about the world around them as they go about their daily lives. How many people could tell you exactly what is happening in each television soap opera or which so-called soppy celebrity is divorcing which, but they could not possibly tell you which species of common garden bird is sitting in a tree or which type of common tree it is sitting in. No wonder religion is just accepted as fact. We must all stop just accepting things and must start thinking about and questioning everything around us. It is what is around us in the real world that matters, not any superstitions or invented television nonsense.

A few weeks ago, I clumsily dropped a cup onto the tiled floor of my kitchen and it broke. The break and the scattered pieces were fact but that to me was not enough. Why did the cup break? It would be easy enough to answer this question with, 'Because it hit the floor', but why did hitting the floor break the cup? What were the forces involved? I pondered the situation and then worked it out. Obviously, the cup fell from my hand and was propelled towards the floor by the force of gravity and as it travelled, this was the only force acting upon it and it was fine, but when the first part of the cup reached the floor, that part came to a very sudden halt. That piece of cup was still fine and survived the impact but then, because that piece had stopped and the rest of the cup was still travelling towards the floor, the item had to disintegrate and go shooting off in all directions.

But did it matter just how and why the cup broke? Should I have been satisfied with the fact that it broke because it hit the floor? Yes, it did matter how it broke because my mind had asked a question and that mind needed an answer. This is what life is all about: questioning. We need to question all the time because by questioning and answering those questions, we learn. As we learn we gain more knowledge and as we gain more knowledge we learn to question more. My nan just accepted the thunderbolt problem but had she questioned it in the slightest, she would have learned that opening windows was a waste of time. All it did was let in the rain which accompanied the storm. She would also have learned that the old superstition of hiding the silver was rubbish but it did mean actual silver, not anything that was shiny, such as her butter knives or soup spoons. She didn't learn though, for two reasons. One was, she never thought and the other was, she never listened. My grandparents were simple but harmless folk.

So what is heaven, where is it, who gets to go there and what do we do when we get there?

In the above question I said when 'we' get there. That statement was wrong, of course, because as I have absolutely no belief in any religious god, of any faith whatsoever, I would be barred from the place anyway because they would class me as an atheist and a non-believer. I am altogether a complete sinner and a dreadful person. Doesn't this raise a thought or two, though?

Am I correct in saying that religionists can sin in the week but have their sins absolved and forgiven in church on a Sunday? Am I also correct in saying that sinners can repent of their sins on their death-beds so that they can get into heaven? Can a mass murderer see a bus coming towards him and shout to God for forgiveness just before he is flattened by it and then enter heaven? When you think about it, isn't this a little unfair? If this is the case then a religionist can murder, rape, rob, pillage and plunder to their heart's content and then say, 'Oops! Sorry, God,' on their death-bed and be allowed into heaven and yet an atheist who has led a perfectly good life, only ever loving and doing good deeds for his fellow human companions, is barred at the gates and is sent to hell to burn for all eternity. That's nice! What about children of religionists, who are not old enough or wise enough to have made up their own minds which path to follow? If they die, do they automatically go to heaven? If so, do the innocent children of atheist parentage go straight to hell?

Is this why religious parents seem to rush so wholeheartedly to indoctrinate their young children? Is it this or do they do it before the child has any chance of thinking differently for themselves?

When we die we go to heaven, they say, but what part of us goes to heaven? When we die we are either buried or cremated. If we dig up an ancient grave, we will still see bones or bone fragments. We know that when we die our bodies are buried or cremated to stop us rotting and spreading disease so if we do not go to heaven as a physical entity, then what part of us does go there and is heaven then not a physical entity or place itself?

They say our souls go to heaven and not our bodies, but then I have also read many accounts of heaven which give a physical description. What is a soul though? Is it something that is planted within us by God at our conception? Some say our soul is what we are and it is in our head. It is true that in our head is what we are but that is not due to something extra planted there, is it? It is due to the way our brains function. There are seven billion of us on our little planet and we are all different. That is not because there were seven billion different souls made separately and implanted by a god. It is because every single brain is different and is wired differently and it is our brain that determines whether we are thinkers, non-thinkers, happy, sad, serious, frivolous, heterosexual or gay, or generally good or bad people. If someone had a bad soul inside them would that mean they did bad things and if so, why were they given a bad soul in the first place? If I were an atheist I would not be allowed into heaven but if I was made by God, then isn't the fact I am an atheist his fault anyway? He made me so how could he possibly judge me? Religion says we should not judge each other but isn't this a touch hypocritical when, in the end, we are all supposed to be judged by God at the pearly gates?

Let me give a description of heaven from what I have read and learned.

Firstly, a dictionary description:

A place regarded in various religions as the abode of God or the gods and the angels, and of the good after death, often traditionally depicted as being above the sky. Those who practised good deeds would receive the reward of a place in heaven.

If we didn't think about the above description then we would, again, just accept it, but look at what it says. It says, 'Traditionally depicted as being above the sky.' How can anything possibly be above the sky? The sky is endless. When we look up we see the sky, we see stars and we see into the universe. We will never see the sky end and heaven begin. Anyway, where is 'Above the sky'? We are all told people go up to heaven. Which way is up? If you went up from America, you would end up in a totally different place to where you would if you went up from Africa or France or England. You see, already in this simple explanation of heaven, there is no sense or logic.

A more descriptive description:

A river, clear as crystal, will flow from the throne of God and of the lamb (Jesus) down the middle of the city. On each side of the river there will be a tree of life, yielding twelve kinds of fruit every month. The streets will be pure gold, like transparent glass. The walls of the city will be adorned with every kind of jewel; emerald, onyx, amethyst, topaz etc. There will be no need for the sun or moon, and no need for a temple or church. The presence of the Lord will be its light.

What can we say about this? Not too much, really. It doesn't give a single fact that makes any sense. Why would the streets need to be made of pure gold? Why would the walls of the city need to be adorned with jewels? Is this because these are the kind of things the writer thinks we should aspire to? Don't we have enough trouble here on earth with people aspiring to such falseness already? Why would there need to be trees yielding twelve kinds of fruit every month? Then, as this is the city of heaven, why would it need walls? Oh yes! That's to keep us atheists out, isn't it? We do have ladders, you know! And giving a little more thought to the description, they have a stream running down the middle of the city but they do not have a sun. Without the sun, how does the water evaporate, then condense, and then form into rain to keep the stream topped up and flowing? Where does the water come from and where does it go? The presence of the Lord will be its light, they say. I hope he's got a good torch.

Again, this comes back to the problem of thought. Whoever made up this description of heaven obviously gave it no thought whatsoever and yet they expected others to believe it. The worrying thought is, did they actually believe it to be real and true themselves as they wrote it? Answer, yes, and you have to admit they were a little insane and answer, no, and you must come to the same conclusion.

Let's try and find something a little more realistic.

Apparently there are actually three heavens. I have always heard if you are good you will go to heaven. Not, if you are good you will go to one of the three heavens.

It seems the apostle Paul was caught up in the third heaven so where are the first two? They say the first heaven is the sky or firmament, where the clouds are. The second heaven is where the stars are (That's big) and the third heaven's position has not been given. Perhaps that's the one above the sky, the one with all the gold and jewels and the twelve fruits.

So are there three different heavens so that there are resting places along the way. Perhaps we all turn into angels and have to flap our new wings hard to get there and need places to rest. Makes sense, doesn't it? Does it?

Biblical description of heaven:

There is a constant chant of holy angels that are continually proclaiming Holy, Holy, Holy over the throne of God. The mercy seat in heaven where the god sits is surrounded by magnificent angels full of glory and power that proclaim and bless the holy name of God without ceasing. Some of these are described as beasts, full of eyes, with six wings and neither rest day or night in proclaiming the holiness of God.

I'm sorry but my first reaction to this is, What! What mind ever thought that up? And worst of all, who actually believes it?

So poor old God is sitting on his 'mercy seat' while magnificent angels chant, 'Holy, holy, holy,' on and on forever without ceasing and some of these angels are beasts which are full of eyes and have six wings. With all the chanting, I doubt if God can ever get to sleep and if he did, whatever would he dream about after being surrounded by such strange and possibly very ugly creatures? It all seems a bit of a nightmare to me and for him.

Thinking seriously, what is it all about? If there was to be a heaven or heavens, then surely a perfectly reasonable description of it could be given. All I have found are totally nonsensical and fanciful ideas that have sprung out of very simple and yet very fervid minds. We are enticed with the theory that if we are good we will go to heaven. Wouldn't it be good to know what we are struggling towards and what our lives will actually be like when we get there?

Why can't they say heaven is a wonderful place, a bit like the plains of Africa where we are surrounded in the sunshine by wildlife and all manner of good food and drink? When we go there we live in total peace and harmony with everyone else (apart from atheists) and we never have to work and worry about paying bills. No-one ever goes hungry, no-one ever goes to war, no-one is ever murdered, raped, pillaged or plundered and we all live happily ever after with love all around us, with the pubs opening twenty-four hours a day and free ice creams and doughnuts in the afternoons. If they promised all that even I would have to carefully reconsider my position but nothing concrete is promised, is it? And that is because in no real world can there ever be such a place.

When we read the Bible or the Interweb we see all manner of things about angels, but what are angels and how do they come about?

Firstly, I said, perhaps we turn into angels and fly to heaven but it seems not. My research has now told me that although people talk about their relatives becoming angels and sitting on clouds watching over them, humans do not actually turn into angels as they are, in fact, a totally different species that was made by God. They were made to use as messengers and had no physical attributes unless they are sent by God to give a message and the recipient needs to talk to them. Angels do not marry or have children so are either created as God needs them or they never die. Evidently, angels can be cherubim, dominions, powers, principalities, seraphim, archangels or even good or bad angels, but if they are angels, why are there bad ones? It seems God tested the angels and those that were not faithful to him were called bad angels and were cast into hell. The question has to be asked, why are there so many different kinds of angels?

Evidently all angels operate at a different frequency. Why didn't I think of that? How obvious was that? It seems each person is different and needs an angel which matches their frequency in order to pass on messages. A cherub has a calming form while a dominion helps others through giving encouraging thoughts. A seraph usually moves slowly but can also appear in a flash, whereas principalities go around in threes to make sure they have enough power. Archangels emit a glow of divine consciousness while the smaller angels tend to group together to help those higher up in the hierarchy. It's all so simple really, isn't it? It's all so simple but not real at all, is it? Please have the logic to agree. Could I be wrong on even this? Surely not.

I also said that it would be good if heaven was like the plains of Africa and those there would be surrounded by animals, but I have heard it said that animals do not have souls and therefore do not go to heaven. Isn't that rather biased towards vegetarians? What are the meat eaters going to eat? Why should we have souls and other animals haven't? I know the Bible seems to put us above all other creatures but this is quite an arrogant view. We may be all different shapes and sizes but, in the end, we are all the same. We are no better than a cat or a caterpillar or a duck or a duck-billed platypus.

Recently I read on Facebook the question, 'Do pets go to heaven?'

The answers to the question all seemed positive so if this is true, the person who said animals do not go to heaven was obviously wrong. The trouble with all this is that none of it is real and therefore no one knows any real answers; therefore, various contradicting stories abound. One person replied to the question, 'Do animals go to heaven?' by answering that they did and they all waited patiently for us at the 'Rainbow Gate'. The what? It all seems like a game of Chinese whispers, with each person not passing on exactly the same story. It then gets blown out of all proportion as piece upon piece gets added and twisted. In Chinese whispers it is all a game, but in religion people treat it seriously and sadly, actually believe it all every step of the way. Sadly, as I am a noisy atheist, all my dead budgerigars, dogs, tortoises, rabbits, cats and pigs will sit there at the gate, waiting in vain for their master's arrival.

After talking to many people of various backgrounds I have come to the conclusion that many if not most people are truly frightened of death and the thought of God, angels, heaven and everlasting life may be something unlikely but is still something to cling onto, because if it all could be true then death wouldn't exist and their worry would be gone. Fair enough, I suppose, but they cannot possibly truly believe it all, though, can they? If they were truly convinced of heaven and life ever after then the worry of dying would not be there, but the worry is there and it is haunting their lives. How, though, can we all live on for ever and ever? We can't, can we? There cannot possibly be any such thing as eternal life because there can be no such thing as an eternity. Even the planet we live on will, one day, cease to exist. Nothing can last forever. We have to look at life in a totally different and realistic way.

Let me give you an example:

On a clear night, get away from the television and go outside to look at the moon. Then, when you see it, don't just see it as a white flat thing in the sky. See it for what it really is, a huge ball of rock orbiting the earth at a distance of two hundred and fifty thousand miles. It is not just a shape sitting there. It is a body in its own right. Understand that it is travelling around us. Then, once you have grasped that and have seen the sheer enormity of it, then think and realise that you are standing on another, far larger ball of rock and that ball of rock is orbiting the sun. As you stand there looking up, you may feel still and quite serene but then contemplate the fact you are standing on a planet which is, in fact, turning on its own axis at a thousand miles per hour and is travelling around the sun at a vast sixty-seven thousand miles per hour, with nothing above it or below it apart from space. Then add to this the fact that the sun is also orbiting the centre of our own galaxy, the Milky Way, which is some a hundred thousand light years away. Think of all this and try to contemplate that light travels at a speed of 186,000 miles each second and yet it takes 100,000 years to reach from the centre of our galaxy to us, and then you get to see just a little something, a tiny inkling of the mind-blowing enormity and complexity of the universe that we live in and are only a tiny, tiny part of.

Look at the stars in the vastness of the sky and don't even bother thinking about counting them. There are literally countless billions of them. Look at them and think, just how many of them could possibly be supporting life as does our star, the sun? Look at them and contemplate the thought of someone somewhere possibly standing on another planet looking back and thinking just the same thoughts that you are.

Once you have looked at the stars, try and contemplate the fact that, although there are countless billions of stars emitting light out there, there was a time when the whole of the universe was black. There was not the smallest twinkle of light anywhere for a billion years or more.

After the Big Bang, the universe was filled with a mass of gasses but there were no stars. Then matter started to form but it took many, many years for gravity to pull this matter together to form stars. Try to imagine that, in the vastness of the universe, tiny specks of matter were very gradually formed and drawn together and this carried on slowly but surely, until this matter had become of a large enough mass to form a star which then erupted with the light we see today. This happened gradually throughout the universe until we saw the huge and wondrous spectacle we see above us now.

The universe is 13.7 billion years old and it is so vast that some of the light we see today is the first light that star ever emitted. It has taken that long for the light from it to reach us.

I will move along because, here, I am turning this book into *Wonderment* again.

We live on a fantastic planet which is full of fantastic things. We need to fully appreciate it all instead of bothering with superstitions. We need to get away from this dark and edgy world of gods and angels and heaven, hell, torment, pain and punishment. We need to ditch worrying about living our lives to suit an imaginary friend in the sky. We need to live our lives for ourselves and to the very fullest of our capabilities and then, at the end of it all, we would have no fear of dying. We could all lie on our deathbeds and think, 'Bring it on'.

It would not bother us in the slightest because we would realise we have been given the sheer beauty of life, have grasped it and have lived it well. We would also realise that our planet managed perfectly well without us for its first 4.5 billion years and once we die it will continue in the same vein for the same amount of time again. I have no fear of death, heaven or hell whatsoever. I think I will, in the end, probably just be glad of the rest.

We don't need to live forever and we have no real need for heaven. As I have said, we are lucky to live on a fantastic planet which is full of fantastic things. If we took away war and hatred (much of it religious, I have to say) and any superstition and lived our lives just by loving each other, caring for each other and the world we live on and giving just a little more than we take, we would have absolutely no need for heaven because we would have our own real heaven right here on earth.

Hell

So what about this other place, the place where I'm condemned to go? Me. My name is already on his list for being a non-believer but it is not only atheists who go to hell. It seems anyone who breaks any one of the Ten Commandments drawn up by God and his secretary, Moses, ends up there as well.

(We shall discuss the Ten Commandments in depth later.)

So can we not commit a sin and then ask for forgiveness on our death bed? It all seems a little contradictory to me. The Ten Commandments lay down the law of God but if we can repent our sins before we die then what is the point of the commandments anyway? Confusing, isn't it? If we commit just one sin, do we go to hell? If so, then why stop at one? Why not commit a million sins and go to the same place with the same punishment?

Even as a tiny child I was told of hell and its consequences. But why? Was it just a way of making me behave myself?

'If you do this or that you will go to hell!'

What a way of controlling your child. Brainwashing him into thinking he would suffer burning for all eternity just because he was picking his nose or was looking at a photograph of a woman in her underwear in a mail order catalogue. (The things we used to do eh?) In a way, you could look at it all and smile, as I am now, but if you think deeper, what is happening is tantamount to child abuse. They were looking to God and the devil as kind of babysitters to make sure you behaved yourself while your parents were not with you.

(Thanks for that one, Ricky Gervais).

It's a good job we didn't listen because boy, did we have some fun! What is the point of your parents telling you forcefully that you must never do this or that when, if they had ever just added a little thought into the mix, they would have realised that because you had been told so strongly and forcefully, all you were going to do was rebel and do it all the more anyway.

If we break any of the Ten Commandments we go to hell. If we do this, we go to hell. If we do that we go to hell. It is a wonder anyone ever gets to heaven at all. Is the place empty? I'm an atheist, I have stolen a few sweets as a child, I have committed adultery in my earlier years, I have taken the Lord God's name in vain, I have not kept the Sabbath day holy, I have coveted my neighbour's wife and his goods. I have no chance of heaven as my final destination but who has? How many people, apart from perhaps Noah and his family, have never done anything wrong? The promise of heaven may be great to any 'perfect' person but how bloody boring must their lives be here?

What about a person who has devoted almost their entire life to charity but has once, as a child, 'forgotten' to pay for a penny sweet? Are they condemned to hell? And what about someone who has devoted his life to the Roman Catholic Church but has, along the way, raped children who were supposed to be in his care? Does God judge them by the life devoted to him or the misdemeanour that has occurred? And as this has happened within the church and has probably been hidden by the church does it make it easier for God to accept it? Where does God stand on all this and where does he draw the line?

So what of the Ten Commandments? Let's take a look at them.

1. Thou shalt have no other God but me.

Isn't this one just a little ironic? Here is a god who is seen to be 'the one and only god' but he is saying we shouldn't have any other god but him. If he is the only one, then how can we have another? It seems even God, the one and the only one, is a little apprehensive and insecure about his position. We have much insecurity in today's society but it seems this may have been passed down from God. But, thinking about it though, we do not have God's blood in us, do we? We only have genes and dust from Adam and Eve. From his description in the Bible God was a fully functioning man though, so why did he invent Adam? Why didn't he just invent Eve and then we could all truly be called the children of God? Perhaps, in making Eve it would have been too painful having to remove his own rib. I don't know. Was this god a jealous god? It is like someone saying, in a childish manner, that they are your friend but you shouldn't really have any other friends? Believe me, I have seen this more than once, even in the real world and even in adults. What kind of friend would demand this? In the end, would they be a true friend at all.

37

2. Thou shalt not take the Lord God's name in vain.

How many of us have never failed this one? What is probably the most common phrase used these days? It's, 'Oh my God!' or 'OMG!' I think, like the hula-hoop or chewing gum, the phrase originated in the US and has now become pandemic. Are we saying and, indeed believing, that if we say, 'Oh My God' or, 'Jesus Christ' or, 'For God's Sake', we are to be burned forever?

3. Remember the Sabbath day and keep it holy.

So many people have to work on Sundays these days. Carers cannot just abandon those entrusted to them. Hospital workers cannot leave their patients to die. Even farmers have to make the most of their good Sundays at harvest-time in order to gather in their crops. Their animals must also be fed and cared for every Sunday. Vicars and priests have to work on Sundays as well, otherwise their churches would be empty and a waste of time.

So are carers, nurses, farmers, vicars, priests and all those who work in Tesco condemned to hell just for trying their best to provide a service to others and a living for themselves? Are they to be condemned to hell for being caring people? Again, can you smell the irony?

4. Honour your father and your mother.

Fair enough, I suppose. My father was not great at his job but I did and still do honour him. He may not have been a terrific father but it was he who bred me and if it wasn't for him I simply would not have been here. My mother couldn't come out and say she loved us but we did know, but what if parents were not like this? What if parents actually physically, sexually or mentally abused their children. Should we still honour them rather than go to hell? Could you possibly blame a ten-year-old boy and send him to hell for dishonouring a father who beat him every day?

Should we stone to death a child who is 'stubborn and rebellious to his father'? Deuteronomy 21:18-21.

5. *Thou shalt not kill.*

Of course, we should not kill and perhaps we would deserve to suffer the consequences if we did but do we need this written in a Bible for us to realise it is not the thing to do? Surely this is common sense. Do we look at a person and say to ourselves, we would kill that person if it wasn't banned in the Bible? Or, if God wasn't watching I would blast that person to pieces? Of course we don't. If we did think such things we would surely need far more help than just the Bible. Killing is wrong and we all know that but, then again, the worst punishment God can think of is to burn you in hell for all eternity and there is no difference in punishment in his mind for mass murder or stealing a single sweet. It seems if you are going to sin you may as well do it for the worst crime you can think of. If you are going to steal a single sweet than you may as well rob a bank at the same time.

Stealing and murder are in the Ten Commandments but what of kidnapping, or beating up poor defenceless old ladies? They are not listed so is it all right to do it? Of course it isn't. Perhaps this is why so many priests have raped children instead of being something great that they could look up to and put their trust in. Could it be that they think, as it is not mentioned in the Ten Commandments it could be a fair and just thing to do? There isn't an eleventh Commandment that says 'Thou shalt not sodomise those in thy care.' Perhaps there should be. Did God and Moses slip up there?

Doesn't this point to the Bible not being needed as a source of morality? Not raping children is not one of the ten commandments but we all know it is wrong. Isn't morality just a matter of common sense, intelligence and reality? We will talk of it in detail later in its own chapter.

6. *Thou shalt not commit adultery.*

Wouldn't it be wonderful, perfect in fact, to be in your teens, meet the love of your life, get married and stay so much in love for the next sixty years that you could never even dream of having sex with another person? I know it does happen and if it has happened to you then all I can say to you is, it is lovely and well done and good wishes but it doesn't always happen, does it? How many of us have been unfaithful, either because of a relationship turning sour, a lack of sexual fulfilment within that relationship or a matter of a simple uncontrollable amount of hormones? In my case it was a little of each. It was all a long time ago and things have settled down and I am truly happy and contented. I know I am not the only one who has committed this 'dreadful sin'. There are millions of us who have done this and are all condemned to fire and torture? Adultery is not a good thing and of course we should not do it but is it really this bad? Does it warrant such a severe penalty? If God was watching me as I was in the act of committing adultery, then why did he not tell me to stop? Why was he watching such personal behaviour anyway?

7. *Thou shalt not steal.*

What amount of stealing does this mean? Is it really fair to lump all thieves in the same boat? Is a child stealing a sweet just as guilty as someone who cons an eighty-year-old widow out of her life savings? Is a starving child who steals a loaf of bread just as guilty as an oaf who beats a pensioner to a pulp in order to steal her pension? It seems under God's eyes anyone who is not as perfect as him is classed as scum or dross or both. But was God himself so perfect? Wasn't he the one who murdered every man, woman and child in the world apart from Noah and his family? And isn't it this great and wonderful God who would condemn a five-year-old to hell because he went scrumping? I feel the Bible does hold far too many double standards and contradictions.

8. *Thou shalt not bear false witness.*

Bearing false witness automatically brings to mind the swearing on a Bible in court. It has been done for years and years but the practice had always bothered and perplexed me. The first reason for my being perplexed is, again, this fear of God thing. Swearing on the Bible must say that once we have done it we are to be afraid of the consequences so we will surely tell the truth, but as I have said before, if this God chap is so loving and benevolent why should we fear him? The other reason for my distrust in swearing on the Bible is the fact that if it is so important to do it and it matters so much, why can't we just

41

believe whatever the person swearing on it says afterwards? 'No, your Honour, I didn't murder that man and you know I didn't.' 'How do I know?' 'I just swore on the Bible, didn't I?' 'Oh yes, how silly of me. Of course you did. Off you go then.' 'Cheers. See you again next week.'

If swearing on the Bible is so important and relevant, then we should rely wholly upon it. Then we would save the government a fortune and it could spend the extra money on really important things like waging another war or something.

The problem here is that swearing on the Bible doesn't work at all, does it? So what is the point of doing it?

I think 'false witness' means to tell lies in court and also it means to lie in general. Blimey! How many of us have never told a lie? As we go on it seems there must be fewer and fewer people in heaven.

On an Interweb page, this commandment also includes the following: lying, gossiping, slandering, back-biting, spreading rumours, deceit, extortion, railing, slander, defrauding, breaking promises, craftiness, hypocrisy, dishonesty, whispering, idle words, withholding of the truth, double tongued, bragging, boasting, flattery, exaggeration of the truth, whining and speaking evil of others.

I think more than a few of us are more than little guilty there.

What sort of lie would see us dragged off kicking and screaming to the furnaces of Hades? Does it have to be a full-blown lie or just a little one? What about someone who has arranged a surprise fiftieth birthday party for her husband but tells him she hasn't? Is this lying, deceiving bitch to be carted off, screaming? Come on, please let's get real!

9. *Thou shalt not covet thy neighbour's wife.*

I got this one muddled once and tried to 'convert' my neighbour's wife. It didn't work. She's still a Christian.

So how do you covet your neighbour's wife?

It is funny how when I just looked at the exact meaning of 'covet' in biblical terms I came across the following sentence. *The ten commandments can never be kept by anyone except Jesus Christ who kept them perfectly.*

So is it only Jesus Christ who lives in heaven? The rest of us are just a bunch of sinners and are all plopped into hell together. So why did God build heaven and everything in it when its only resident is a carpenter from Nazareth? God, he must be bored on his own. Whoops! I have just taken the Lord God's name in vain again.

To 'covet' thy neighbour's wife is to have a wrongful desire towards her. In this context I suppose the word 'neighbour' means any fellow human being, not just the chap next door. I also presume this can mean your neighbour's husband as well. How many of us have never had a wrongful desire towards a neighbour's husband or wife? Still, if it is only Jesus who got to heaven then does it matter what we think? What is a wrongful desire though? Surely it doesn't matter what we think or desire, providing we never put our thoughts into actions. If I had ever turned all my wrongful thoughts into actions I would have been worn out years ago.

I gave a list in Commandment No 8 but that seems nothing compared with what is included in this one: Coveting, Lust, Envy, Drunkenness, Sorcery, Materialism, Wantonness, Sensuality, Gambling, Revelry, Attachment to riches or material goods, Lawsuits against Christians, Emulations, Extortion,

Desire for money, Desire for power, Desire for sex (relating to immorality), Anger at others' good fortune, Desiring things of others, Flirting or Playing with temptation.

I love the one about lawsuits against Christians. Does this mean a Christian can commit a crime against you and you must simply allow it to happen for fear of eternal burning?

10. The shalt not covet thy neighbour's goods.

If my neighbour buys a new Range Rover or a nice sports car am I never to feel envious? Of course I'm envious. Envious, that is, as opposed to jealous. I do like to make a clear distinction between the two. Envy is a natural and wholly constructive feeling. You can be envious of your neighbour's Range Rover but still go and congratulate him on his purchase without it biting you hard inside, whereas jealousy breeds bitterness and contempt. In my childhood I saw much jealousy. My mother used to dislike some people because they were 'house-proud'. That was another of her thoughts and sayings that I couldn't understand. She was actually jealous because someone had a cleaner and tidier house than her. We were told that certain people were snobs because they had this and they had that. Again it was only pure jealousy. My big worry is that many adults do still show jealousy towards others instead of congratulating them for their efforts and achievements. I have even experienced this in adults due to me becoming an author. I am nothing special because of it, but most do congratulate me on my efforts but some, even family, do avoid talking about it altogether because of sheer jealousy. They talk about anything else, but not my writing. Sad, isn't it? But that's life these days.

Of course we covet our neighbours' goods. It is a healthy thing and if it is dealt with logically and healthily it can only make us try harder to aspire more to their good fortune and, perhaps, make us work hard to achieve those goals ourselves.

We have been through all the Ten Commandments and we now realise that it is only Jesus that got into heaven so the rest of us are condemned to hell, so as we are all going there let's take a look at what it is, where it is and what it has in store for us abhorrent creatures.

Firstly, we are always told we go up to heaven but down to hell, so hell must be a purpose-built place somewhere underground. On a couple of websites so far, all I have come across is that hell will be a place of weeping and the gnashing of teeth. This sounds like the British House of Commons to me. Let's look a little deeper.

In a description of hell, I have read that what is written is 'documented evidence' of hell and if I read it I could be putting myself in serious danger. If that's the fact, then why tempt people to read it by writing it in the first place? I took the gamble, took my life in my hands and dared to look. Oh, I do love to live dangerously.

It says: 'Hell is below the ground and the great pit would only have to be less than 100 miles in diameter to house all the 40 billion people that have ever lived.' ('This is assuming their bodies after death were the same size as they were before.')

The figure for dead people is complete guesswork. I have read of figures up to 140 billion and some also say there are more humans alive today than have ever died. They say this space would be plenty for everyone with room to spare. I have just used a rough calculation based on simple mathematics and this says each of the forty billion residents of hell would receive just under half a square inch of space so it must be assumed that hell is in fact set out on many floors or levels and must be vast. There must be literally thousands of floors and as we are all there for all eternity then it must be getting more and more crowded. Does everyone just get their space or do they have separate sleeping quarters? And what of toilets? There must be millions of them and all plumbed in. Food would be another huge consideration. Somehow these people die but are then given new bodies in hell. If not, there would be nothing to burn. It is said that their skin is burned off and then once it has regrown it is burned off again, so their bodies must receive sustenance in order to regrow the skin. But what do they eat and who does the cooking? Perhaps they have even more floors on which to grow cattle or sheep or vegetables, but where does the necessary light come from? The food doesn't come from 'up above', does it? Because if it did surely there would be some evidence of it happening. 'What are you doing above that hole with those ropes and pulleys and chunks of meat and baskets of parsnips?' 'Oh, nothing really. Just passing them down to hell.' 'Ah, I see. Don't worry. I won't tell anyone.'

Of course, heating and cooking the food would never be a problem, would it? There is plenty of heat down there and after spending a day or two having their flesh burned off I would think the victim would be only too glad to tuck into a nice cool, fresh salad anyway. I doubt if BBQs or hog-roasts would be too appealing. They would probably bring back unhappy memories of when it was them on the spit.

And then there would be staffing problems. I have never seen an advertisement in my local supermarket or newspaper saying: 'Staff wanted in hell. Must like heat and burning people. A chance to meet many famous dictators, despots, authors, priests and celebrities. Good rates of pay and no work on a Sunday.'

Maybe I am totally wrong here. Maybe the population of hell do all their own dirty work. They are allocated jobs and as an incentive to work maybe they receive burning on a slightly less regular basis by working hard. It makes sense, doesn't it? 'Look, if you clean the toilets you will only get burned once this month rather than four times.'

The incentive would work, I think, and whatever job you did you would be sure of receiving a good tan.

I am being totally frivolous here, I know, but what else can I be when the whole thing is so completely and utterly preposterous and yet people really do worry about it all and let it affect them for the whole of their lives? Please be realistic.

Some say that the fearsome noise from a volcano is actually the screams of tormented souls in hell and someone else said that hell is for 'people who like parties' but they must remember that some of the people they would be partying with were not very nice. I've been to a few parties like that myself.

Jesus Christ says about hell, 'Where their worm dieth not and the fire is not quenched.'

It seems this worm is in fact the carcass of the person, which does not die but regenerates ready for the next burning session.

So if we transgress in the slightest, either by taking a few sweets or taking the Lord God's name in vain or we convert our neighbour's wife or we work on the Sabbath we are all condemned to eternal burning and torture. The God who made us the way we are will see us punished for all eternity for being the way he made us and the only person who will possibly escape this dreadful torture is Jesus Christ himself. Even that must be seen as being a little nepotistic, as he was or is the son of God. We are burned and tortured and tortured and burned and then burned again but, in the end, we never complain because, in our hearts, don't we just know that God loves all of us so dearly?

As a conclusion to this piece, we have to admit that there is absolutely no evidence for heaven or hell and the stories we read and hear of them are ridiculous to say the least. We will never live in a city paved in gold or live underground with our skins being burned off for all eternity, will we? There is so much horror promised to sinners by the Bible, so much torture that no sin on earth could ever justify it and that, I think, is why many people do still believe in it all. It is because, plainly and simply, they are truly afraid not to.

As I stated at the beginning of the book, I am a member of various religious and non-religious discussion groups on Facebook and do enjoy debating. It can very frustrating when some, on both sides, can only argue through temper and insults because of their lack of knowledge. They do not have a good, intelligent and logical answer so all they can do is rant and make fun of those with some degree of intelligence. It does make me cringe sometimes when someone who has probably not even read the Bible properly sincerely thinks they know more than all the top scientists put together. Many of them have absolutely no idea at all about even the topic they are trying to debate. A classic example of this is the meme which shows an intricate sand castle on a beach and the caption says this is what atheists believe happens all by itself. They haven't the intelligence to even separate evolution from erosion.

Back to my point. If I were to post a question on a religious page such as, why did Jesus have to die for our sins? many people would try and answer it. They would give their honest opinions on the subject because they have learned it from the Bible or Bible teachers but there have been four questions that I have posted that not one person has replied to with any answer at all. In fact, some of the questions, I feel, were possibly deleted by those running the group in order to avoid embarrassment.

The questions were:

1. If evolution never happened, then the God of the Bible had to have made all the animals in the world in just 24 hours. If we accept there are approximately eight million animal species on our planet and he had to have made at least two of each, he would have to have made 185 animals each second of that day. How did he do this?

No answer.

2. It is generally accepted these days that corporal punishment is frowned upon strongly in the western world. The harshest acceptable punishment that can be applied to children seems to be sitting the child for a few minutes on 'the naughty step'. Could anyone from any religion please explain to me why light corporal punishment is so frowned upon and yet parents can, in the name of religion, still have the end of a male child's penis cut off with no remorse or comeback?

No answer.

3. Genuine question out of interest. Religious people are sure that people such as me are condemned to hell. Before I go there I would like to know just where it is, what it is like and what happens there. I felt that, although I am a sinner and am therefore destined to go to hell, surely I have some small right to be told what I'm letting myself in for.

No answer so I reversed the question.

4. I asked the above question but I realise that as you are all religious and have faith and trust in God and Jesus, you will not know anything about hell. As you are all going to heaven could you please tell me where that is, what it is like and what happens there?

Again – no answers.

Heaven and hell are two of the fundamental aspects of religion but it seems that although people promote them strongly and vehemently, they do not actually know a real thing about them and doesn't that make you wonder? It does me. The only explanation I have ever seen given about what happens in hell is the simple fact that if you are sent there you are 'separated from God' and that, in itself, is a terrible punishment. As I am an atheist I have been separated from him for many years so, to me, if this is the case, life will just go on as normal.

A little light-hearted triviality

Why do Christians go to church and pray to God on a Sunday when they are fully aware that it is his day off?

Ephesians 5:24
As the church is subject unto Christ, so let the wives be to their own husbands in every way.

Is this the morality we should be leading our lives by?

No woman should ever be subject to her husband's will and ways.

In no way can this sort of behaviour ever lead to any kind of full, and loving relationship.

Revelation

In a spare moment, some time ago I just picked up a New Testament Bible and opened it quite randomly. It fell open at Revelation. I then sat and read and was quite astonished. I could not believe what I was seeing and reading. With all seriousness, I tried and tried, totally and utterly, to take it all in seriously but to this day I have to swear the author of the piece must have been high on magic mushrooms or some other strong narcotic substance. That sort of wild and vivid imagination surely must have been stimulated by something. It was written some time ago and, even today, some believe it to be true, but if it was written today and was asserted as being true we would all laugh, surely? It is far more fictitious and fanciful than any *Harry Potter* or horror film. In fact, it makes *Nightmare on Elm Street* look like *Tales of the Riverbank* or *Postman Pat*.

Ironically there will be those among you who will totally disregard my writing as wrong, and even complete nonsense, but how can anyone do this and yet still believe what is to follow?

The New Testament seems to suddenly have gone from being what I would perceive as trivial and harmless nonsensical stories to being an explosion of the writer's mind. He seems to have suddenly turned into the Incredible Hulk. Whoever upset him that much? Or was it the mushrooms? We'll look at what it says but I will not copy it all out. It is there if you should wish to read it in its entirety and I would strongly suggest you should. If you do read it and find it at all plausible then I'm afraid you and I are on 'totally different buses', as they say. It is the revelation of Jesus Christ; which God gave him to show his servants what must soon take place. It is said that it offers comfort and encouragement to Christians to show them God was still in control. Where the 'comfort' comes in I do not know. Forces of evil were trying to rule the world and *Revelation* shows they would all ultimately be destroyed. It is all quite good reading but I am just going to pick out the highlights. Mind you, there are a lot of them. I cannot see a single word of it being true, but, as with all religion, I do love it and find it fascinating. Totally weird but still fascinating.

I will add here that yes, I do think the world, our world, is coming to something of a vast dilemma and anarchy is not far off but I do not quite think we are heading for the following.

Revelation:

God says to the orator (John): *Write therefore what you have seen, what is now and what will take place later. The mystery of the seven stars that you saw in my right hand and of the seven golden lamp stands is this: The seven stars are the angels of the seven churches and the seven lamp stands are the seven churches.*

See what I mean? He is actually holding seven stars in his hand. And why the seven lamp stands? Why do the stars represent the angels and why do the lamp stands represent the churches? If he wants to use angels and churches why doesn't he just use angels and churches? He can hold whole stars in his hand. Surely churches and angels would not be a problem? How do you possibly hold a star in your hand? You cannot, can you? Again, this shows the naivety of the writers of the passage. To them, in Bible writing times, stars were just the small twinkling things in the sky and to them, it would be possible and simple to hold them in your hand. They had absolutely no idea, did they? Science and common logic have since proved them wrong again and even the most fervent believer of religion will admit today that stars are not just small twinkling things. They are vast and hot. Our sun is only a relatively small star but it is many, many times greater than the earth and it is not hard to see that the thought, these days, of holding it in your hand has to be mindless and preposterous. This is the Lord God Almighty though, they say. He can do anything. He can hold not just one in his hand but seven. The author has to be on something, doesn't he?

God, then to the Church in Thyatira: *Nevertheless, I have this against you: You tolerate that woman Jezebel, who calls herself a prophetess. By her teaching she misleads my servants into sexual immorality and the eating of food sacrificed to idols. I have given her time to repent of her immorality but she is unwilling. So I will cast her on a bed of suffering, and I will make those who commit adultery with her suffer intensely, unless they repent of her ways. I will strike her children dead.*

This piece then goes on with God saying, *He will rule them with an iron sceptre; he will dash them to pieces like pottery.*

Once again, the Bible is talking about sex and violence. It seems sex is immoral in the Bible but its writers certainly do seem to show a keen interest. They mention it at every available opportunity. Jezebel was to be cast onto a bed of suffering and anyone who lay with her would suffer intensely. Surely it was God the creator who gave the human population the ability and want to enjoy sex and if that was so, why was it so insanely wrong to do it? And why was any of this the fault of Jezebel's children? It wasn't, but God wanted to strike them dead anyway. As with everything else, I bet he still loved them deeply though, didn't he?

In the centre, around the throne, were four living creatures, and they were covered with eyes, in front and behind. The first living creature was like a lion, the second was like an ox, the third had a face like a man, the fourth was like a flying eagle. Each of the four living creatures had six wings and was covered with eyes all around, even under his wings.

So we have four living creatures and each of them had six wings and loads of eyes, even under their wings. See what I mean about being high? I've been drunk a few times but have never been on a drug-induced high but I can easily imagine these kind of thoughts could manifest whilst on one.

And now it starts getting interesting as we move on to the Lamb, the Scroll and the Seven Seals. The Scroll was sealed with seven seals but no one could be found who could break the seals so the orator wept and wept. Bless him! It must have been terrible but luckily, just then, the Lion of the tribe of Judah, the Root of David appeared and he had a go and, lo and behold, he could break open the seven seals but before the seals were broken, ten times ten thousand angels (that's a hundred thousand angels) were heard singing. I bet the song was *All things bright and beautiful* again. They seem to sing that everywhere.

The first of the seven seals was opened and a white horse appeared. Its rider holding a bow, and he was given a crown, and he rode out as a conqueror bent on conquest. (Here we go with the violence again.)

The second seal was opened and another horse came out, a fiery red one. Its rider was given power to take peace from earth and make men slay each other. (More violence.)

For some reason, when the third seal was opened there was only a man on a black horse who had a set of scales in his hand. He was going on about, 'A quart of wheat for a day's wages'.

The fourth seal brought out a pale horse and its rider was named Death, and Hades was following close behind him. They were given the power over a fourth of the world to kill by the sword, famine and plague, and by the wild beasts of the earth. (You guessed it. More violence.)

The fifth seal was opened and the souls of those who had been slain because of the words of God were seen under the altar. The souls called out to the Lord and asked him how long it would be before he judged the inhabitants of the earth to avenge their blood. They were given a white robe each and were told to wait. Fair enough.

The sixth seal was opened and there was quite a spectacle. There was a great earthquake. The sun turned black like sackcloth made of goat hair, the whole moon turned red, and the stars in the sky fell to earth as late figs dropped from a fig tree when shaken by a strong wind. The sky receded like a scroll, rolling up, and every mountain and island was removed from its place. How amazing but how totally unlikely and absolutely ridiculous? That trip really is taking hold now, isn't it?

Adam and Eve and Noah and his ark were unbelievable but gentle stories laid down by naive writers, but this really is good.

No, it isn't, is it? Try as I may, I cannot help thinking it has to be complete rubbish, garbage in fact. These writers were so ill-educated that they obviously thought all this could happen. Even the most uneducated of us today knows just how big stars are compared with the earth and we all know they cannot simply fall to earth; and how did they possible think the sun could turn black like sackcloth? In their primitive little minds, they even saw the sky as probably a painting on a canvas which could roll up, but what we have to think is that despite the earth being 4.5 billion years old, this writing was put down after the supposed birth of Jesus Christ and that was only two thousand years ago. Isn't it amazing, just what some of us have learned in this relatively short span of time since? I do say 'some of us'.

When the seventh seal was opened there was silence in the heaven for about half an hour. Then the seven angels who stand before God were given seven trumpets. They might have known this would cause trouble. Why give seven naughty angels a trumpet each when you know they will cause problems? They weren't about to simply play pretty tunes, were they? I bet they didn't even have a risk assessment for what was about to come.

The first angel sounded his trumpet and there came hail and fire mixed with blood and it was hurled down upon the earth. (You see, I told you there would be trouble.) With this one blast of his trumpet a third of the earth was burned up, and all of the green grass was burned up. Yes, all this through the blowing of a single trumpet. Mind boggling, isn't it?

Despite all the chaos caused by the first trumpeter, the second angel then blew his trumpet. He wasn't about to play *Silent Night, Holy Night,* was he? He blew and something like a huge mountain, all ablaze, was thrown into the sea. A third of the sea turned to blood, a third of the living creatures in the sea died and a third of the ships were destroyed.

There was now utter chaos in the world but still only two trumpets had been sounded and there were five left. People must have been dreading the third but it happened, of course. The angel blew and as it sounded a great star, blazing like a torch, fell from the sky on a third of the rivers and on the springs of water. The name of the star was Wormwood. A third of the waters turned bitter, and many people died from the waters that had become bitter.

Panic must have ensued. Everyone knew the rest of the trumpets had to be sounded, but what devastation would they bring? Oh dear!

The fourth trumpet was sounded and a third of the sun was struck, a third of the moon, and a third of the stars, so a third of them turned dark. A third of the day was without light, and also a third of the night. (Think about that one.)

The fifth angel sounded his trumpet and another star fell from the sky to the earth. The star was given the key to the Abyss. When he opened the Abyss, smoke rose from it like the smoke from a gigantic furnace. The sun and sky were darkened by the smoke from the Abyss and out of the smoke came locusts who were given the power of scorpions. They were told not to harm the grass of the earth or any plant or tree, (Wasn't all the grass destroyed by the first trumpeter?) but only to harm those who did not have the seal of God on their foreheads. As God was obviously in a good mood at that point he said the locusts were not allowed to kill these people but could only torture them for five months. (That was generous of him.) He said they should torture them so well that they should seek death but not be able to find it. How lovely. What a kind and benevolent person he was. We ought to pray to him.

The sixth angel then sounded his trumpet and God said the four angels who were bound at the great river Euphrates should be released. Now that seemed a good gesture but no. With God being God, he had other ideas. He wanted them to kill a third of mankind. They were supposed to have had two hundred million mounted troops, so I suppose numbers were on their side and they had a bit of an advantage.

Everyone heaved a huge sigh of relief because there was only one trumpet left to be sounded, but what would it bring? Would it bring more stars falling from heaven? Would it bring more earthquakes or more pestilence or death? No, it didn't. It brought forth voices from heaven which praised the Lord God to the highest. Such peace after such devastation! But to cap things off it was followed by flashes of lightning, peals of thunder, an earthquake and a great hailstorm.

So what can we gather from the sounding of the seven trumpets? Firstly, we must realise that even in the most fervent religious mind surely no one could possibly believe it ever happened. Anyone who can possibly see this as truth, to my mind, has problems. Or is it me? Let's look at some figures and happenings.

So what little mishaps have been caused so far? It seems the earth has suffered the following:

We have a conqueror bent on conquest.
    Men made to slay each other.
    Killing by sword, famine, plague and wild beasts.
    Great earthquakes.

The sun turned black, the moon turned red and stars fell to earth.

The sky rolled up.

Hail of fire mixed with blood.

One third of the earth burned up and all its grass.

A huge mountain ablaze and thrown into the sea.

A third of the sea turned to blood.

A third of the sea creatures killed.

A third of all ships destroyed.

A great star fell from the sky turning the water bitter.

A third of the sun, moon and stars were struck and turned dark.

A third of the day was without light and so was a third of the night.

Another star fell to earth.

Smoke erupted and locusts tortured people for five months.

A third of mankind were murdered.

All topped off with a good old earthquake and hailstorm.

The first thing I must say here is I am chuckling to myself at, 'A third of the night was without light'. Is it just a little simple of me here to point out that not just a third of the night should be without light? If it had light wouldn't it be called 'day'? And if a third of the day was without light wouldn't that be called 'night'? So I presume all they had to do here was alter their clocks to compensate.

All the above terrible things have happened and have been caused by God. But why? What was the need for such drastic actions? Perhaps if his actions had been less drastic it wouldn't have made for such a good read. And why, in God's mind, did every question and slight problem have to be answered with extreme megalomaniacal violence? In this instance, the only consequence for the earth would have been total annihilation. An annihilation from which it could never have recovered. Still, we as humans must have listened because we are still the same, aren't we? Even now, nothing is ever done with measured action as we do love causing strife, agony, carnage, hatred, hostility and war wherever possible.

You may think this is the end of all the troubles, but no. Don't be silly. This is the Bible so there is plenty more to come yet. We now come to the Woman and the Dragon. I want to quote the first piece as it is brilliant.

A great and wondrous sign appeared in heaven: a woman clothed with the sun, with the moon under her feet and a crown of twelve stars on her head. She was pregnant and cried out in pain as she was about to give birth. Then another sign appeared in heaven: an enormous red dragon with seven heads and ten horns and seven crowns on his heads. His tail swept a third of the stars out of the sky and flung them to earth. The dragon stood in front of the woman who was about to give birth, so that he might devour her child the moment it was born.

Boy, the author's trip is still biting hard! We've now got a woman standing on the moon, wearing the sun, who is about to give birth and has a red dragon with seven heads and ten horns waiting to eat her baby. That shit must be heavy, man!

But it doesn't happen, does it? Good job really. The woman actually gives birth to, 'A son, a male child, who will rule all the nations with an iron sceptre'. Her baby wasn't eaten but it was snatched from her by God. That was nice of him, wasn't it? She lost her baby but as compensation she fled to a place in the desert where she was taken care of for 1,260 days. See, life isn't all bad, is it? Or is it? It transpired that a great war then broke out in heaven and the dragon then ended up being thrown down to earth so he pursued the woman who had given birth but guess what? She was given the two wings of the great eagle, so that she might fly to the place prepared for her in the desert where she would now be cared for, for a time, times and half a time, out of the serpent's reach. But things were still not safe for the woman despite her new eagle wings, because the dragon spewed water from its mouth to try and sweep her away with a torrent. Things looked precarious for the woman but then her luck changed again, because the earth helped her by opening its mouth and swallowing the river that the dragon had spewed. The dragon was jolly upset at this and decided he would go off and make war with the rest of her offspring. As you would. I bet he was jolly angry.

Now we have a beast out of the sea. Whatever next? Perhaps it was just a fish or a crab, or starfish or lobster or something. No, it wasn't, was it? Don't be daft. It had ten horns and seven heads, with ten crowns on his horns, and each head had a blasphemous name. It resembled a leopard, but had feet like those of a bear and a mouth like that of a lion. One of the heads of the beast seemed to have a fatal wound. (It was lucky he had another six then, wasn't it?)

Like Eve's friend the snake, this beast was given a mouth to utter proud words and blasphemies and to exercise its authority for forty-two months. It seems its power would enable it to make war against the saints and to conquer them. All the inhabitants of the earth that were left after the stars falling, the plagues, the night turning to day etc. had to worship it. It was said that 'If anyone is to be killed by the sword then with the sword he shall be killed.' Well, at least that bit is plain enough. I suppose today if you are to die in a plane crash then in a plane crash it will be. Or if you are to die of malnutrition then of malnutrition it will be.

Next we seem to swiftly move on to the Beast of the Earth. No, this will not be a badger or mouse or fluffy bunny, will it? This one had two horns like a lamb and spoke like a dragon. This beast performed great and miraculous signs, even causing fire to come down from heaven to earth in full view of men. (Goodness! In full view of men! That's amazing.) It was given power to give breath to the image of the first beast, so that it could speak and cause all who refused to worship the image to be killed. (More violence.)

The Lamb and the 144,000.

The Lamb stood on Mount Zion and with him the 144,000 who had his name and his Father's name written on their foreheads. Then they heard the sound of harps playing a song which only the 144,000 could hear. That was nice for them and you would think then that this piece was quite pleasant but to add a little spice to it, it seems the 144,000 were those who did not 'defile themselves with women', for they kept themselves pure. What has the Bible got against women and sex?

The Three Angels.

Now this sounds pleasant, three angels, but you guessed it, it isn't pleasant at all. It seems the first angel just said, 'Fear God and give him glory, because the hour of judgement has come.

Worship him who made the heavens, the earth, the sea and the water.'

That one wasn't too bad.

The second angel followed and said, 'Fallen! Fallen is Babylon the Great, which made all the nations drink the maddening wine of her adulteries.'

That wasn't too bad either but then the third angel chipped in and went and spoiled it.

He said, in a loud voice, 'If anyone worships the beast and his image and receives his mark on his forehead or on the hand, he too will drink of the wine of God's fury, which has been poured full strength into the cup of his wrath. He will be tormented with burning sulphur in the presence of the holy angels and of the Lamb.'

So even the angels were threatening violence, but this time with burning sulphur. Where does all this hatred come from? No wonder we see so much in society today. Isn't it funny how we say things like, 'Oh, you are an angel', or, 'She has the charms of an angel', when in fact angels are not always the nicest of people at all.

We then have the Harvest of the Earth before coming on to more naughty angels and these ones had plagues. There were seven of them and each had his own particular plague. They were dressed in clean, shining linen and wore golden sashes around their chests. Then one of the four living creatures (they're back on the scene) gave the seven angels seven golden bowls filled with the wrath of God.

The Seven Bowls of God's Wrath.

The angels were told to go and pour out their bowls. The first angel did and ugly and painful sores broke out of people. (Teenage acne?)

The second angel poured out his bowl on the sea and it turned into blood again and every living thing in the sea died. Hadn't they all been killed before or was it just a third of them?

The third then followed and turned the inland waters to blood.

The fourth angel then proceeded to pour out his bowl on the sun. (How do you pour out a bowl of something on the sun?) This gave the sun power to scorch people with fire. 'They were seared by the intense heat and they cursed the name of God'. I should think they did after even more violence was forced upon them.

The fifth angel's bowl made men gnaw their own tongues in agony, which was still not very nice but at least it was different and showed some imagination.

The sixth angel then poured out his bowl and the great river Euphrates dried up. What was in these bowls of God's wrath? It wasn't Coco-Pops, was it?

When the seventh angel poured out his Coco-Pops, sorry, bowl, every island fled away and the mountains could not be found. From the sky huge hailstones of about a hundred pounds fell upon men. It is a mystery, isn't it? Where were those naughty mountains hiding? Perhaps the angels counted to fifty and then shouted, "Here we come. Ready or not!"

The Woman and the Beast.

It says: *Then the angel carried me away in the Spirit into a desert. There I saw a woman sitting on a scarlet beast that was covered in blasphemous names and had seven heads and ten horns. The woman was dressed in purple and scarlet, and was glittering with gold, precious stones and pearls. She held a golden cup in her hand, filled with abominable things and the filth of her adulteries.*

There was so much utter carnage being caused. People were dying by the sword or plague. Stars were falling to the earth and water was turning to blood so why, with all this happening, is the author so interested in what people were wearing? This lady was wearing purple and scarlet and was glittering with gold. It is a bit like Jesus being crucified, but it didn't matter because someone in the audience had a nice bright frock on. And why did all these creatures had multiple heads and horns? What significance did that hold? Hang on though. It seems the ten horns are ten kings who have not yet received a kingdom. Of course. What a thicko I am! Duh!

Apparently, the beast with the ten horns will hate the prostitute. She will be left naked and ruined; it will eat her flesh and burn her with fire. I bet she'd charge extra for that.

The Rider on the White Horse.

And I saw an angel standing in the sun, who cried in a loud voice to all the birds flying in mid-air, 'Come, gather together for the great supper of God, so you may eat the flesh of kings, generals, and mighty men, of horses and their riders, and of the flesh of all people, free and slave, small and great.'

Obviously just killing people wasn't enough. It would be a far better story if everyone and their horse was fed to the birds. Now we can imagine all sorts of wonderful things happening.

And then they went on to have more fights until many more were killed and the birds gorged themselves.

Satan's Doom.

It seems Satan had been in prison for 1,000 years and when he was released he deceived people from all corners of the earth to gather them for battle. In number they were like the sand on the seashore. He surrounded the camp of God's people but fire came down from heaven and devoured them. And the devil who had deceived them, was thrown into the lake of burning sulphur, where the beast and the false prophet had been thrown. They would be tormented day and night for ever and ever.

Why did Satan try to take on God? Didn't he know God could do anything? He wasn't going to be beaten, was he? And didn't God make everything? If he did, he obviously made Satan. So if he made him, couldn't he just as easily make him disappear if he wished?

The Dead are Judged.

Then I saw a great white throne and him who was seated on it. Earth and sky fled from his presence, and there was no place from them. And I saw the dead, great and small, standing before the throne, and books were opened. Another book was opened, which is the book of life. The dead were judged according to what they had done as recorded in the books. The sea gave up the dead that were in it, and Death and Hades gave up the dead that were in them, and each person was judged according to what they had done. Then Death and Hades were thrown into the lake of fire. The lake of fire is the second death. If anyone's name was not found written in the book of life, he was thrown into the lake of fire.

More benevolence, I see. In my New Testament, Revelation goes on for over thirty pages and it is just one huge horror story, an immensely imaginative story of lust, blood and death.

The New Jerusalem.

It seems this is where a new heaven and a new earth appear, so perhaps things are getting better, but no. It says that the cowardly, the unbelieving, the vile, the murderers, the sexually immoral, those who practice magic arts, the idolators and all liars – their place will be in the fiery lake of burning sulphur. This is their second death. So things are carrying on much the same as usual, then? What would we do without that burning sulphur? Life just wouldn't be the same, would it?

It seems, after all this, Jesus came, they all said Amen and then they all lived happily ever after.

I have been told the story of Revelation is the telling to Jesus what would happen in the future but it is all told in past tense. I'm getting even more confused now. I have also been told that the story is allegorical and can therefore be taken whichever way anyone wants. 'It is there to be interpreted.'

Again, we are coming back to my book idea as mentioned in the preface. If I say 3+3=7 then how can I possibly ask people to interpret it as being six? Someone has said to me that all the stars that were said to have fallen to earth could well have been meteors. I say if they were meteors, then call them meteors. We don't say, 'The little cat laughed to see such fun and the plate ran away with the spoon,' do we? But perhaps it is supposed the be that way but I have failed to interpret it. Am I living my life in a too simplistic and realistic way? Do I demand too much logic in my life? Perhaps 3+3 does equal 7.

It is said that Revelation is 'God's disclosure of himself and His will to His creatures'. If God wanted to disclose himself then why didn't he just do it? And if he wanted to disclose his will then why didn't he just do that as well? Surely he could have thought up some small Revelation rather than destroy the world. I think he was in a particularly bad mood that day, things got a little out of hand and he went over the top a bit. If God wanted to disclose himself, then it has to be said, why doesn't he do it now? It would save a hell of a lot of arguing and heartache.

The author of this could have made up a nice little vignette and told a few words of how God disclosed himself. Why did he need all this other crazy stuff unless he was, indeed, on something? Still, what was said here could easily have been told plainly in just a couple of pages and as TV's Mrs Brown said, 'If most of it wasn't made up it would only be a pamphlet.'

In the past there have been thousands upon thousands of gods that have been worshipped. Why is it today that people only worship their chosen one? This is, by the way, only one more than me. They are only one god away from being atheists.

Young Earth

Scientists believe and have proof that the earth is 4.5 billion years old and yet some religionists swear it is only a 'young earth', one which is under ten thousand years old. Firstly, before I do my best to debunk their theory, I will try to explain why they think this is so when there are so many facts that contradict it utterly.

As I said in *Wonderment*, some religionists say that a God day is far longer than an earth day. Again, why don't they say what they mean? In reality a day is a day. It is just that, a day. It is the time the earth takes to revolve once on its own axis. In reality it can be no more or no less. In Genesis it says God created the earth in six days and rested on the seventh. That is why we are supposed to keep the Sabbath holy. It doesn't say God created the earth in six days which are really supposed to be three quarters of a billion years long and then he rested for the next three quarters of a billion years because those days were very long and he was completely and utterly pooped. We call Sunday the Sabbath and some say it is Saturday. The Sabbath is not every seventh three quarters of a billion years. If that was the case, we could all be resting now and what a rest it would be! I think we have all noticed that the Sabbath happens once each week and not just once in many countless lifetimes.

'Young earth' believers say the earth is somewhere between 5,700 and 10,000 years old and they come to this conclusion because the Bible was written as actual history and was to be understood as actual history. The piece below endeavours to explain it.

That the time from the beginning of the universe to the creation of humans was the six days recorded in Genesis 1. And that from the time of the creation of man to the birth of Abraham was approximately 1,950 years, as recorded in the Biblical Genealogies. Given Biblical and other data for calculating a date for Abraham, we can calculate that the universe and earth were created approximately 6,000 years ago.

So here they are not saying a God day is a long one. They are taking Genesis as literal fact and man was created on a Saturday and then along came Abraham a couple of thousand years later. They then say that by using other data they know the universe and earth were formed six thousand years ago. How simple! Again, it negates any need for thought or wonder at all. 'There it is, six thousand years and we have proven it in a four-line paragraph. Simple!'

To understand and take this as fact and taking genealogy into account, we have to believe that on pre-flood earth, it seems most lived for up to a thousand years. Noah was over nine hundred when he died and so was Adam.

When we look at the true, amazing and wondrous universe we live in surely it deserves more thought than just a few lines of description. But no, in the eyes of these people it is as simple as that and that is all there is to it. If we were to just take this on board and accept it, we then lose any and all passion for life.

We lose the complete complexity of the evolution of the universe and all the gigantic forces within it. We lose the death of stars and the new beginnings of others. We lose red giant stars and we lose white dwarfs. We lose black holes and galaxies and nebulae and supernovae. We lose the wonder of where the universe came from and where it is going and, most sadly of all, we lose the need to think, to think for ourselves, educate ourselves and live life to the full, luxuriating in the knowledge we have gained.

These 'young earth creationists' say the earth was formed and then the universe and according to them, there is only a few days between them age-wise. Again, it takes out every wonder there is and has ever been and every thought that has ever been contemplated. Of course, the earth and all the stars are not the same age. The universe was nine billion years old before our sun even came into existence. It wasn't made a couple of days later just to throw light on the earth, an earth which God had already shone light upon from another magical source. Our earth is just a tiny and very insignificant speck of dust at the edge of a small galaxy set in a vast and almost unimaginable and wondrous universe. It can never be held as being the centre of and the entire meaning of the universe and everything it holds. It can never be this or anything remotely like it. That thought would be completely mindless and would show gratuitous arrogance, to say the least. It can never be held as the centre of anything apart from our existence. I feel if we have the capabilities to even try to imagine all this then we start to lose the need for and the point of religious and other superstitions. Our minds, no matter how great they are, can never fully comprehend it all but surely, with just a little thought, we can see beyond our own noses and see beyond the thought imprisonment that religion induces.

Can we possibly say that, just by adding together people's ages from the Bible, we can judge the age of the earth? Especially when some of these people are said to have lived up to an amazing and imaginative one thousand years old? I say these people are not just wrong. They are preposterously and mind-blowingly wrong and are not thinking at all. With minds closed this tightly, there is no wonder they believe God was around, on his own, living in nothing, and then decided to create the world just so that he would have people who he could threaten with all kinds of torture and hardship if they did not pray to him continuously. They believe Adam was made out of dust and his wife had a pet talking snake. They believe Noah, a 480-year-old man, built a boat that could house 16 million animals and all their needs for a year. They believe the earth was then flooded with as much water as it held already without giving a single iota of thought as to where that water was to come from or where it was to go afterwards. They also believe that Noah was 600 years old when he set all the animals free to make their merry way back to their own far-flung countries. Noah and his very ageing family were then to repopulate the globe. Am I wrong to say again, please wake up and smell the irony?

As with everything else they believe, their only source of evidence is the Bible and that is all they need, but that is just a book which holds no evidence whatsoever for any of its claims. It is a book full of falsities. It cannot prove the existence of God and it does not have a single atom of proof for anything he is ever supposed to have said or done. It can prove nothing and yet, in a debate, it is soon and almost always quoted by theists. They use it to prove things to atheists and yet it is the atheists they are arguing with who have no belief in what it says and therefore cannot accept the argument. How can they use a book that atheists do not believe in to prove what atheists do not believe?

What I would like to do here, though, is give a few examples of plain and simple evidence that the universe cannot possibly be this young. I am not going to go into radio carbon dating or anything highbrow. I just want to talk about everyday things that all of us can see around us and understand if we are willing to apply just a modicum of thought and logic.

1. We know most of the dinosaurs died out during the K-pg event some 60 million years ago and by doing a simple sum we can calculate that this period of time is one seventy-fifth of the time the earth has been in existence. If we then use the same calculation for when the dinosaurs died out in the, 'young earth' way of thinking, we come to the simple conclusion they actually died out eighty years ago. This is my way of thinking, but if the earth is as young as they say when do they think the dinosaurs did die out? Would their theory even actually allow dinosaurs to have existed in the first place? Do they deny it? If it all happened this quickly, do they think dinosaurs and humans lived alongside each other? After all, animals were made on a Friday and we were made on a Saturday. We and dinosaurs must have lived alongside each other unless they became extinct before midnight on the day thcy wcrc madc. If thcy died out this eighty years ago, then even my mother-in-law would remember them. Come to think of it, she might even be one of them. Sorry, Mother.

2. It is a generally understood and accepted fact that the earth once held a giant land mass called   Pangaea and that this land mass then broke up and drifted apart because of the movement of the earth's crust. Science has told us with irrefutable proof that the continents of America and Africa were once joined

together. Pangaea formed about 300 million years ago and broke up again 100 million years ago. It has taken this long for the Atlantic Ocean to become as wide as it is today. Let's say the Atlantic Ocean is an average of 3,000 miles wide and it has been getting wider ever since day one of the creation of the young earth. This would mean it has been growing in distance every single year by half a mile. In reality, it actually spreads between two and five centimetres each year, which seems more likely to me.

3. We cannot say that just because there are sea shells left high and dry on the tops of mountains, they must have been left there when Noah's flood subsided. Especially when we know a flood of this magnitude could never have happened. They have been deposited there by continental drift which has caused land to move and, in the case of mountains, they obviously moved upwards and what were old sea beds were eventually to become the tops or sides of mountains. This has happened over millions upon millions of years and never over just 6,000.

4. Fossil records show the whole history of animal life. The Burgess Shale fossil beds date back 500 million years and contain very ancient species. In no way could these fossils have formed in just 6,000 years. Complete fossil mineralisation usually takes hundreds of thousands of years. And why do we find different fossils in different rock strata? If all animals were created at once then surely we would find them all dying within roughly the same period and they would then all be fossilised together. Human and dinosaur fossils would be lying side by side. We have found so many fossils now that we can see their progression through evolution and we know that, through a vast number of years, they have formed and have gradually become new species. This does not happen in 6,000 years either.

5. Again, through science we know that the moon was once part of the earth and it was blasted out in a gigantic explosive collision between two bodies. We know this happened, so at what point in the young earth time do they think this happened?

6. Look at the Grand Canyon. Was that carved out in 6,000 years? And the same goes for the Badlands of America, the African Great Rift Valley and even the coastline of Britain. There used to just be land between England and Holland. We know this because we are hauling up mammoth bones. When do these people think this flooded? Was it during Queen Victoria's time?

7. The galaxies of the universe are seen to be moving rapidly away from each other and this can only be attributed to the Big Bang. If they are travelling and have travelled this far, how have they managed it in this short span of time? We now see galaxies that are billions of light years away from us. We look at them and, because they are so far away, the light they emit has taken so long to reach us we actually see them as they were shortly after the Big Bang. We certainly do not see them as they were six thousand years ago.

8. Even looking at things from a Biblical point of view, Jesus was born 2,000 years ago, which means that only 4,000 years had passed between the very creation of the earth and his birth. It says that in the beginning the earth was without form. How did it come from no form at all to the forming of the great Roman empire in just 4,000 years? And in the times of Jesus, was Mount Everest only two-thirds the height it is today and was the Atlantic Ocean a third narrower? Come to think of it, were all the galaxies we have talked about a third closer?

9. We have found several Hominid species and all but one has died out. In the young earth theory where in the timescale did we lose *Australopithecus Afarensis, Homo Floresiensis, Homo Erectus, Homo Heidelbergensis, Homo Sahelanthropus* etc? Were they just fly-by-night species that lasted a few years or even months or weeks?

10. On to my favourite, Noah's Ark. There was so much salt water on the earth at the time of the great flood that everything would have either been killed by salt or would have been washed away by the necessary rains. The very core of life would have been crushed completely and utterly under the unimaginable pressure of water above it. In no way could Noah have just landed, set all his charges free, set up his vineyard and got drunk before his son saw him naked within his tent. The earth would have taken millions upon millions of years to recover. Again, the Bible is stating one thing and then trying to make people believe another.

11. Science says that humans originated in Africa and perhaps just one tribe managed to leave that continent and then colonise the rest of the world. It seems totally remarkable to me that the rest of the world was populated in just 70,000 years. How likely is it that Adam and Eve went from just two people to 7,000,000,000 in just 6,000 years? I would sincerely state that it was not likely; more like totally and utterly impossible.

These are just a few simple and clear reasons why the earth is the 4.5 billion years old that science says it is and can never be just the 6,000 years that some want us to believe. The problem here is that no matter how they try to argue their case, they can only look silly in doing so. But, on the other hand, they know that if they give up the argument they either lose another part of their religion, or their whole religion, so they continue behaving and arguing in what has to be said is an almost childlike fashion. What amazes me is that, although this is pure fantasy, they do give arguments which, to them, make perfect sense and it is almost worthless trying to argue back. Like many people, they convince themselves and are therefore correct, no matter what anyone else says. Their minds are closed and all logic is repelled. Some arguments are so preposterous that retaliating is all but futile in every way as no logic can ever sink in.

What we have to do is what I tried to teach in *Wonderment* and that is, accept reality for what it is: real. There were times when most people thought all this god and holy stuff was totally real and they did so because there was nothing else. There was no science to contradict it and life was tough but now I feel we have many of the real and true answers and don't need religion any more. As I am writing this I am once again sitting in the bay window of the house in Port Isaac, Cornwall, where I wrote some of my last book. This little fishing village has seen its fair share of tragedies in the past, with some of its folk being lost at sea. Can you wonder why they were so keen on religion when they always had to wonder if their loved ones were coming home from the sea or whether the very thing that put food on their table had taken them for good?

Yes, religion did have its place and yes, people did need it (and some still do) but we are learning more and more and are needing religion less and less. I feel we were wrong to believe it, but what is the harm in admitting we were wrong? I feel we need to get real, open our eyes and move on. The earth is not just six thousand years old and admitting the fact can be no sin. We admit things and learn by our mistakes. If we are to believe what we hear from some religionists, then the earth is six thousand years old and everything was made in six days.

Science says the earth is four billion five hundred million years old and life has been evolving for three billion five hundred million of those years. We modern humans have been on the planet for two hundred thousand years so if science is correct, then we took four billion, four hundred and ninety-nine million, eight hundred thousand years to evolve. In my mind, this is far more likely than the religious account of six days. Dinosaurs were made on a Friday and we were made on the Saturday? Is it me?

Do folk really and truly believe these six thousand years or do their minds see it as a span of time that they can see and understand? If you think about it, it must be far easier to put everything in its own little time pigeon-hole within this space, rather than have to imagine this time multiplied by seven hundred and fifty thousand. How much simpler must six thousand years seem?

Question.

We have seen people beheading others, including children, in the name of religion and in certain countries it is fine to marry and have sex with little girls and yet God does not interfere. Women are completely subjugated within many religions and children, male and female, are mutilated sexually, seemingly with God's consent. So the question has to be: 'Why is it fine to behead someone or marry and have sex with a child or to subjugate women or mutilate children, and yet some of the people who do this are not allowed to eat a bacon sandwich?'

Where is there any slight amount of rationale and realism in this? Am I dreadful in the fact I must be missing something?

The Lord, Abraham and Lot

In Genesis 17 a covenant was given by God to Abraham and the covenant concerned the cutting off of the end of every male's penis. This, to my mind, is a barbaric act and is completely mindless and futile. It can hold no necessity whatsoever in any real person's mind and absolutely no advantage can be gained from it. The practice has to be pathetic and could well, in my mind, infringe upon a person's human rights. There can be no even slight reason for this in any way and I have covered it in full in *Wonderment*.

In this book, I would like to move on to Genesis 18 and 19 as they also tell quite a story, one which I feel is quite indicative of Bible writers. When I say 'writers' I do mean that the Bible was written by several people and was written long after any event it covers. I'm sorry but I cannot countenance the fact that some say it was actually written by God or Moses, or God dictating to Moses.

Genesis 18. The Three Visitors.

Abraham was sitting quite nonchalantly near some big trees in Mamre and whilst he was sitting, the Lord appeared to him. Of course Abraham was not shocked by this as visits by God seemed quite a regular occurrence, but then he saw three men standing nearby so he rushed over to them and bent low to the ground. It seems a little odd that the Lord himself had just appeared to him and he didn't bat an eyelid, but then he rushed over and bowed to three strangers and left the poor old Lord standing there talking to himself.

He grovelled to the strangers and offered to have some water brought so that they could wash their feet, and he said he would get them some food so they could be refreshed before they went on their way. They agreed, so Abraham went into his tent and told his wife to make some bread and he then got his servant to kill and prepare a tender calf. The food was prepared and all the men ate veal, curds and whey and bread under a tree. Abraham was jolly kind, wasn't he? Here were complete strangers and he had no idea who they were or what they were up to but he took them in and fed them well. But this is the Bible. Shouldn't Abraham have known that something awful must have been heading his way? They ate well, but was Abraham's wife Sarah not allowed food, or was she just not allowed to eat with the men? Perhaps she just chose to eat hers in the tent where it was cooler.

Anyway, the visitors had not seen Sarah so they asked where she was and Abraham said she was in the tent. (Who did they think prepared their meal?) They then said that they would return in a year's time and Sarah would, by then, have had a son. (Yes, another son. There were women about but their births were hardly ever mentioned.)

Now, Sarah was listening to them at the entrance to the tent which was behind them. So there she was, eavesdropping on the men's conversation. My question here is, how come she was plenty close enough to hear what was said and had been kind enough to prepare food for the guests and yet she hadn't even been introduced to them? If only in a small way, the Bible is being misogynistic and sexist here again.

Sarah was not too keen on the idea of becoming a mother again and who can blame her? If we cast our minds back to Genesis 17 we will remember that Abraham was 99 years old, then when he had to cut all those bits off. Can you wonder why Sarah gave a little laugh at the suggestion of her becoming pregnant? She was not that much younger herself. Apparently, the Lord was bemused and couldn't make out why Sarah had laughed. He was a little displeased and ask Abraham if he thought anything was too hard for the Lord. Then he repeated that Sarah would have a son. It might have been a nice, warm and kind gesture if they had allowed Sarah out of her tent and asked her if she did want another child but no, the Lord had spoken and he had to have his own way again. Poor old Sarah didn't like the Lord's tone of voice and she became frightened and said she hadn't laughed but the Lord knew differently. 'Oh yes you did!' he said.

When the men had eaten the veal and bread and curds and whey they got up to leave and then looked down towards Sodom. The Lord had plans for this city and he wondered whether he should tell Abraham. But what were these plans? Was he going to install running water and sanitation? Was he going to put in a one-way traffic system to help stop donkey congestion? Was he going to build top class hospitals or an aqueduct? No, quite simply and in his usual way, he was going to destroy it, destroy the whole city. Things don't change, do they?

The men turned toward Sodom and Abraham stood watching, but then he went over to them and asked if they were going to destroy the city with everyone in it. He said that not everyone there were sinners and should the Lord destroy the righteous as well? He obviously hadn't looked back to and learned from Noah's flood. It didn't matter then what good any of the human population had done or how religious, loving, kind and caring they were. Apart from Noah and his family they were all destroyed. Every last man, woman child and baby. Anyway, he started to plead with the Lord and said, would he spare the city if fifty righteous people were found in it? The Lord said yes, so Abraham then began to lower his bid down to forty and then thirty and then twenty and then ten righteous people and each time he said a number, the Lord agreed but I think he was only kidding, because we find in the next part that he destroyed it anyway.

Genesis 19. Sodom and Gomorrah destroyed.

This part of the Bible story says that the two angels arrived in Sodom in the evening. As it is entitled *Sodom and Gomorrah* I can only assume the party split up and the other man went with the Lord to destroy Gomorrah. We'll see. I suppose 'Sodom' was probably what the Lord said about the people of the city.

Anyway, the two angels arrived in Sodom and Lot was sitting in the gateway of the city and when he saw them, he got up and bowed down with his face to the ground. He told them to turn aside to his house, where they would wash their feet and stay until morning. That was another kind gesture to make to two strangers. And why did they always have to wash their feet? It seems everyone was doing it. Perhaps it was all the sand and sandals. The angels said they would not bother him but would spend the night in the square but Lot insisted and invited them in and they accepted. Lot then prepared a meal for them and baked bread without yeast. I'm sorry, I am no expert on when these events were supposed to have taken place but how – again apart from the fact it is written – can we possibly know this happened at all, let alone the fact Lot actually baked bread without yeast in it? No one knows this. No one could know this.

Moving on, things are about to become sinister because before they all went to bed, all the men of the city gathered like a mob at Lot's door and when he asked them what they wanted at that time of night they said, 'Where are the men who came to you tonight? Bring them out to us so that we can have sex with them!' There were old men and young alike and suddenly they all had this all-consuming desire to have sex with angels. Where did the writers of the Bible conjure this up from? What were their little minds like? And can you have sex with an angel anyway? As I said in my part about Heaven, it seems angels are not human. Do they have the necessary parts to have sex? It is said angels do not breed so were they sexually capable? Perhaps if men in biblical times treated their wives like angels rather than just objects they would have no need for angelic fornication at all. Why would a whole city see two strangers enter a man's house and then suddenly turn this rampant? Was it the Middle Eastern heat?

All this was bad enough but then Lot, being the fully accommodating fellow he was, hatched a cunning plan and his idea was simple. 'No, my friends,' he said to the men. 'Don't do this wicked thing. Look. I have two daughters who have never slept with a man. Let me bring them to you, and you can do what you like with them. But don't do anything to these men, for they have come under the protection of my roof.'

So what can we make of this. Firstly, I see it as just another way for the writers to bring sex into the Bible, but what of Lot?

Yes, he had invited these angels under his roof and yes, he felt he should protect them. That was an honourable enough thought but to coldly and simply offer them his sweet and innocent daughters so that they could be raped and defiled in whatever grotesque and totally depraved way was wished by a gang of angel-hungry lunatics was probably not the most fatherly thing he had ever done, was it? No one would do this. Not even in the name of religion, would they?

It turned out Lot's offer of his two virgin daughters was not enough for the horde anyway. They seemed hell bent on having sex with angels and tried to break down his door. Luckily for Lot, he didn't live in a tent as most people seemed to then. Lot was pulled away from the door by the angels and they then set about making all the men at the door go blind. A little over the top, don't you think? If they had magic powers shouldn't they have just magicked the men to go home to muse upon their bad behaviour rather than use violence? So the angels were saved and so were Lot's sweet daughters but as we find out a little later, they were not quite as sweet and innocent as Lot had made them out to be.

Then the angels asked Lot if he had any other family in the city and if he had, he ought to get them out because they were going to destroy the city. I would think Lot was gutted. There he was, playing host to what he thought were charming angels who obviously had loads and loads of sex-appeal and he had even tried to save them by offering up his dear virgin daughters to the horde, but in the end all the angels wanted to do was destroy the city he lived in and played host in.

Lot then went to visit the two men who were betrothed to his daughters as he wanted them to get out of the village, but they thought he was joking. I bet he didn't tell them he had offered their future wives to be ravished by all the males of the city. He might not have been too popular.

Early the next day, the two angels told Lot to take his daughters out of the city and when he hesitated, the angels grabbed his hand and the hands of his wife and two daughters and guided them out of the city. And so Lot has a wife as well, does he? Obviously she wasn't worth a mention up until now either. I bet she would have had something to say about her daughters being given up to a mob. It's a wonder Lot didn't offer her as well but perhaps, like Abraham's wife, she was getting on for one hundred years old at the time and was probably glad of the rest. I don't know. They were told to all flee for their lives and not to look back.

But Lot didn't want to flee to the mountains. He wanted to go to a place called Zoar instead and the angels agreed he could. Then the Lord rained down burning sulphur on Sodom and Gomorrah from the heavens. What is it about this burning sulphur? It seems the Lord absolutely loved the stuff. The cities were destroyed as were all the people in them. (I see the Lord was being kind and benevolent again.) They all died, which was plain enough but what was to befall Lot's wife took some imagination. If you remember, they were causally told not to look back but no seriousness was attributed to this statement, but Lot's wife did look back. She wasn't rebuked or given a little slap on the wrist, was she? Oh no, this is the Bible, so no trivial punishment could be handed out. She had been a naughty lady and had upset God. This innocent lady, who had just fled her city, her home and all in it to run away with a husband who had tried to give up their daughters to be gang raped, simply looked nostalgically back at what had been her home and refuge and suddenly there she was, turned into a pillar of salt. A what?

Why? I bet Lot quickly turned around and sold her to the local chip shop.

The Bible never mentions any grief for his wife on Lot's behalf, but it simply says he and his daughters left Zoar and went to live in the mountains where they were to live in a cave. In their isolation, the girls began to think. It was a woman's duty to bring forth children (probably sons) but there in the mountains no men were to be found or seen, so they too hatched their own cunning plan. They decided to get their father drunk and then have sex with him. See, I told you they weren't too innocent didn't I? On consecutive nights they got their father so drunk that he didn't even know he had impregnated his daughters. It's a wonder he could impregnate anything after being that drunk but it seems he did and they both gave birth to sons. (See, I told you so.)

So this is Genesis 18 and 19 and what can we make of it? Again the Lord is venting his anger and destroying things and sex is being brought into the story willy nilly. It is brought in whenever possible and with the gusto the Bible writers' minds demand in order to quench themselves and their obvious sexual desires and frustrations.

This book is written from my mind's viewpoint and my opinion, and in my opinion it cannot possibly be any true historical reference. What does this story say and why does it say it? What is it supposed to mean? Again, if it was written today no one would believe it and yet this is part of a book which still holds sway with many millions of today's people. It is a book which many of the world's inhabitants actually do believe totally and live their lives by. Once again, I feel it has to be totally wrong but once again I have to ask the question, is it indeed wrong or is it me?

Question.

From the very beginning of time, the Bible tells us that God spoke to everyone about everything. He spoke to Adam and Eve. He spoke to Noah. He spoke to Abraham. He spoke aloud and quite articulately but just when did he stop speaking aloud and why did he do it? If there is this all-powerful and omnipresent being, why doesn't he speak aloud today so that we do not have to doubt his existence? Just a few words would suffice. 'Hello, subjects. This is your God speaking. I love you all. Go to church on Sunday.'

Something like that would do.

A dark thought in my mind is this though. In the past he has murdered so many and tortured so many others that, just perhaps, he is frightened to show his face. This is a thought from my mind but if we are to believe everything we read in the Bible then this could well be the case. A lady once accused me of, 'Only believing in reality'. Am I being too realistic again?

Genesis 20

I know we have covered Genesis in some detail but I thought we would move on again, to Genesis 20-22 as it is another great little story.

Now Abraham moved into a region of the Negev and lived in a region between Kadesh and Shur and for a while he stayed in Gerar and there Abraham said of his wife Sarah, 'She is my sister.'

Then Abimelek, who was the king of Gerar, sent for her and took her.

Abraham did like to move about a bit and here he was in Gerar and it seems the King of Gerar was quickly made aware of his presence, because he hurriedly sent for Abraham's wife. But why? Was he so sex crazed that he had to have every woman who entered the city? Do we visit London and have our wives kidnapped immediately by Prince Philip? And, without wishing to be disrespectful to Abraham or Sarah at all, Sarah was probably a lovely lady but she was getting on for 100 years old. Was she such a sought-after prize? According to the Bible she was still fertile but I doubt, no offence to her, if she was all too alluring. There is nothing wrong with older women and I do still find my wife very attractive but this lady was very elderly and surely if the king had the power to take any woman in the city that he wanted, he would have picked someone slightly less old and more nubile. Still, according to the story he did take her so let's get on with the story.

But Abimelek was about to get his comeuppance because God came to him in a dream and said Abimelek was as good as dead because he had taken a married woman.

Now, poor old Abimelek, although he was a little hasty in his choice of women, did not know his victim was married because that sneaky Abraham had told him a fib. He had told him Sarah was his sister. It seems a little naughty of Abraham to have told this fib as he was so righteous and all that but it seems this was just another cunning plan because, as we will see, he comes out of it all in the end with quite a haul. But he had lied. He had broken one of the Ten Commandments. Should he have been rewarded for it?

Abilmelek quickly told the Lord that he had been tricked. He explained that Abraham had said Sarah was his sister and Sarah had said Abraham was her brother. He didn't know, did he? He pleaded with God not to kill him because of a misunderstanding. He said he had done it all with a clear conscience and clean hands. He had, I suppose, but how do you just kidnap women, quite at random, with a clear conscience and clean hands?

Then God confessed that he knew Abimelek had a clean conscience and clear hands (or the other way around) because it was he who had kept Abilmelek from having sex with Sarah. See, he was in on the act too. It was a cunning plan devised between him and Abraham and it worked. God instructed Abilmelek to return Sarah to Abraham and then he would live and be prayed for. This seems a little strange if you think about it. Here is God telling Abilmelek to go to Abraham so that Abraham could pray to God for him, but God was already there with Abimelek, wasn't he? Why didn't he just grant him his wishes there and then? Perhaps it was because the story needed Abimelek to go to Abraham so that the prize for the cunning plan could be delivered. The next morning Abilmelek summoned all his officials and he told them what had happened and just how close he had come to being killed and they were all very afraid. I should think they were because God was about and no one knew what was in store when he was.

Being king, Abilmelek didn't return Sarah to her husband; he called for Abraham to collect her which he did. He must have looked smug when he turned up, knowing his plan was about to come to fruition. 'What have you done to us? How have I wronged you that you have brought such great guilt upon me and my kingdom?' Abilmelek said, starting the conversation. 'You have done things to me that should never be done. What is your reason for doing this?'

I like the bit where Abilmelek says Abraham has done things to him that should never be done. Hadn't he just kidnapped Abraham's wife as soon as she entered the city? Who was he to talk of right and wrong?

Abraham replied that he felt there was no fear of God in the city and so he would have been killed because of his wife. Question: If he realised this then why, unless he had his plan, did he enter the city in the first place? He explained that he had only half lied because Sarah was indeed his sister, but only a half-sister as they only shared a father. He said he had told Sarah that she could show her love for him by telling everyone that he was her brother. It makes little sense to me but then it obviously worked for them. It obviously made sense to Abilmelek as well because he immediately had sheep and cattle and male and female servants brought to Abraham as gifts. See, the plan is working. Abilmelek also said his land was before Abraham and he could live where he liked. A small farm with a large house would have been handy to house all the new animals and servants.

Then Abilmelek turned to Sarah and said he was to give her husband 1,000 shekels of silver to cover the offence against her. So poor old Sarah had been kidnapped and if it hadn't been for God's intervention she would have been ravished by a sex-crazed king, but as recompense for her being so cruelly wronged, the compensation was awarded to her husband. Yes, typical biblical logic again.

Sarah had been returned to her husband. All was well and God and Abraham's plan had worked and Abraham had become much wealthier, so Abraham prayed to God. God lifted his curse and healed Abilmelek, his wife and their female slaves so that they could have children again because the Lord had kept all in Abilmelek's household from conceiving children until Sarah was returned. It says Abilmelek was healed as well. Could be have children as well, then? Or did he have something else wrong with him? A nasty cold perhaps or meningitis?

And so, this is the story of Abraham and Abilmelek. Again, it cannot be true but it is delightful. And, also again, do we take it as a true account of ancient history or do we have to see it as allegorical and have to interpret it as we wish? Perhaps my mind is too plain and simple because I plainly and simply interpret it as God and Abraham hatching a dastardly plan for Abraham to get rich, but the key to the plan is the possible sacrifice of Abraham's dear 90-year-old or so wife, Sarah.

Abraham wanted to get rich so desperately that he offered his wife in order to obtain his wishes. Also, am I being too cynical here? But if God was so all-powerful and could do anything and Abraham meant so much to him, why did he not just magic up the sheep and cattle and shekels and servants for him in the first place? This would have prevented all sorts of dastardly deeds and would have made Sarah's kidnapping totally unnecessary. This is my interpretation of events but yours may well be different.

The Bible states that adultery is a terrible thing, but in the next chapter of Genesis we see that Abraham has a son by Hagar, one of his servants, and the son is blessed by God. It seems we are dealing with double standards again.

Abraham than went on to almost slaughter his son Isaac just because God had told him to. He got as far as binding his son on an altar, ready to give him up as a burnt offering. As with circumcising all the males in his household, Abraham was even willing to do this without the slightest of question as to why? Put yourself in Abraham's position. You have a son and that son is obviously hugely loved by you, but then God tells you to go and tie him to an alter and kill him. Would you do it? Well, maybe some are so insanely religious that they just might. If you think you could possibly be tempted then, sorry, but I suggest you seek help immediately.

Nahor's sons

A short passage from Genesis 22. *Some time later Abraham was told, 'Mikah is also a mother; she has borne sons to your brother Nahor. Uz the first born, Buz his brother, Kemuel (the father of Aram), Kesed, Hazo, Pildash, Jidlaph and Bethuel.' 23. Bethuel became the father of Rebekah. Milkah bore these eight sons to Abraham's brother Nahor. 24. His concubine, whose name was Reumah, also had sons: Tebah, Gaham, Tahash and Maakah.*

It seems Abraham hasn't seen his brother Nahor for some time because he is only just being told of the birth of all these people. In the time they have not been in touch, Nahor's wife has given birth to Kemuel and he in turn has fathered Aram but this is not my point of quoting this little piece. Its point is, once again, here we are with a total of twelve sons being born but only the mention of one token daughter, Rebekah. And as with his brother Abraham, it seems Nahor was partial to adultery as well, because four of his sons were by his concubine, Reumah.

Deuteronomy 22

This section of the Bible relates to virginity. In the Bible, all brides were supposed to be virgins. I think we will be talking about that sex thing again.

13. If a man takes a wife and go in unto her and hate her.

This is such a short sentence but it says so much. Firstly, we are talking of a marriage union between a man and a woman and, supposedly, both are consenting to the union. They are deeply in love and have just had a wonderful ceremony which has been blessed by God and then on the wedding night they go to bed and fall passionately into each other's arms and make love.

The trouble here is that they do not make love, do they? He 'Goes in unto her!' How eloquent and romantic that is.

And then, 'He hates her'. At first I took this literally. He has married her and now he just hates her but no. He realises she was not a virgin after all and this is why he hates her. Oh dear, what a terrible woman!

14. And give occasions of speech against her, and bring up an evil name upon her, and say, I took this woman, and when I came to her, I found her not a maid.

Firstly, he has found his wife not to be a virgin. Fair enough, if this is what she claimed to be but what of him? It does not question the fact, was he a virgin? Again, it is the men who are unquestioned while the women have to fit to their strict stereotype of a 'biblical wife'. He may have had dozens of past lovers but that's okay. He seems to talk openly against her and call her an evil name but if it was he who was not the virgin then he would probably force his wife not to say anything against him for fear of punishment. I wonder how many 'non-virgins' had previously married and then had been in trouble because he was the cause of their non-virginity. Only speculating here.

15. Then shall the father of the damsel, and her mother take and bring forth tokens of the damsel's virginity unto the elders of the city in the gate.

So the mother and father of the lady involved now have the onus put upon them to prove their daughter's chastity. They have to bring forth 'tokens of her virginity'. I'm sorry but I am thinking hard and cannot work this one out. Am I being stupid? What is a token of virginity? How can you have such a thing? Maybe they brought forth her diary which read:

September 12th. No sex today.

September 13th. No sex today.

September 14th. No sex today.

September 15th. Thought a little about sex but still didn't have any. And so on.

Perhaps they could bring forth a chastity belt or a signed statement to say that she never ever left the house and no male visitors ever called. Could they swear and sign a form to say she had been locked in her bedroom for the past twenty years? If you understand this better than me then that's good. Well done.

16. And the damsel's father shall say unto the elders, I gave my daughter unto this man and he hateth her.

This is obviously a very serious crime as it has gone as high as the city elders but, then again, in those days anything to do with sex was serious and something good to gossip about.

17. And, lo, he has given occasions of speech against her, saying I found not thy daughter a maid; and yet these are the tokens of my daughter's virginity. And they shall spread the cloth before the elders of the city.

I must say I am a little lost here again. What are these tokens of virginity and how and why would they 'Spread the cloth before the elders of the city'? Is the spreading of the cloth another way of saying they give their evidence of their daughter's chastity? They are spreading their evidence before them? But why would a cloth be seen as evidence? Help me out, someone.

18. And the elders of that city shall take the man and chastise him.

The case is before the elders of the city and it seems if the damsel's virginity is proven then her husband will be chastised. We find out in the next piece just how he is to be chastised. I am already thinking that, perhaps, his wife may be punished just a little harder if it is proven she was not actually a virgin. We will have to wait and see.

19. And they shall amerce him an hundred shekels of silver, and give them unto the father of the damsel because he has brought up an evil name upon a virgin of Israel: and she shall be his wife: He may not put her away all the days of his life.

Fair enough, I suppose. The man has wronged his wife and is to be fined the usual one hundred shekels of silver and this would be given to her father. Again, she is the one who has been wronged but the compensation is to be given to someone else. All she gets out of the situation is to stay married to the man who totally distrusted her on the very first day of their marriage and what a basis of a good marriage that is. And, moreover, it seems she is stuck with him for the rest of his or her life. I bet the father took the one hundred shekels as well. Surely if they were a newly married couple that amount of money would have come in very handy, probably as a down payment for a mortgage. Still, we don't want to make a woman's life too comfortable, do we? She is just a woman, after all.

20. But if this thing be true, and the tokens of virginity be not found for the damsel.

Whoops! Here we go. I bet she is in for it.

21. Then they shall bring out the damsel to the door of her father's house, and the men of the city shall stone her with stones that she dies, because she has wrought folly in Israel, to play the whore in her father's house: so shalt though put evil way from among you.

I said she was in for it and it was obvious, wasn't it? This is the misogynistic Bible. If she was found to be a virgin then her husband was to be fined a few shekels, but if she was not a virgin then all the men of the city would throw stones at her until she was dead. What brain would ever think of such a punishment? And I can hear you say it still happens today. It does and it is ridiculous. Ridiculous, inhuman and totally pathetic. Why would anyone, other than a complete fool, want to do it? What sort of human being could throw the stones? The trouble is, they would and they would even thoroughly enjoy doing so.

Also here, have you noticed again it is the men of the city who do this? Not the women. It is the men when, more than likely, it was one of them who had sex with her in the first place. I bet even he would enjoy throwing rocks. Humans are supposed to be closely related to apes. I would think the apes would be ashamed to admit it.

The passage says she has wrought folly in Israel and has been a whore in her father's house. Why again is it so dreadful to give in to the sexual urges her God had given her? And what of the man responsible? Did he stand up and say, 'Sorry, elders it was me', or did he just carry on throwing his stones? It seems in the next excerpt that there is some redress to the situation.

22. If a man be found lying with a woman married to a husband, then they shall both of them die, both the man that lay with the woman and the woman. So shalt thou put away evil from Israel.

Well, it seems there is some equality in biblical life after all but, as I have said before, is not being a virgin on a lady's wedding night or committing adultery deserving of such utterly barbaric punishment? Especially when their God made sex such a completely pleasurable thing.

23/24. If a damsel that is a virgin be betrothed unto a husband, and a man find her in the city, and lie with her;

Then ye shall bring them both unto the gate of that city, and ye shall stone them with stones that they die; the damsel, because she cried not, being in the city; and the man because he had humbled his neighbour's wife: so you shall put away evil from among you.

Just a thought here. Didn't God later go on to impregnate another man's wife?

25. But if a man finds a betrothed damsel in a field, and the man force her, and lie with her then the man only that lay with her shall die.

Fair enough, I suppose. A little justice for the women at last. It's a wonder they didn't stone her for leading him on.

26. But unto the damsel thou shalt do nothing; there is in the damsel no sin worthy of death: for as when a man rises against his neighbour and slayeth him, even so is this matter.

Makes sense.

27. For he found her in the field, and the betrothed damsel cried, and there was none to save her.

Again, this makes sense but I can't help thinking about the minds of the writers of it. Is finding a damsel in a field and having sex with her just one of their little fantasies?

28/29. If a man finds a damsel that is a virgin, which is not betrothed, and lay hold on her and lie with her, and they be found;

Then the man that lay with her shall give unto the damsel's father fifty shekels of silver, and she shall be his wife: For he has humbled her, he may not put her away all of his days.

How lovely this is. It reminds me of the old saying, 'Get your coat, girl. You're pulled!'

Perhaps we should look at this from the damsel's point of view. Here she is, being a good girl and not giving in to the temptation of sex when, all of a sudden, this stranger lays hold of her and rapes her. Suddenly her life is in turmoil. She has just been terribly violated and with the laws as they were at the time, you may think the perpetrator would be stoned to death or something just as horrible. But no. Again, this is the Bible so things are not quite as logical and straightforward as they could be. The man has violated and ruined the lady's life and what is his terrible punishment? He has to give her father fifty shekels of silver. So, the man who accuses his wife of not being a virgin when, in fact, she was, is fined one hundred shekels but the man who rapes a virgin is only fined fifty. Once more in this story, it is the girl who has been raped but it is the father who reaps the reward and, as if this wasn't enough, the girl then has to marry her attacker and live with him for the rest of her life. I can't see this as being another loving, tender and caring relationship, can you?

30. A man shall not take his father's wife, nor discover his father's skirt.

For a man to take his father's wife would mean either she was his mother or his step-mother. If she was his mother, then this would make good sense but if his step-mother was young and alluring then the temptation may be there. It would not really be morally correct to take either and this part of the excerpt is plain and simple but the last few words are making my mind boggle. 'He shall not discover his father's skirt?' What does this mean? Does it mean he has suspicions that his father is a transvestite and he mustn't go looking for any women's clothing because he would be disappointed in his father if he found evidence to back up his theory? Colloquially the word 'skirt' has been used to mean woman. Perhaps a son should not look into his father's extramarital affairs. I don't know.

Once again, this passage from the Bible is very reminiscent of most others. It portrays women as second-class citizens and brings in sex with abandonment. How can a woman be stoned to death for not being a virgin on her wedding night? What would that do for today's society? There would be no one left and piles of bloodied rocks everywhere. And let's look at it from another perspective. Let's say I was a young man and I met a beautiful girl and fell head over heels in love with her. She is a good, wholesome virgin but she promises me that once we are married she will be a nymphomaniac in bed and will satisfy my every wish, need and even each and every kinky desire. Of course, I am taken in by this and look forward to my honeymoon with great longing. We eventually marry after a couple of years of celibacy and then the night comes. I brush my teeth, freshen up after the day's ceremonies and activities and walk eagerly to the bedroom where she is waiting, only to find she is too shy to take off her coat and is one hundred percent frigid and actually hates even the thought of sex. I am not saying we should have sex with everyone we meet, but finding out you and your wife are sexually compatible before you get married is quite a wise thing to do. I would also add that this part of my story would be the same for the wife if it was the other way around.

To fall in love is beautiful and a big part of that falling in love has to be the physical side of things, as there is absolutely no better way of showing that love than through actually making love. Sex doesn't always have to be the be all and end all of every relationship but in the relationships of most young people, it is a vital part and has to be right. I have thought long and hard about the next statement but I do feel I have to include it. It is something once said to me, years ago, by an old country gentleman.

"Well, boy," he said. "Before you get married you gotta make sure it fits."

Crude, I know but true, if only in meaning you have to make sure your needs and desires are compatible. In a good, warm, loving marriage you could be together for sixty years. Isn't it best to make sure things are right before you commit to it? And lastly, if we all wanted to and had to marry virgins then I think most of us would still be single and, being men, it would be our own fault if our chosen partners weren't. Someone had to have taken their virginity away.

It would be easy to say that sexual morality has slipped too far these days and perhaps, in some instances, this would be totally correct, but I do feel we cannot live in a modern society and still uphold ideas and ideals that were written down by Bronze Age thinkers. The world moves on and, to a certain and healthy extent, we must follow it.

Through the death of my late wife I had to remarry at the age of fifty-three. Where was I going to find a virgin at that age? It reminds me of a song by a man called Reckless Eric which was entitled, *I'd go the whole wide world - just to find her.* I think I would have had to have done.

God made Adam from dust.

Just how do you make a fully functioning brain, heart, lungs, liver or reproductive system out of dust?

Also, if God made Adam from dust so easily, then why did he bother ripping poor old Adam's rib out to make Eve? Surely there was plenty more dust around?

If Adam was made of dust then so are we, if we are supposed to be his descendants. I know for a fact that we are made out of hydrogen, carbon, oxygen, nitrogen and calcium plus a few other minerals. If we were made of dust and it became windy, wouldn't we blow away?

Genesis 38

I know we have been and are still covering Genesis but here is another wonderful story I would like to talk about, the story of Judah and Tamar.

Judah left his brothers and went to stay with a man of Adullam named Hirah. While he was there he met the daughter of a Canaanite man named Shua. He married her and made love to her. She became pregnant and gave birth to a son (Here we go again) named Er. Then she conceived again and gave birth to another son called Onan, followed by another called Shelah.

Judah went on to get a wife for Er, his firstborn, but things started to get a bit messy. Er married Tamar, the lady chosen by his father and you may think they would live happily ever after, but no. Again, this is the Bible so as Er was wicked in the Lord's sight, the Lord put him to death, which is probably fair enough in the eyes of the Lord but it led to poor old Tamar being a widow, so Judah turned to Onan and said, 'Sleep with your brother's wife and fulfil your duty to her as a brother-in-law to raise up offspring for your brother.'

But Onan knew that the child would not be his, so whenever he slept with his brother's wife, he spilled his semen on the ground to keep from providing offspring for his brother.

Of course, what he did was wicked in the eyes of the Lord so he killed him as well.

Onan's brother was dead so, it seems in those days, it was a brother's duty to impregnate his sister-in-law. It doesn't mention if Onan was married, so we cannot judge him, but why was he worried that any child produced from the union would not be his? Who else would be the father? Perhaps he felt any child would still belong to his dead brother. Whatever his reasons were, he took steps to make sure the lady did not become pregnant and was put to death. In his own mind he was just using logic. Was this a crime? In God's eyes it was and it was not just a crime. It was, again, a crime worthy of capital punishment.

It seemed Tamar was something of a jinx, as she had very quickly played a part in the death of two of Judah's sons, so Judah told her to go away and live with her father. He hadn't given up on her completely, though, because he had plans for her and another son, Shelah, when he was old enough. Perhaps with all these sons being born to everyone, girls were rare and Judah thought while he had Tamar in his family he had better use her.

After a while Judah's wife, the daughter of Shua, died, so after a period of grieving, Judah went off with a friend to Timnah to see the men who were shearing his sheep and when Tamar was told of this she took off her widow's clothes, covered herself in a veil to disguise herself and sat down at the entrance of Enaim, which is on the road to Timnah, for she saw that although Shelah had grown up he had not been given to her as a husband.

Her little plan was flawed though and it took a nasty twist, because Judah saw her and thought she was a prostitute because her face was covered. It seemed he was delighted and jumped at the chance and asked her to have sex with him. (Again, why does everything come down to sex?) One may think that her father-in-law wanting sex with her could possibly offend and even disgust her in some way but no: she asked him what he had to offer. I suppose you may as well keep it in the family. Judah said he would get her a young goat from his flock. He also gave her his seal and its cord and his staff as a pledge until the goat arrived and it seems Tamar was well pleased, so she slept with him and she became pregnant and then went off to put her widow's clothes back on.

Judah sent her the goat but those delivering it could not find her, so she had prostituted herself to her father-in-law but was not going to receive full payment and when Judah asked around of the shrine prostitute, everyone told him that there were none in the area, so Judah was puzzled but then, three months later, he was told that his daughter-in-law had prostituted herself and she was pregnant. He was the father and you might think he would be slightly sympathetic to her cause but no. He demanded that she was brought out and burned to death. Lovely.

But it seemed Judah still hadn't worked it out somehow and was unaware it was she he had slept with, so Tamar told everyone the father of the child was the person who owned the seal and cord and the staff that she showed. Then Judah realised his mistake and said she was holier than him and he didn't sleep with her again.

To give the story a happy ending, Tamar gave birth to not one son but two. Where did all the women come from?

Again, as with most other stories, this is a charming and totally inane and naive piece of literature but, in my mind, it cannot be true. Can it?

Childhood Diseases

I have seen reports where children have had cancer and if they manage to recover from it, those involved with them sincerely thank God and praise him on high. Am I wrong here again when I say, wasn't it God who created cancer in the first place? If God created everything, then he created cancer in children. Below is a list of other things God must have created for children:

Deafness

Blindness

Cerebral Palsy

Bodily Deformities

Spina Bifida

Meningitis

Malaria

Heart Defects

Asthma

Cystic Fibrosis

Down's syndrome

Juvenile arthritis

Autism

Dwarfism

Hydrocephalus

I could go on and on and on but I think I have made my point. And weren't many of those children who recovered in hospital, being treated by modern medicines and professional, educated, dedicated and gifted staff who understood science? Would the children have survived if they had just been left at home with a prayer being offered at their bedside? Can we say if they live, then God made them better and if they die, it must have been the work of the devil? Wouldn't that be just a little too simplistic? How is it that more and more children are surviving awful diseases and illnesses as science progresses? Surely it has to be because of science and not just because God is beginning to care more?

Ezekiel.

Just as I was thinking of trying to get away from talking about sex in the Bible I came across this. Is this what we should be reading and following? Let me explain with Ezekiel 23. *Two Adulterous Sisters.* I will say that I have read several differing allegorical statements as to just what this story means but, as I say, they are differing versions which leads anyone to think that the reader has to make up their own minds what the writing does actually portray. I am a plain and realistic person and my mind can only see what is written. If that is not the case, then why do they not write what is meant in the first place? Someone could hang a painting in a gallery which is simply a white background with a random splash of red paint in the middle and in viewing it one person may say it is a, 'Representation of the Japanese flag which, because the red is in disarray, states that the Japanese government and its people are in turmoil', while another may say, 'It is the blood of the Christian martyrs which has been shed upon a virgin land'. I would be inclined to say it was a random splash of red paint on a white background. Am I wrong? Am I, as a person, indeed too realistic and simplistic?

Am I truly missing something that others get great knowledge from?

23: 1-5. The word of the lord came to me: Son of man, there were two women, daughters of the same mother. They became prostitutes in Egypt, engaging in prostitution from their youth. In that land, their breasts were fondled and their virgin bosoms were caressed. The older was named Oholah, and her sister was named Oholibah. They were mine and gave birth to sons and daughters. Oholah is Samaria, and Oholibah is Jerusalem.

These two sisters, or half-sisters, were prostitutes, which makes me wonder. The lady in Deuteronomy 22 who, if she told her husband she was a virgin when she wasn't, was called a whore and would have been stoned to death and yet these sisters are clearly and openly prostitutes and it seems fine with everyone. Why is that?

Perhaps the rest of the story will tell us of some huge moral or enlightenment, or something intense. Perhaps it purveys some great course that we should follow. A course which we should live our lives by, but no. This is the Bible, which is supposed to be read by everyone with a leaning towards religion and these people do include children. There seems, to me, to be no great moral or message at all. All it is is sex. What possible need could there ever be to write about these two females having their breasts fondled and their virgin bosoms caressed? Again, am I being stupid? Is there something here that I just do not understand? Am I too stupid to comprehend? This sort of thing was included in the story of *Lady Chatterley's Lover* and that was deeply frowned upon in 1928 when it was only a story. The contents of this piece are supposed to be fact and yet it seems it is accepted with open arms. Am I wrong in saying I see it as a blatant way to put more sex in this 'holy' book and I see that as a problem?

Another problem arises in the story in that it says their 'virgin bosoms were caressed'. They were prostitutes and sold themselves to men. Did they just start by selling their bosoms to be caressed, because if they sold themselves fully it would only have been one customer who would have had the chance to caress their 'virgin' bosoms?

It says, 'They were mine', but whose were they? I am missing something here, I know. Is this person their father or is it God? Is it their pimp, perhaps?

No. Looking at it and studying it more closely, I realise that the narrator is, in fact, Ezekiel himself. He is acknowledged as being a Hebrew prophet. Why he is saying, 'They were mine', though, I do not know. Was he their pimp or was he their father or master, perhaps? Many will judge me here and say I should know but in this instance, if it is obvious and I cannot see it then I am ignorant of the facts and I do apologise and will get on with the story.

This is quite a long passage (probably because of all the sexual hype involved) so I shall not write it all out but I shall try and summarise it in my own words.

Oholah lusted after her lovers, the Assyrians. They were warriors, governors and commanders who were clothed in blue. They were all young, handsome men who rode horses. She gave herself to all the elite of the Assyrians and defiled herself with all the idols of everyone she lusted after. She carried on her prostitution as she had in Egypt, where all the young men slept with her, caressed her virgin bosom and poured out their lust on her.

So this is a little bit more about Oholah. It seems she was quite a girl and had one hell of a sex-drive. She had it and obviously made a good living out of it. What is bothering me, though, is the piece which reads that she, 'Defiled herself with all the idols of everyone she lusted after'. She obviously had sex with her customers but how did she 'defile herself with their idols'? I see an 'idol' as an image or carving. A doll perhaps. Is the story's writer getting carried away here? I think I shall just move on without going to deeply into matters and my thoughts, as my thoughts are becoming, possibly, a little too vivid.

It goes on to say that 'I' delivered her into the hands of her lovers, the Assyrians. (Perhaps Ezekiel was her pimp.) They stripped her naked, took away her sons and daughters and killed her with the sword.

Poor old Oholah had worked so hard touring and giving pleasure to her Assyrian clients and then what happened? They showed their great respect by killing her.

Her sister Obolibah happened to see this and you would think any normal woman would have been horrified and would mourn the loss of her dear sister dreadfully, but no, not this one. Evidently the whole incident just made her even more depraved and she, too, lusted after the same men.

Sex is a strange old thing. You would think, with what had happened, she would stay well clear but no. She needed sex and this looked like the place to get it so she too defiled herself with them before carrying on her prostitution still further. She saw figures of Chaldeans painted on a wall and decided she had to have them as well, so she sent for them.

Then the Babylonians came to her and defiled her in their lust but afterwards, she didn't seem too happy about it so she turned away from them in disgust. As time marched by she became more and more promiscuous, especially as she thought about her earlier days in Egypt, where '*She had lusted after her lovers whose genitals were like those of donkeys and whose emission was like that of horses*'.

WHAT!

This is the Bible. This is what children are taught. Come on! What has this nonsense ever got to do with life, history, religion, God, or any morality? Why does this stuff have to be included if not purely and only to fulfil the fetish of the writer involved? Can this be seen as some kind of teaching for us? Perhaps it is just purely allegorical and the conclusion has to be drawn by us individually. I must say that my conclusion is my conclusion, and my conclusion says, sorry, but it has to be absolute nonsense. It can have nothing whatsoever to do with anything. Well, nothing outside of some randy mind, that is.

On with the story.

Maybe she had been a little over the top with all her lustings because the Lord thought he had better speak to her. He told her he would stir up her lovers against her and we must remember, there were a few of them. There were the Babylonians, the Childeans, the men of Pekod, Shoa and Koa and all the Assyrians. He said they would come against her with weapons, chariots and wagons and with a throng of people with small and large shields and helmets. I don't think she would have held out too much hope of a victory as she was slightly outnumbered especially if they had small *and* large shields. There would be thousands of men against one woman. What possible relevance did the size of their shields have?

He said she would be punished by their standards and he would direct his jealous anger towards her. But why was it jealous anger? She was a sex-crazed prostitute, for goodness' sake. What was there to be jealous of? And what was it to be 'punished by their standards'? They had all paid to have sex with her, and was she the only prostitute they had ever paid for? I very much doubt it and I very much doubt if their standards were too high either.

He went on to say they would cut off her noses and ears. This seems wrong as she only has one nose but it seems he is now talking to a group of people, as it goes on to say that those left after this would fall by the sword. The Lord then goes on to say her sons and daughters would be taken from her so perhaps this is the group he was talking about when he mentioned noses. He said that anyone else that was left would be consumed by fire. She was to be stripped of her clothes and fine jewellery. The Lord finished his speech by saying that she would be left stark naked so that all could see what she had been. From the sound of it, to most people, men at least, this would have been a sight that was nothing new.

I really do want to discuss other things in the Bible and get away from sex totally but it is everywhere and I find it very difficult to reconcile the fact. To my mind it does nothing for the book at all. If anything, it simply detracts from any good message that the book tries to deliver. I will look and have a think though. Surely I can find some nice, harmless little story to talk about without upsetting the children.

As children we are all told of the Bible and, at first, we believe it because we have been told to do so by adults and these are the wise people we are supposed to look up to and learn from. So many people just grow up still believing the Bible is the true word of God and it is factual. How many do actually read it, though? Because I find the more I read it, the more fanciful it seems to become. Perhaps it is just me again but the fact is, if the Bible is not fact then it has to be fiction, just like *Lady Chatterley's Lover*, a book which, to my mind, is far less harmful to those who read it. At least we do not believe it and then try to live our lives by it.

As a child I was sent to Sunday school. There we learned the simple and harmless stories of the Nativity and Jesus' life and we also learned of Adam and Eve and Noah's ark, with all the colourful animals happily going on board two by two. Isn't it strange that we were never told of the customers of prostitutes who were hung like donkeys and had the emissions of horses? Perhaps they were a little frightened of us thinking there may have been a slight possibility that the Bible was not quite fully true. Of course, you are correct. Sexual explicitness is not for children but if that is the case, then why is it in the Bible?

Here I would like to quote a lovely lady who posted a true story on Facebook and did not fully understand what she had witnessed. She said, 'A beautiful woman I knew died a long and painful death. She was a religious person. Family said God was giving her a final test before she went to heaven.

'My non-religious friend had a long and painful death. Religious family said he was being punished for all his earthly sins. This is what is amazing about religion, you get to make it up as you go along.

Thank you for your permission to quote.

Another post I did not quite get or agree with is this one: 'If we allow gays to marry then they will be stealing our girlfriends.'

Think about it.

Jesus

I said in the first chapter of this book that heaven and hell are a central part of the Bible, but another huge and even greater part has to be Jesus. Without Jesus, the whole thing would probably collapse. The birth of Jesus and the New Testament probably refreshed everyone's thoughts on religion. He became the central part of a reinvigorated story, so let's look at how he came to be and what effect his life has had, both on the Bible and the world we live in.

The first thing to say is that when we talk about God and Genesis, no one is really sure when it was all supposed to have happened. As I have said, if science is to be believed, the earth's origins date back 4.5 billion years yet 'young earth' believers say it is only a history of some 6,000 years. The birth of Jesus is said to have only been 2,000 years ago, at the time of the Roman Empire. We have much knowledge of the latter and as it is not that long ago, it suggests to my mind that, yes, Jesus could possibly have existed although, once again, there is no proof whatsoever, apart from what is written in the Bible. With me being a fervent atheist (but one who is willing to be taught) you may be surprised by my possible belief in this, but I do think Jesus could easily have been a real person. But then again, Paul Daniels (RIP) and David Blaine are real people, but it doesn't mean their magic is real, does it?

Before we go on to his actual story I shall give you my totally cynical theory. Please remember the fact that I am totally cynical and this is only my theory. It is from my mind and in no way am I saying it is true. Several have closely echoed my thoughts but I am never going to shout from a roof top or from behind a sandwich board that this is what actually happened, as I have absolutely no evidence. (That sounds familiar.)

Mary was betrothed to Joseph and he, being a Christian and following his beliefs and Bible doctrine, had not made love to her. He wanted her to be a virgin until their wedding night. It is against the odds this would happen today, but who could blame him then for being such a gentleman?

Science had not progressed too far by these times and almost everyone thought and readily agreed that gods were the answer to everything and who could blame them? There was nothing else to contradict their thoughts. If, when they turned to Christianity, they were told that God created man on a Saturday what argument was there to question it? If the Bible pointed to the earth being just 4,000 years old, then it was 4,000 years old. No one had the thought, tools or education to refute it. The Bible was all they had. Understanding was in its infancy and although the Romans were good at constructing villas, building roads, making wine and crucifying people, it would be some years before people started to question why and how everything really happened. A bird would be in the sky because a god put it there. A mountain was there and had always been there in that same state. The continents and oceans were set and static and life was just life because they never, ever needed or felt the need to wonder differently. Religion was religion and gods were gods and people felt they needed someone or something to follow. Having something to look up to and pray to helped them aspire to better things as their lives were hard. For some Romans, life was good. They had the power to take whatever they wished and desired but for most, it was a tough existence and if help had to come from prayer, then so be it. The problem arose when, for example, a good harvest was prayed for and then it happened, and if it happened it must have meant their prayers had been answered, so they prayed again for this and everything else. The fact that particular year had seen just the right amount of rain and sunshine at just the right times never came into their heads. They had prayed and their prayers had been answered and that was that.

At first, they believed in many different gods. They had no better understanding and the thought of a god or two or many helping them along their way could not harm but could, in their minds, only be quite beneficial. They had:

Saturn: The King of Gods. He was the god of seed-sowing and had the Romans hold the festival of Saturnalia to honour and celebrate him.

Jupiter: Jupiter was Saturn's son and was the god of the sky. He later took over from his father and was the most important god.

Juno: This was Jupiter's wife and she was the goddess of, and looked after, women.

Neptune: Neptune was the god of the sea and was also Jupiter's brother.

Minerva: Was the goddess of wisdom and women's work such as weaving.

Mars: The god of war, although he was originally the god of farming.

Venus. She was the goddess of love and was the lover of Mars.

Diana: The goddess of the moon.

Fortuna: The goddess of luck.

Janus: The god of gates and doors. (I love that one.)

Bellona: Goddess of war.

Laetitia: Minor Roman goddess of gaiety.

Mercury: The god of thieves, commerce and travellers. Also, the messenger of the gods.

Pluto: The god of death and the riches under the earth.

Proserpina: Pluto's wife and goddess of the underworld.

Vulcan: The god of fire and blacksmiths.

Cupid: God of love.

Bacchus: The god of wine, parties, festivals, madness and merriment.

Vesta: Virgin goddess of home and hearth.

Terra: Goddess of the earth.

Victoria: The goddess of victory.

Lupa: Immortal Roman wolf goddess.

Apollo: The god of the sun. He rides the sun chariot.

Ceres: The god of farming and agriculture.

These are not all of the Roman gods but it does indicate that the Romans looked for help wherever they could. Also, with such a vast number of gods, just perhaps it can be seen why, eventually, many condensed it down to just one, a Christian one. It was simpler. The Greeks also had their own set of gods.

Christianity didn't establish itself throughout the Roman empire overnight. At first it was frowned upon and many lost their lives because of their religion. They were used as scapegoats for deeds they had not done and many saw horrible deaths. The Romans were quite a bloodthirsty bunch and often saw death as entertainment. As we know, Christians were thrown to the lions or forced to fight gladiators and it was quite obvious who was going to win, especially when the Christians were either unarmed or very lightly armed whilst up against a fully armed and trained killer. Lions were often kept hungry and would kill their rivals and partially eat them before the show was ended. Some were killed 'mercifully' by being beheaded with a sword which was, at least, quick. There is evidence, evidently, that the emperor Nero actually had Christians covered in pitch before being crucified. They would then be set alight to light up gardens when parties were held. These tortures seem extreme and they were, but what bothers me is that the lust for it still remains today and all kinds of evidence can be found of this throughout the world.

One of the farthest corners of the Roman Empire was Judaea, which was a land of religious fervour and ancient traditions. It was a land that had been ruled by the Romans for decades and the resentment of its people grew and grew. They were a people with their own ideas, traditions and identities and found it hard to take the fact that their lives were cast down and so sorely trodden upon by their masters. They were lost, frustrated and angry.

This is where I come, eventually, to my cynical theory. Chaos ruled and there was Mary, about to be married to Joseph when she found she was pregnant but her husband-to-be had not made love to her. She was in dire trouble, so what did she do? What could she do? She couldn't just go up to Joseph and say,

'Sorry, but I've been a bit naughty and have become pregnant by someone else,' could she?

Even in those days it had to have happened to many women. Her punishment and shame would have been far too much, so she thought and thought and eventually came up with a plan. Just think, in these times, as can still happen today in some parts of the world, she stood a good chance of being stoned to death for adultery. What would you do? She told Joseph her pregnancy was an immaculate conception and the father was not him but was in fact the Lord God Almighty. What a way out and who was Joseph to argue with the Lord? Eureka! It had happened and he had to accept it. What else could he do? If he railed against it what would his punishment have been? It was not the best scenario for him but he knew and understood how God worked and feared the consequences of refuting it or ranting against it. He couldn't even leave his wife for fear of God seeing it as abandonment so he went along with it all almost wholeheartedly.

It all did bother him to some extent though, because that night he had a dream in which he was convinced that God told him about what had happened. God said, 'Joseph, thou son of David, fear not to take unto thee Mary thy wife for that which is conceived in her is of the Holy Ghost. And she shall bring forth a son and thou shalt call his name Jesus. For he shall save his people from their sins.'

So that was it. His mind was satisfied. Mary had become pregnant, Joseph hadn't particularly liked the fact but was frightened to question it, but then it had all become clear in a dream. Joseph married Mary and a few months later little Jesus was born. He wasn't just born though, was he? It seems he was told of the immaculate conception story and later in his life, if my theory holds water, he capitalised on it fully.

As I have said, this is purely my cynical take on the matter and in no way, without proof or evidence, am I professing it is the truth but to my enquiring mind, I do find it logical and a few others have agreed.

Let's just say Jesus was born. I have no proof of my theory but, in reality, the Bible cannot show proof either so for now we will just say he was born and existed.

Jesus, the son of David.

In my plain way of thinking, I'm sorry, but I am lost already. Joseph would be his guardian but it was God who made Mary pregnant, so how could Jesus now be the son of David?

The Bible's explanation.

St Matthew

Chapter One

6. David was the King and he begat Solomon of her that had been the wife or Urias.

7. And Solomon begat Roboam and Roboam he begat Abia; And Abia begat Asa.

8. And Asa begat Josaphat and Josaphat begat Joram and Joram begat Ozias;

9. And Ozias begat Joatham and Joatham begat Achaz and Achaz begat Ezekias.

10. And Ezekias begat Manasses; And Manasses begat Amon; And Amon begat Josias;

11. And Josias begat Jechonias; And his brethren about the time they were carried away by Babylon.

12. And after they were brought to Babylon Jechonias begat Salathiel; and Salathiel begat Zorobabel.

13. And Zorobabel begat Abiud; and Abiud begat Eliakin; And Eliakin begat Azor.

14. And Azor begat Sadoc; and Sadoc begat Achin; and Achin begat Eliud.

15. And Eliud begat Eleazar; and Eleazar begat Matthan; and Matthan begat Jacob.

16. And Jacob begat Joseph the husband of Mary of whom was born Jesus.

So Jesus being the 'Son of David' isn't quite straightforward. David was in fact a very early ancestor of Joseph and Joseph wasn't even Jesus' real father. If my calculations are correct Jesus was the G-g-g-g-g-g-grandson of David through the family line of the man who was not actually his father.

I think we will have to look at it in a different way. It seems Jesus Christ (the Messiah) was the fulfilment of the prophecy of the seed of David. Jesus was the promised Messiah which meant he had to have been of the lineage of David. Jesus was the direct descendant of David through Joseph, his guardian.

To me, it is not much clearer this way but to save any arguments or hassle, I shall just refer to him as Jesus.

I'm sorry, but just a thought here. Let's say a young woman went to her fiancé today and said she was pregnant by the Lord God through an immaculate conception. Do you think he would believe her? Yes, come to think of it, some probably would and they would probably be mighty proud of the fact as well, despite all the sceptics and admonishments.

The birth of Jesus.

We all know the story of the nativity and I even played the part of Mary, just a few years ago in a care home, to entertain a group of elderly and frail people. I had no real belief in what I was portraying but they had and they thoroughly enjoyed it. It made an otherwise boring afternoon into something for them to enjoy. I may not believe but some do and they are welcome and entitled to their beliefs. These people seemed to need theirs and at their age there was nothing wrong in the fact at all.

Mary was heavily pregnant with Jesus when she and Joseph had to travel to Bethlehem because of a Roman census, but when they arrived after a long and uncomfortable journey, with Joseph walking and Mary sitting on a donkey the place was busy (No, it wasn't busy because it was Christmas) and all the accommodation was booked so, in desperation, they took up the offer of a night in a stable behind an inn. It wasn't to be just any old night though, because during it Mary gave birth to Jesus and he was laid in a manger for his bed.

It seems news spread quickly because three wise men from the east would visit him, saying, 'Where is he that is born King of the Jews? For we have seen his star in the east and have come to worship him.'

Herod the king had heard of the birth and he was troubled, and all of Jerusalem with him. He gathered together all his top people and asked them to find where Jesus was so that, he too, could go and worship him. When they all heard what the king had said, three wise men departed and followed a star which they saw in the east. It went before them until it stood still over where the child was. When they saw the star, they rejoiced with exceedingly great joy.

They reached the stable and found Mary and her child inside and they fell down and worshipped him before giving him gifts of gold, frankincense and myrrh. But it seems they had been warned not to return to Herod so they departed to their own country by another way.

After they had gone, the Angel of the Lord appeared to Joseph in another dream and told him to take the mother and child and flee into Egypt and stay there until word was brought, because Herod would seek the young child and destroy him. Naturally, Joseph did as he was told again. They stayed there until after the death of Herod and then the Lord called them out of Egypt.

But before Herod died, he saw that he had been mocked by the three wise men and was very angry and sent people to slay all the children that were in Bethlehem, and in the coasts thereof, from two years old and under.

So Jesus was born but already there was strife surrounding him. There is no concrete evidence of the actual birth of Jesus. We do not see it written down anywhere and we do not have a birth certificate. Much of what we have is either written in the Bible or has been passed down through word of mouth but as I say, I am willing to say he did probably exist. There he was, born in a stable and laid in a manger for his bed and these people came to visit him. To my mind it does not seem logical that a star could have guided people to his whereabouts. No star would travel through the sky and then suddenly stop. The story says the star 'stood' over the place where Jesus was. In my mind, I think this is perhaps just an unfortunate use of the word 'stood' as I can imagine it standing there and pointing. In reality, though, stars cannot just stop. They are seen to be travelling across the night sky due to the rotation of the earth. If the star stopped then it had to have been because the earth had stopped, which is also unlikely, to say the least.

Without thinking, anyone could probably miss the point here and ask why the people sent by Herod did not return to him? I know it said they were told not to in a message from

God, but what was the message and why was King Herod suddenly so angry? He went from wanting to see Jesus and praise him on high to suddenly wanting to destroy him. He was bluffing, of course. The birth of Jesus posed a threat to his power so he wanted him gone. His anger was such that he ordered his people to kill every child under the age of two. Jesus had just been born and Herod's wrath had been stirred. He wanted the child destroyed because of his own insecurities, but why destroy every child under two years old? As I say, Jesus had just been born, so he was a baby. How could a two-year-old possibly be him? Again, I feel the Bible is being a little dramatic here and the lust for death is rearing its ugly head again.

Anyway, Herod did die and Joseph was told to take his family into the land of Israel, but fearing Herod's son, who had inherited his father's reign, Joseph headed for Galilee where he dwelt in a city called Nazareth.

It seems Jesus grew up quickly, as the King James version of the Bible gives no account of his childhood. The next time we see him is when he meets John the Baptist and asks him to baptise him, but John has already heard of Jesus and refuses, saying that as Jesus is the powerful and holy one it should be Jesus who baptises him.

So, Joseph took his family to Nazareth and that is where Jesus grew up, but it seems word of his position in life had been spread and he soon amassed followers. As I had said before, the region was under Roman rule and the population felt downtrodden and oppressed. They needed someone to follow and receive hope from and there was Jesus, who they could see as a guiding light. I have tried hard not to think of the film *The*

Life of Brian whilst writing this, but I will give in to temptation here and quote a character played by John Cleese.

Graham Chapman (Brian): 'I'm not the Messiah.'

John Cleese: 'I say you are, Lord, and I should know. I've followed a few.'

Jesus was baptised and when he came up from the water, the heavens opened and he saw the Spirit of God descending like a dove lighting upon him. And lo, a voice from heaven, saying 'This is my beloved son, in whom I am well pleased.'

I am trying here again but I fail to see in any real world how the heavens can open and a spirit can descend like a dove, but there you go.

It seems God was well pleased with Jesus but he didn't trust him fully yet because he had him led up into the wilderness to be tempted by the devil.

Firstly, Jesus fasted for forty days and forty nights and afterwards he was hungry. And when the tempter came to him, he said, 'If thou be the Son of God, command that these stones be bread.'

But he answered and said, 'It is written. Man, shalt not live by bread alone, but by every word that proceedeth out of the mouth of God.'

And then the devil took him up into the holy city, and setteth him on a pinnacle of a temple and said to him, 'If thou be the son of God cast thyself down for it is written, "He shall give his angels charge concerning thee; and in their hands they shall bear thee up, lest at any time thou dash thy foot against a stone".' Jesus refused, of course. He told the devil it was written and he would not tempt the Lord thy God.

Again, the devil taketh him up into an exceeding high mountain, and sheweth him all the kingdoms of the world, and the glory of them and said unto him, 'All these things will I give thee if thou will fall down and worship me.'

Jesus was having none of it and said, 'Get thee hence, Satan; for it is written, "Thou shalt worship the Lord thy God, and him only shalt thou serve".'

So Jesus was not tempted and the devil left, but Jesus had heard bad news. John had been imprisoned so he went to Galilee.

I'm sorry to have to bring up this old chestnut again but once more, we are hearing that God said this, Jesus said that and the devil said something else. We have no account for anything that was said unless the scribe who actually wrote it was with them at the time and witnessing and writing every word as it was spoken. Maybe he or she was. We will look into the actual writing of the Bible later. In Genesis it is said that God said, 'Let there be light'. Who was he speaking to and who was recording it? He was on his own.

Also, as with the fact we have no idea what God or Jesus said, we have no idea what they looked like. We see pictures of Jesus everywhere but they are all different and what amazes me is the fact he is usually portrayed as being white.

I was always taught that God hated the devil but again I am wrong, because here we see them working alongside each other in order to prove Jesus' loyalty to God. The devil had tried his best but Jesus was as good as God had hoped; but then again, God had made him so of course he was good. If God was so brilliant, why did he make a human being (as himself) and then feel he had to test him?

To move on a little, Jesus preached wherever and whenever possible and gathered together his disciples. Word spread of his greatness and soon his fame spread throughout all Syria, and they brought unto him all the sick people that were taken with divers diseases and torments and those which were possessed with devils, and those which were lunatic, and those that had the palsy, and he healed then.

It is early in the morning and my brain is not quite awake. For a few moments I sat here thinking, what are divers' diseases? The only one I could think of what the bends. Then I realised the word was divers or diverse.

Once again, my mind goes back to children and their suffering. If God and Jesus can cure illnesses such as torments, possession and palsy just like that, why do they allow poor innocent children to suffer so dreadfully today? Here they are, curing people of insanity and yet they leave toddlers to die in agony? Once again, is it me? Also, once again, where do these accounts of healing come from? Was the writer there as a witness? Once again, I feel, the only evidence we have is the fact that, 'It is written'.

Digressing here and being frivolous, my stupid mind goes to a story someone once told me of a person in a wheelchair who travelled to Lourdes to be cured. He was so excited as he was wheeled into the waters and everyone prayed for him but when he came out the other side he was still exactly in the same condition, but at least his wheelchair did have four new tyres. Sorry.

Great multitudes then followed Jesus so he went up onto a mountain with his disciples and he opened his mouth and taught them and said just about everyone was blessed. He gave a long and rousing speech which was gratefully received by his followers and when he came down from the mountain he was followed by many, including a leper and the leper worshipped him and said, 'Lord if thou wilt, thou canst you make me clean?'

Jesus did, the man was cleansed and he became well, an ex-leper.

Jesus then went on to cure many more and then a scribe came to him and said he would follow him. So there was a scribe. Was this the one who would record every detail? Others said they would follow him but one man asked for time to go and bury his father but Jesus said no. He said, 'Let the dead bury their dead.'

How can the dead bury the dead? I suppose this is meant to be allegorical again. But why was this man's father dead? This man was willing to follow Jesus, go wherever Jesus went and possibly devote his life to him. If Jesus could cure all these other people just like that would it have been too big a jump to just bring the man's father back to life?

The man's father stayed dead and Jesus and his followers boarded a ship but a mighty tempest blew up and everyone feared for their lives, but Jesus slept through most of it before being woken by his disciples, who told him of their fears but he just said, 'Why are ye fearful? Oh ye of little faith.'

He then rose from his bed and rebuked the winds and the sea and there was great calm. He simply told the sea off and it behaved. I know people are going to say I am wrong and they will say something which is totally correct in their own minds, but this is not really likely, is it? And thinking back again, if he could do something this great which was totally against the forces of nature, why couldn't he just bring back to life the man's father? Didn't he later bring back to life a ruler's daughter? He 'rebuked the sea and it behaved'. Come on, this is nature. You can't even rebuke a teenager and get it to behave, let alone a tempest.

Later, Jesus was being followed again by a great horde of about five thousand men beside women and children and when it was evening, they realised they were in the desert with no food, so Jesus took the five loaves and two fishes which they had with them, blessed them and fed everyone and when everyone's hunger was satisfied, there were twelve baskets left over.

I'm sorry to go on again, but how likely is this? It is said he later went on to do the same for another 4,000 people. This time it is said he had seven loaves and a few little fishes. More loaves and fishes and less people, but it still isn't possible, is it? And if it is this possible and simple, then why do we have so many starving children today? Not just hungry but starving.

I don't want to go on and on because this is not my way of writing, but Jesus went on feeding and healing and being tempted but then the true nature and reason for his birth was to be shown. This is another central part of the Bible and its stories but when we read different accounts of it, things do differ slightly. From what I can make of it, and please correct me if I am wrong, the whole purpose of Jesus was to be put on earth by God to be tortured and crucified to atone for the original sin of Adam and Eve. By giving his own son like this, he was forgiving the sins of everyone. Jesus, the son of God, was to be flogged and nailed to a cross to forgive others their sins. WHY? Why would a father see his son (or himself) so viciously tortured just so that he could forgive others? This father was the Almighty God. He could do anything. Why didn't he just keep his son and tell everyone they were forgiven? Again, I am going to be told I am making no sense but what sense does this make? Any?

Someone once quoted the following to me: 'Atheists are the way they are because God sending himself to sacrifice himself to himself to save us all from himself is a bit much for a logically thinking person.'

It is said that Jesus was arrested because he claimed to be the King of the Jews and the Jewish high priest and elders accused him of blasphemy and arrived at the decision to put him to death. (Any excuse.) They couldn't do this, though, without the approval of Rome so they took him to Pontius Pilate, the Roman governor in Judea. Pilate found him innocent but he feared the crowds and thought he had better let them decide Jesus' fate and, of course, they all shouted, 'Crucify Him!' so that was that. Pilate was the governor and he found Jesus innocent but he had him crucified anyway. The world doesn't change, does it?

This was God's plan though, wasn't it? He wanted Jesus crucified so no matter what the Jews or Pilate or the crowd thought, it had to happen anyway. It was in the script, wasn't it? It makes a better story this way, doesn't it? I suppose it does.

As was common in those days with crucifixion, people were not satisfied with just nailing someone up. Oh no, humans are too bestial for that. No, quoting The Life of Brian again, *'Crucifixion is a doddle.'*

Jesus was to be flogged repeatedly with a leather-thonged whip which had small pieces of metal or bone tied at the end of each thong, which caused deep flesh wounds as they struck. Evidently, he was spat upon as well, which, although degrading, was probably not quite as painful as the flogging. A crown of thorns was put upon his head before he was led to be crucified but as he was too weak to carry his cross, someone else stepped in to carry it for him. There was humanity after all.

Once at the crucifixion site it is said that large nails would have been driven through his wrists and ankles, which was how they fastened him to the cross. Confused? Yes, so am I? We are told of stigmata, which is a representation of the hand injuries suffered by Jesus, and yet we are saying he was nailed through the wrists. From what I have been told, the Romans did crucify people by nailing them through the wrists so why is it a generally held belief that Jesus was nailed through the hands? Someone out there must know.

After about the ninth hour Jesus gave out a cry, saying, '*Eli Eli Lama Sabachthani*?', which means, 'My God, my God, why hast thou forsaken me?'

He then cried again, with a voice that yielded up the ghost, and the veil of the temple was rent in twain (ripped in two) from top to bottom and an earthquake split the rocks. Graves were opened and many of the saints inside arose and came out of their graves.

As an act of kindness, some Romans broke the legs of those being crucified so that they would die quicker. That was good and charitable of them, wasn't it? How kind. They didn't do this to Jesus though, because by the time they came to him he was dead already so they just pierced his side. He was taken down by sunset, wrapped in a clean cloth and laid in his tomb.

His cry split a temple in two, caused an earthquake and opened up graves from which saints came back to life. Reality?

I have read that those who questioned Jesus' words sealed their own fate and that means those of us who question now are doing to the same thing. Are we who look for logic and reality all doomed?

Jesus was dead. Or was he? It seemed not because, on a Monday, Mary Magdalene and Mary the mother of Jesus went with spices to prepare his body but when they reached the tomb, the door was open and a man inside told them that Jesus had risen from the dead. According to St Mark 16 'They were affrighted'. What a lovely word. The women shook and ran from the tomb because they were again, affrighted.

At first no one actually believed he had risen but gradually he appeared to people and they began to believe the miracle. He appeared to his disciples and told them to go out and preach the good news to everyone. He said that everyone who had been baptised would be saved but everyone who had not would be punished.

Here again we have this 'all-loving' person telling people to go out and punish those who had not been baptised. Why is the whole Bible bent of punishment and violence? I say it is because it was written by humans and humans are bent on violence and hate, even today.

And when the Lord had finished speaking to them he was taken up into heaven and sat at the right hand of God. Then the disciples went out and preached everywhere. The Lord worked with them. And he backed up his words with the signs that went with it.

This is the story of Jesus and in places it is my personal interpretation of it. Jesus was sent to earth to be used as a tool to forgive original sin and was thus crucified. If the world is 6,000 years old, then Jesus was sacrificed for a simple mistake made by a man made from dust, a woman made out of a bone and a talking serpent some four thousand years before. If it happened, then it seems illogical as God could just have forgiven anyway, but many do believe it is all completely true and is the word of God.

If I am wrong once again, then I am wrong, but it all seems illogical to me. A virgin woman is made pregnant by a god and her husband-to-be gets told it is okay, by God, in a dream. It just happens they have to go Bethlehem for a census at the precise time she is about to give birth and it just happens the only accommodation is a stable with a manger for his bed. Poor old Mary didn't have a say in the matter at all, but then again this is the Bible and she was a woman. There was no television or telephones or even Facebook, but somehow everyone knew of the birth and three wise men followed a star which 'stood' over the stable.

Baby Jesus would grow up and become a great leader and, although he was just a carpenter, he could heal the sick, bring people back to life and feed thousands with just a few loaves and some small fish. He sadly ended his first life by being flogged to within an inch of his life and then being nailed up on a cross, before dying and then being raised from the dead again.

All in all, and as with so many other Bible stories, (apart from the ones just about sex) this is a truly beautiful piece of writing which holds a huge part in the history of us, but is it and can it ever possibly be held as a true and worthwhile piece of our factual history? I say no, but many of you will disagree and say I am totally wrong and to you I say, that's fine with me. The views in this book are mine and are from my own mind which will not allow me to believe it. I cannot even watch a *Harry Potter* film because it is too far-fetched but those stories are brilliant for children and are in no way supposed to be real.

Numbers 15:32 *And while the children of Israel were in the wilderness, they found a man that gathered sticks upon the Sabbath day. And they that found him gathering sticks brought him unto Moses and Aaron, and unto all the congregation. And they put him in ward, because it was not declared what should be done to him.*

I don't suppose they had gas or electricity laid on in those days, so here was a man gathering sticks, presumably for cooking his family's dinner and he was spotted. The climate in the area was warm and I presume he didn't need heat, so cooking had to be the purpose of the sticks. It may have become cold at night, I suppose, but let's just say he was going to use them for cooking. It was the Sabbath and although he could have had a salad, he thought a hot meal was preferable. He was obviously a proud man and was doing his best for his family but instead of applauding him for it, he was dragged off to be judged and punished. This naughty man had sinned by gathering sticks on the Sabbath. He hadn't been caught fornicating or masturbating or being a homosexual or murdering or robbing, raping or pillaging had he so you would think his punishment would be light. He hadn't even really sinned. All he was doing was collecting sticks to cook his dinner, which wasn't really work was it? Did 'resting on the Sabbath' mean doing absolutely nothing? Anyway he did a little something and he was to be punished. Perhaps they would tell him off or fine him a few shekels but no. Let's see.

And the Lord said unto Moses the man shall be surely put to death. All the congregation shall stone him with stones without the camp. And all the congregation brought him without the camp and stoned him with stones, and he died as the Lord commanded Moses.

I don't suppose that surprised you at all, did it? This is the Bible, isn't it?

We are supposed to get our morals from the Bible. What sort of moral is this? If anyone does anything on the Sabbath they must have stones thrown at them until they are dead. And what kind of person could do this to a fellow human being for such a misdemeanour?

Again, is it me? I'm sure many will say I am wrong but sorry, I just cannot see it.

The Tiger's Tale

I have entitled this chapter *The Tiger's Tale* and I shall talk about tigers within it, but it is more a general view on evolution. I know I covered evolution quite fully in *Wonderment* but I thought I would go into just a few more aspects here in more detail and to illustrate it and the Bible's view I shall also be covering my old favourite story, Noah's Ark, just a little more as well.

As we know, it is said in the Bible that God created all the animals on a Friday and as I have said before, he had one busy day as there were over eight million different species of animal to create. He could not have made just one of each species either because, as we all know, it takes two to breed so this makes sixteen million animals. If we do a simple sum here we see that he actually made a hundred and eighty-five animals in every second of that twenty-four-hour period; animals ranging from bees to badgers and from winkles to whales and dodos to diplodocus.

Even if we could say this was possible for this all-knowing and all-doing God, the figures are still, in fact, totally incorrect, inadequate and vastly understated. If we think about it, God could not have made just two of every animal. Even if he could possibly have made two of the top predators they would need to eat, so a greater number of their prey would have to have been made and the numbers would have grown as we travelled down the food chain. What would be the point of making two ants and two anteaters? If the anteaters ate just one ant each then the ants would become extinct and because the ants were extinct, then so would the anteaters become extinct as they had nothing left to eat. You can't have anteaters without ants or bee-eaters without bees.

Some say I am wrong and he only had to make one type of deer, one type of fish, one type of bat and one type of big cat. This would be much simpler for him but then the argument against evolution flies totally out of the window because where have all the other types come from? Today it is estimated we have over one thousand two hundred species of bat in the world. If he only made one and there is no evolution, where did the others come from? If evolution could have started after creation, then what is wrong with it happening instead of creation? But then again, it does seem easier for religionists to understand one type of bat turning into another when their minds cannot possibly tackle one species of animal turning, eventually, into another separate species entirely. This is obviously more difficult to contemplate but it did happen. It took millions upon millions of years but happen it did and we now have fossil records to prove the fact. For instance, my favourite, Lucy, (an Australopithecus Afarensis) is a 3.5 million-year-old fossil of a female of her species of hominid. She was a link between apes and man. It all takes some studying and you have to do it with a totally open mind, but it is all there for us to be amazed at and I think, for our own sakes, amazed is what we should be.

There is something else that I have not brought into the equation as well. When I say there are eight million different species of animal on the planet, it is a fact, but what we have today is only a tiny, tiny fraction of what there has ever been. Science tells us what we see today is only between 0.01% and 0.1% of what has ever lived. If all the animals that have existed were made by God on the same day, then my figure of sixteen million in twenty-four hours is wholly wrong and completely inadequate. If we have eight million species today and that is only 0.1% of what has ever lived, then there had to be eight billion made in the same twenty-four-hour period. This means there were a hundred and eighty-five thousand made each second. If the figure is 0.01% then we have to add yet another naught onto the figures. Even if we say God did exist and did do wondrous things, we have to admit this was a bit spectacular. It is easy to blindly believe that he did this but if we really and truly open our minds and think, we have to come to the conclusion that, in reality, it could not have happened at all. Some would still say it did happen though. They refute the tiniest part of evolution that they cannot understand and then use that tiny part to say that evolution could never have happened. They do this but, at the same time, they accept that a god did it all with just magic and a miracle, and how do you argue with minds that can only think in this way? In their way of thinking it would also have meant that dinosaurs were made at the same time as everything else so they all coexisted. Dinosaurs were made on a Friday and we humans were made on a Saturday, so unless dinosaurs died out on the same evening they were created, then they and man must have lived together. This is a theory that cannot hold because we know that modern man has only been on the earth for two hundred thousand years and the large dinosaurs died out sixty million years ago. In reality, there was quite a gap. If all the animals were made together on the same day, they would have all been dying at roughly the same time and there would be fossils of every one in the same rock strata, but there are not.

What does it take to 'make' an animal?

Here is where I bring in my tiger. The tiger is one of the world's greatest predators and one of the most beautiful of all the animals and it could possibly be seen as the T-rex of today. It is a truly glorious and magnificent creature which anyone and everyone should hold in absolute awe. You look at it and it is so gorgeous that you immediately want to go over and give it a huge hug, but you know if you did it would, more than likely, be the last thing in your life that you ever saw and hugged. I have only seen tigers on film but I have seen lions in the wild and the feeling was much the same, although I would say tigers are just that little bit more handsome. Sorry, lions.

If we take creation to be true then we have to believe that God thought to himself, 'I'm going to make a striped animal that will live on meat and will keep the population of deer in check. How do I design it?'

Before I go into the design of the tiger, I want to point out that God didn't actually have to design all the animals on the day he made them, did he? That would be far-fetched. Before he made the universe, he had nothing to do for an entire eternity and would have had all the time in the world to have drawn up his designs. Drawn then up in his mind, that is, because he had, up to that point, created nothing so a pencil and a piece of paper had to be out of the question.

When we look at a tiger we see sheer beauty, but if we look closer we see a vastly powerful and complex creature which holds the high position of being at the very top of its food chain. To function and keep in that position here are a few things the animal needs:

1.The ability to breed. (A hugely complex reproductive system which is obviously completely different in males and females.)

2.The ability to give birth to and suckle its young.

3.A brain to work out how to live successfully and to raise its family.

4.Eyes to see its family, its prey and its surroundings.

5.Ears to hear its prey and any threats to itself or its family.

6.A nose to detect the smell of its prey.

7.Lungs to breathe in order to give it oxygen.

8.A heart to circulate blood and deliver that oxygen.

9.Large teeth and claws to catch and dismantle its prey.

10.A digestive system to take the goodness from that prey.

11.A bowel to eject matter left over.

12.A urinary tract to dispose of liquid waste.

13.Striped fur to help camouflage it in amongst the undergrowth whilst hunting.

14.A complex skeleton to hold and manoeuvre its frame, which could weigh up to 300 kg.

15.Muscle and sinew to move.

16.All this, plus kidneys, liver, tongue etc.

A mammal foetus generally develops gradually within its mother's womb and grows by extracting goodness from its mother via the placenta and umbilical cord. It is inside its mother for varying amounts of time depending upon which mammal it is, but in the case of a tiger this is about 105 days.

It takes this time for a tiger foetus to develop and that is after the tiger has mated and the necessary genes for life have been passed on so just imagine, with your eyes, heart and mind fully open, how difficult it must have been for God to create one in a tiny fraction of a second. He had no genes to work with. Adam was made from dust and Eve was made from one of Adam's ribs, so was this the case for the tiger and his partner? Just how do you make a tiger from dust? The simple answer is, you don't, so God had to have another way.

I am going to try and delve imaginatively into God's brain here and look at his design process. Neither I nor anyone else knows how God thought but it must have been something like this.

(Firstly, we have accepted for a while that God existed and then discount continental drift and ice ages etc. We will have to accept that the world has always been as we see it today.)

God looked at his work and saw that it was good. He looked at Asia and saw that it was warm and lush with vegetation, which would encourage the growth in numbers of various species of herbivores including deer, and if he didn't do something about it those deer would run rampant and destroy his good work, so he realised there had to be predators which could control their numbers for him. He had already designed the civet, the marbled cat and the clouded leopard, but he thought what he really needed here was the largest cat in the world and envisaged the tiger, so he sat down and thought.

The tiger was a cat just like the others so he needed two hundred and thirty bones, all of different sizes and purposes. This animal, he decided, would be about nine feet in length and about three feet in height so it would need a far superior muscle mass to the likes of a civet. (I use feet because this was in pre-metric times.) Its eyes had to be good to see every movement of its prey so he decided they needed to be six times better than the human eye he had already envisaged for use on Saturday. Its claws would need to be up to five inches long and had to be retractable, otherwise it could not run to catch its prey. It would need thirty teeth which would have to be of various shapes, sizes and lengths to suit different tasks and he decided that the fur of the animal needed to be striped to provide camouflage and should be placed at somewhere between two thousand and three thousand hairs per square centimetre, (Whoops! Gone metric.) depending upon which species it would be, because he had complicated things by deciding to create more than one type.

Just how do you make these decisions and how do you make these things? How do you decide how many hairs per square centimetre an animal should have and how do you decide what traits that animal should have, to match and live in a particular environment? How do you make a single hair, let alone a body full of them and then an eye or a brain or a heart or lungs? What equation do you use to work out the loss of body heat due to the ambient temperature outside it and how do you know which type of fur insulates best against that particular loss? If he used the same fur that he gave to a polar bear, the tiger would die of heat stroke and if he didn't use enough hair, then the tiger would die of either cold or exposure.

A heart consists of muscle to pump blood, chambers to hold blood and complex valves to regulate the flow and direction of that blood. It has to beat within a certain range per minute and it has to work continuously and efficiently throughout the whole life of the recipient. If it stops at all, the animal dies. It is not as complex as the eye or the brain but, (think about it for a second), how could it be made from dust? Ridiculous? Is it me?

In several arguments I have heard or read, the person arguing says the eye is such a complex organ it could not have possibly come about by evolution. The answer has to be this is far more likely than it being developed by God, again from dust. If we get a speck of dust in our eye it hurts and irritates like hell. Would that extra speck of dust matter in the slightest if the eye was made from dust already? The eye, like everything else, evolved step by extremely tiny step over many millions of years. The first eye was very simple and just gave the owner of it the ability to differentiate between light and dark, which isn't much but it is better than nothing. At least it gave its owner the ability to spot something moving in front of it and if they fled from this movement it could have saved them from predation and would then further the continued existence of their family and their species. This simple eye then developed into an eye with dish-like edges which then gave the owner not only the ability to see something, but also gave the ability to tell from which direction light was coming and, therefore, from which direction something is approaching. Again, an improvement. Not only would the animal know to run but it would also know in which direction to run. Through time and evolution, the eye became more advanced as the rim of the 'dish' became greater and eventually developed into something of a 'pin-hole' type eye which gave its owner the ability to see in some detail just what it was looking at. The big breakthrough came with the evolution of the lens, which revolutionised sight. As I say, the better the eye, the better chance you have of seeing your predators coming and the better chance you have of that, the better chance you have of escaping and surviving. It then goes on to the fact that the better you survive, the more you can breed and the more you breed, the better chance you have of passing on your genes to the next generation.

Of course, the better the eye you have, the better you survive and if your next generation happens to be born with an eye very slightly better than yours they then stand an even better chance of surviving than you do. This is how evolution works. We are seen as the superior of all animal species but our eyes are not nearly as good as those of a hawk, an owl or our tiger. If God was so good at making the ultimate eye, then why didn't he just make it and give it to all animals? We as humans have good eyesight, but not nearly as good as some other animals, but then there are still some animals that have very basic eyes. This is not because God decided we should all have different eyes; it is because this is the way evolution works.

It is highly probable that ammonites had pin-hole eyes and we know that their relative today, the nautilus, does have them. We have two eyes and two lenses, as do all mammals, but most spiders have eight eyes. Is that because God designed them or is it because they are this way because of evolution? Why did God think humans could manage very well with two eyes but a spider would, for some reason, need eight? Why did God think we only needed two legs but a spider needed eight?

What has to be considered in all this is that the Bible says that all animals, apart from us, were made on a Friday by God and if we just leave it there and do not think for ourselves, we accept it as fact and, as I said in my previous book, 'There the Wonderment would end.'

With evolution, however, we have to look at it all in a far greater and broader context. Evolution tells us life was not made in one day but over billions of years. With the Bible view of things, the whole earth and universe beyond and all in it was made in six days, whereas science is telling us, with evidence, that the universe is 13.7 billion years old and the earth is 4.5 billion years old. I know I have covered some of this in *Wonderment* but it is so amazingly breath-taking that I feel it deserves a repeat to some extent.

It took nine billion years (9,000,000,000 years) for the sun and earth to develop and it took another billion years (1,000,000,000 years) for the earth to form into a planet which could support even the simplest of simple life forms. It took another three billion, four hundred and ninety-nine million, eight hundred thousand years for us modern humans, Homo sapiens, to evolve. This is what we have to consider. Not if it happened but the sheer amount of time it took to happen. If we see dinosaurs on a Friday and humans on a Saturday then, yes, evolution is totally impossible, but if we see most of the dinosaurs dying out sixty million years before humans developed, then evolution is possible. If 'young earth' creationists are to be believed then the earth is less than ten thousand years old and even in this time evolution would not be at all possible, so you can see why they cling so tightly to their beliefs of creation. It is only when we can possibly contemplate a span of four billion five hundred million years that we can even start to grasp any of evolution's reality. I always thought this was a huge number and it is, but when we look at the world's human population of seven billion, it holds one and a half humans for every year the earth has been around and two humans for every year life has been evolving. That puts things in perspective and is also quite frightening and alarming if we think about it too closely. The problem with us humans is that we can easily compute six days or even six thousand years, but how do we get our heads around four billion five hundred million years? I'm sorry, but it is not easy for a few and is impossible to most. The tiny, tiny increments involved cannot, it seems, be understood either. We, other apes and monkeys, do have a common ancestor but that ancestor lived many millions of years ago. Many theists I have spoken to and argued with seem to think we are trying to say we were all monkeys until just a few years ago. Their minds suffer from a great deal of intransigence and they cannot understand that we are not actually trying to get them to believe that either our grandparents or great uncles were chimpanzees or macaques, but we come from a very early common ancestor that was around way back, in an almost unimaginable and incomprehensible distant past.

In various Facebook groups theists try hard to debunk evolution and I can understand why. If they gave in to evolution, or even contemplated it at all, it would mean their God theory would start to go out of the window so you constantly see false, and often very silly, arguments; arguments which they quite truly believe in their own minds. Charles Darwin's theory of evolution was flawed, they say, because he didn't have all the answers. He did his studies over one and a half centuries ago. Of course, he didn't have all the answers. Science has moved on and has learned much since. It is like saying that all cars are still boxy and black because that was what the Ford Model T looked like in 1910. Darwin was a brilliant thinking man and his work did form the basis of evolution but, as with the motor car, so much has advanced and has been learned since. Science has raced on but still we do not have all the answers and doesn't this show the sheer beauty and majesty of it all? A problem that runs deep is the fact that because people cannot understand evolution, they have to argue that it didn't happen. It would be like me saying complex brain surgery doesn't exist. Of course it exists. The fact is that I simply do not understand what happens. It is no good me trying to deny it. It is me who is wrong, not the brain surgeons. There are many things that we do not understand but if they exist then they exist. No one's mind knows everything but the more we open up those minds and use them, the more we will learn and the less we will have to deny. Dogma only stifles and kills intelligence.

Someone even argued with me about evolution and in the end he felt the only way he could win the argument was to tell me that fossils did not exist. What can you say to that? We have millions of fossils of millions of animals, in many different rock strata from many different ages and from many different parts of the globe. Has someone made them all from plaster of Paris? This is what I gave in to just to stop the debater's nonsensical rantings. If people can only argue whilst trying to think through this amount of stupidity then perhaps it is best, in the end, not to argue.

It is easy to say that God made everything and then close your mind to learning. I vehemently believe that we have a duty to learn and fulfil our lives to the best of our abilities. To say that everything was made by God a few thousand years ago and 'that was that' is almost sad when there is so much in our beautiful universe to wonder about and ponder upon. Try pondering upon this:

You cannot just make an animal and that is the end of it. Even if it were miraculously true that you could, in no way could you just drop that animal into any old environment. All life depends upon the intricately complex ecosystem in which it survives and thrives. If you introduce just one species into an ecosystem that should not be there you cause problems and that ecosystem can fail. It can fail quickly and with drastic effects. Look at the domestic cat. It has been introduced by humans and has brought the numbers of wildlife species down dramatically. They do not just kill mice and birds. They are taking that food supply away from the natural predators that are 'supposed' to be there. The whole ecosystem of an area is totally dependent upon each animal evolving into its own little place or niche. Plants are eaten by insects. Insects are eaten by lizards. Lizards are eaten by snakes. Snakes are eaten by mammals and birds and they are then eaten by their predators. Ecosystems are far more complicated than this but this shows in general terms just how each species relies on the existence of another. In my simple example, it is easy to see that those at the bottom of the ladder would need to vastly outnumber those at the top. All this has come about over multi-millions of years of evolution. In the creation theory, God would have had to have made an absolute minimum of 185 species each second of the day and he would also have had to have designed the whole intricate ecosystem that they were to live in. He would need to have created just the right environment. It would have needed just the right plants, the right amount of light, water and heat and the right numbers of prey animals and their predators. Then these environmental areas would have had to overlap so that one area didn't suddenly become hugely hotter, colder, dryer or wetter than the next area. Great and exhaustive planning would have had to have gone into the environments of every single little area of the whole world, before even a single thought was made as to which animals could live and thrive there. If we put aside the sun being needed for all existence and it needing to be there before the earth was made (but in the creation story it wasn't), we also have to admit that the sun had to be set at just the correct distance from the earth it would sustain. How did God know all this? How did God know about the force of gravity, and how did he know at just what strength this force had to be set throughout the entire universe so as to sustain everything in its rightful and perfect place? He had to work out how far the earth had to be from the sun, but how did he know just how hot the sun would need to be? What great equation would he have used to work this out? It would not have been $e=mc2$.

I said above that if you introduce a species into an ecosystem that should not be there, then that ecosystem becomes unbalanced and unstable. It has happened with the domestic cat and the mink, but which is the most dangerous and disruptive of all animals? Which animal is the only one on the planet that has the brain capacity and therefore the capability of destroying the very planet that sustains us? Yes, you've got it first time. It is us, the humans that were made from dust on the Saturday. We are supposed to be the ones who are the most important. We are held way above all the other animals and have dominion over them but it is we who are destroying ecosystems left, right and centre and it is we who are, quite rapidly and very worryingly, destroying the whole world because of it. To illustrate this, I will talk about Yellowstone Park which is a wonderful natural area. The ecosystem of this area was almost ruined by some clever humans who thought it would be a good idea to slaughter all the wolves the park held. Why? They did, of course, with no real thought whatsoever and the effects were drastic.

With the wolves gone the numbers of their prey species, mainly elk, were able to multiply their numbers greatly. It may have been a happy time for them, not being eaten, but then as their numbers increased, far too many saplings were being eaten by the elk and the trees started to disappear.

Again, man was interfering with nature. The trees were gone and so were all the animals that lived in them. Another major casualty was the beaver, which needs trees in order to build dams and its home. And then, with the dams gone, water flowed from the land too quickly, destroying all the wildlife that lived in slow-moving water.

So, once again, man thought he knew best, but didn't. Wolves have now been reintroduced and the balance is being struck again. Yellowstone's ecosystem is slowly recovering. One single species removed from an ecosystem that took millennia to evolve can cause almost instant destruction. The Yellowstone ecosystem had taken millions of years to come about. In no way was it created on a whim and in an instant by a god who had lived for an eternity in nothing and had nothing to create it with.

We have created global warming and that, in its turn, is changing ecosystems. As soon as an area becomes just a tiny bit warmer, colder, wetter or dryer, the ecosystem of that area changes. We then see other animals moving into the area and still others either moving out or dying out. We have seen those who are supposed to be the most intelligent of us all having giant meetings and great steps forward have been taken to combat it all. I am lying here, of course. They do honestly think they have come to great conclusions and have made great steps forwards but no. Their latest promise to dear old Mother Earth is that they will release only as much carbon dioxide as she can deal with naturally. This would indeed be great if they were to do it now. Believe me, it needs to be done now. They have promised this will happen in the next forty-odd years. Forty-odd years? This is no good, no good in the slightest. If we are to save Mother Earth's life at all, NOW and only NOW will do. It is no good having cancer and saying you will go to see your GP in twenty years' time. If you are to save your life you have to deal with it instantly. Come on, you 'intelligent' people. Please wake up. As with all of the world's problems they are just waiting for that 'hungry lion' to pounce. Donald Trump has now pulled out of the Paris Agreement on climate change. What harm will that do?

I recently asked on a religious discussion site, if evolution does not exist and God made every single animal is twenty-four hours, just how did he do it? I was genuinely interested in hearing answers but I posted the question twice and on neither occasion did I receive any kind of answer. It was not a surprise though. Did I really expect common sense, logic and reasoning? Did I really expect an answer to an unanswerable question? I think, this time, it was me who was being foolish.

If so many people try to trash evolution, (sometimes with much anger) surely they should have a counter argument ready beforehand. Again, if I said 2+2=5 you could put two things in front of me and then another two things and when I counted them I would see there were, in fact, four things and I would be proven wrong. I would realise and accept that 2+2=4. I would have been wrong and I would learn. Never again would I say 2+2=5. I would have seen the evidence. I would strongly suggest that everyone does this but if there does happen to be that someone who seriously thinks 2+2=5 or that they can debunk evolution, they should put all their evidence carefully together and present it to the powers that be. They should write a dissertation and if their evidence is anywhere near as good as they state, then they would completely change the course of science and history, would be totally famous, would make an absolute ton of money and would probably be awarded the Nobel Prize as well. Their name would go down as one of the world's historical greats. So why has nobody done this? They haven't because, plainly and simply, underneath it all, even they realise they have no evidence at all to prove their Bible theory. Believe me, if they could prove it they certainly would jump at the chance and I would love to see it. If they could prove the existence and wonders of their god then they, too, would immediately be treated as one.

'No matter what we say they will still argue and deny as argue and deny they must.'

So, going back to my favourite, dear old Noah. If evolution does not exist, he had at least sixteen million animals on his wooden boat and that is taking into account the fact that there were the same number of animals then as there are today. If, however, the flood was almost at the beginning of creation then he would have also had two of all the animals aboard that have since become extinct, and even if we just take into account that there are 0.1% of the species left today and not 0.01% that have ever existed, then poor old Noah would have had two of nearly eight billion species on board, including our tigers which would have needed quite a few deer to munch and survive on.

In Genesis 7.20 it reads that, in Noah's flood, the mountains were covered and yet it also says, *'Fifteen cubits upward did the waters prevail'.*

People do say the Bible contradicts itself and it sometimes does, but in this instance it is a vast contradiction. Taking a cubit as being the measurement between a man's elbow and the tip of his fingers, this makes the depth of water a maximum of eighteen inches' times fifteen, thus twenty-two and a half feet or seven metres. As you can see, this is a little short of covering the Himalayas. All the animals would have had to have done was walk to slightly higher ground. There are very few places on earth where a flood of this depth would have caused any havoc to life at all.

It is said that the story of the 'Great flood' was taken from a flood which actually happened and with water just at this level it could well have happened locally. Either it was a seven metre flood or it covered the mountains. Both cannot be true. What we have to think about here is that a big flood in the Middle East could well have seemed like it was covering the whole world, as this area was the only world these people knew. They hadn't travelled, had they?

Then again, was the earth flooded to above the tip of Everest or was it flooded just to a depth of seven metres or did the waters prevail to seven metres above Everest? Again, is it all allegorical and I cannot understand it with my simple mind?

I know this is a little unrelated to what I have been saying but I just want to add a little more about the universe before we move on.

The Bible says the earth was created first and then the stars, and the stars were simply there to illuminate the earth at night. If this is true, why did God bother to create so many countless billions of them out there and have them all moving away from each other, causing an ever-expanding universe? We are supposed to be living on the most significant body in the universe but, really, we just live on a tiny planet which sits at the edge of an insignificant galaxy. We and our tiger are not made from dust and are not even one single speck of dust in comparison to it all.

Even most of the strictest and most dedicated of theists uses a computer and the Interweb. They rely upon satellites flying above them to broadcast television programmes and they use them to tell them where to go via their sat navs. They drive in cars and fly on aeroplanes or travel on ships or in trains. They rely upon internal combustion engines for everything that is delivered to them. We rely upon electricity and gas and even their churches do. Even these buildings also rely upon modern sound systems to get their messages across. In their homes theists have telephones, microwaves and central heating. Everyone in the modern world luxuriates in using clean water and eating good food. They take medicines and have scans and X-rays to help them survive. Every ailment is treated by the wonders of science.

It has to be admitted by everyone that we all live by the great and multitudinous gifts of science. Although I did once hear someone say that gravity did not exist, we all must truly admit that science plays an absolutely massive part in our lives and in no way could we live lives anywhere near to what we do today without it. With this said, why is it theists can quickly and openly and whole-heartedly accept all these things from science that better their lives but they cannot allow themselves to just accept one more thing, evolution? It is just like their own personal god. They can easily discount thousands of other gods so why can't they simply discount just one more? It seems they have to hold onto something, anything.

At the moment, even the greatest and brightest of minds cannot come to grips fully with the Big Bang theory. We know what happened the tiniest of tiny fractions after but no one, no matter what brains and intellect they have or how hard they think, can tell us how it actually came about or what, if anything, was there before. Was there anything before? Did time actually start at the Big Bang? Were there and are there other big bangs still happening? I think this is all a wonder in itself but this does give religionists something on which to offer a heartfelt and smug snigger. They say that because we don't know, then God must know because it proves he made everything. No! It proves nothing! What a thing to presume! We seem to think that the universe came from nothing and again, the religionists cheer. They shout that you cannot produce something from nothing and, again, God did it all. Can you imagine and feel the smugness emerging and erupting? Why can't something from nothing?

Yes, we are puzzled. How did it all come from nothing? But if you then smugly say that God did it you have, in reality, to ask the self-same question. How did God make it from nothing? Either way, it came from nothing. In the God theory, even he existed before he created the universe so he actually existed before it, when there was nothing. The Bible is full of stories and suggestions but how can its readers and followers all be so smug when they themselves do not even have answers to even one of the statements involved? There may be theists reading this and hating every word. These words are mine and I feel they make sense but if I am wrong then I would suggest a few of those who hold different views should sit down and put them to paper. If they could produce a book of their thoughts as I have done, a book which answers a few of the questions I have asked recently, I would be hugely interested. My book is entitled, *God, Religion and The Bible. One man's view*. Perhaps one of theirs could be called, *God, Religion and The Bible. What Don't You Understand?* If they could prove me to be the numpty they say I am then I would be very pleased to accept the label.

Two different quotes that I have read:

A theist is someone who has a close and personal relationship with God.

An atheist is someone who has a close and personal relationship with reality.

Sorry, but again I see this as true. Am I wrong?

The Story of Moses

As I have said before, the Bible may or may not be a true historical record of life but it certainly is full of wonderful stories which can be truly believed if one does not think too long or hard.

This is the story of Moses who, again, is central to the Bible's authenticity.

It is a shame that none of the events in the Bible give actual dates. Wouldn't it be good if it said Moses was born in 3,000 BC or something? It would give us a sense of timescale. In the missing out of the year we do not have this sense. Is the omission because no one knows when he was born or is it because he wasn't born at all? Anyway, on to his story:

At the time of his birth, the Hebrews were slaves in Egypt and the Pharaoh was frightened of them. They were numerous and he feared a rebellion so he hatched a plan. He commanded that all newborn Hebrew baby boys should be killed at birth.

Sorry again, but here already is a problem. This supposedly powerful and intelligent man, the Pharaoh, is leading a nation but he wasn't too intelligent, was he? I am not advocating violence here but he had power over the Hebrews and could do anything he wanted. He was their master. Why didn't he make an exhibition of a few male slaves and have them executed in public to warn others not to revolt for fear of the same punishment? By killing off all the newborn male children he was depriving himself of a whole future generation of male slaves and with all the older slaves still there, the problem of a potential revolution was also still there. I would think he was only exacerbating the problem, because surely the mothers and fathers of those babies killed wouldn't be too impressed at losing their offspring and would most probably feel the need to seek strong retribution. Surely the risk of revolt had only been heightened?

Now, Moses' mother also hatched a cunning plan. She decided she would save her son by laying him in a basket and putting him in a river.

I know she was desperate but was this the wisest thing to do? A baby in a flimsy basket in a river? Wouldn't it have made more sense to have sent him away to live with relatives or hide him? Being a slave though, her choices were limited so this was her choice and, luckily, it worked and worked well.

As he lay there in his basket, his older sister Miriam stayed and watched over him until Pharaoh's daughter came down to the river to wash and saw him there. Seeing his safe discovery, Miriam went over to the Pharaoh's daughter and said she knew a woman who could nurse the child. She didn't say who but she meant her and Moses' mother. The Pharaoh's daughter agreed and took the baby home to live with her as her son.

What could have been a very watery end for baby Moses turned out well. Luckily his sister watched over him and luckily the Pharaoh's daughter found him and luckily, she took him home to live as her son, but doesn't this pose a few questions?

Firstly, wasn't it just a little bit of a coincidence that it was the actually the Pharaoh's daughter who found him when it could have been anyone, any old peasant?

She was there to wash in the river. This was the daughter of the ruler and I know they didn't have running water and luxurious showers or bathrooms in those days, but would a lady of this high standing wash in a river in public? Surely water would have been brought to her by servants so that she could disrobe in private? Again, I am open to being wrong.

The next thing that has to be contemplated here is that her father had ordered the murder of all newborn Hebrew babies. Didn't it seem a little odd to them that here was this male child, hidden in a basket in a river, at the same time as the killings were ordered? In the King James version of the story it does say she realised the child was a Hebrew, so why just accept it as her own? And what of her father? Didn't he suspect a little something when the child was brought home? Did he just say, 'Oh well, my daughter. Finders keepers. You've found him so you can keep him.'

He was desperately worried about the Hebrews. Would he have brought one under his own roof without questioning who and what it was? Perhaps his daughter had no children and he was as desperate as she was. Perhaps the thought of the patter of tiny feet around his house and someone calling him Granddad was worth the risk. Did they never suspect the fact that the wet-nurse brought in to feed the child could be its own mother? I suppose, though, that at that time there would have been many childless mothers around because he'd had all their babies murdered.

The years passed by and Moses grew up into a life of great privilege as an Egyptian prince. He had everything he could possibly desire, but then one day his temper came through when he saw an Egyptian who was beating a Hebrew slave. He was rightly annoyed, but probably went a little too far and killed the man. Trouble then brewed as the Pharaoh heard of what had happened and sought to slay Moses, so Moses thought, rather than get into bother, he should run off to another land. He dwelt in the land of Midian and sat down a well. The priest of Midian had seven daughters (What, no sons? That's unusual.) and they went to the well to draw water for their father's flock. Then some shepherds came along and drove them away but Moses came out of the well, rescued the sisters and watered their flock for them. The girls returned to Reuel. Their father was surprised his daughters were home so early and he questioned them about it, so they explained about Moses living down the well, the shepherds and Moses watering the flock. Reuel told them they should not have left Moses in the fields after he had helped them so much and he instructed them to find him and bring him in. They did so (He was probably sitting down the well again) and Moses stayed with Reuel and was given one of his daughters, Zipporah, in marriage and, as with just about every other story, apart from this one, Zipporah gave birth to a son, who they named Gershom. Moses did rather well, didn't he? All he did was water some sheep and he ended up with a wife and child and loads of sisters-in-law. It must have been expensive at Christmas though.

Moses hadn't forgotten that he was a Hebrew and you could understand his revulsion at seeing one of his fellow men being beaten, but why did he risk everything by, in turn, killing the assailant? He was an Egyptian prince and therefore had great powers. Surely he could have devised a punishment that would not have seen him having to flee. But flee he did and found good fortune once again. Our Moses had led quite a charmed life. He was put in a river in a basket and had been taken in by the Pharaoh's daughter to be brought up a prince and, even after murdering an Egyptian and running away, he was found sitting down a well by a priest's daughters and was immediately given one of them as a wife. But, of all the places to sit, why did he sit down a well? Surely a barn or cowshed or stable or even under a tree would have been somewhat drier and more comfortable? Any of these would also seem a little less insane but then again, at least he didn't go thirsty.

During this period, the King of Egypt died and God heard the slaves there moan and cry out to him and while Moses was tending to the flock of Jethro, his father-in-law, the Angel of the Lord appeared to him in a burning bush and Moses went over to the bush to see why it was not being destroyed.

Whooah! Hang on! Go back a bit! Am I being silly here? I have read it again and to my mind it does not make sense. Moses had been given Zipporah as a wife by her father, Reuel, but now he is tending the flock of 'Jethro', his father-in-law. I thought perhaps Zipporah had died and Moses had married again, but it seems Reuel and Jethro are the same person, because it says they were both the Priest of Midian. Having looked the matter up, I see they are both the same person, but the Bible does sometimes give more than one name to the same person. Why is this? The only reasons I can see are either that the writer of this particular piece forgot what he had called the man, or he was just making it up anyway and therefore it didn't really matter either way. Perhaps his name was Reuel but this was short for Jethro or vice versa. Or as my wife has just pointed out, maybe one of his names was just a nickname. She knows everything, you know.

He saw God talking to him from a burning bush. God said, 'Moses, Moses' and Moses replied 'Here I am. Here I am'. No, he didn't. He only said it once. This is something different, I suppose, but why did God feel the need to appear in a burning bush? Why didn't he just come to Moses in a dream or send an angel to talk to him? It does say it was the Angel of the Lord in the bush, but it was God who spoke through him. Isn't the burning bush being used as some sort of symbol of sensationalism? It does show imagination again, I suppose.

Moses walked over to the bush but God told him not to get too close and he also told Moses to remove his sandals because he was standing on holy ground. Moses did as he was told again. I cannot see why it was so important to remove his sandals in a field, but the Bible does say it was suddenly holy ground so who was Moses to argue? His life had been charmed up until then so he didn't want to upset God, did he?

The Lord said he had seen the misery of his people in Egypt and had heard them crying out because of their slavery. He said he had come down to rescue them and put them in a land of milk and honey so he was sending Moses to do it.

At first, he said he had come down to free the slaves and then he told Moses to do it. It was a bit of a cop-out but Moses knew his place and did as he was ordered. God had passed the buck but then, he was in charge and had the authority.

Moses was to go back and free all the Hebrew slaves. If he had cared so much about them why hadn't he done it before, rather than lap up all the luxuries of high Egyptian society whilst he was living his life as a prince as they all suffered? It seems he had suddenly learned the error of his ways though.

God had told him to do so and who then would have crossed God? Everyone knew, only too plainly, what God was capable of.

'Come now therefore', said the Lord. 'I will send thee unto Pharaoh, that thou mayest bring forth my people, the children of Israel, out of Egypt.'

Moses knew he had to go but he questioned God, saying, 'Who am I that I should go unto the Pharaoh, and that I should bring forth my people, the children of Israel, out of Egypt?'

God told Moses that he would be with him and he could use this as a token of his intent. He told Moses that when he had freed the slaves Moses was to serve him upon the mountain where they then were. 'Go and gather the elders of Israel together,' God said. 'And say unto them, the Lord God of your fathers, the God of Abraham, the God of Isaac, the God of Jacob has sent me unto you and will bring you out of the affliction of Egypt.'

Moses had God on his side but still he was very sceptical about his mission, so God decided to give him proof of his powers. He told Moses to throw his rod on the ground and when he did, it turned into a snake. It doesn't say if this one talked or not, but it did show the Lord's power, but it frightened Moses and he backed away from it, but the Lord told him to be brave and grab the snake by the tail and when he did, it turned back into a rod. God then told Moses to put his hand towards his bosom and when he did and brought it away again, it was leprous as snow. God had just given Moses leprosy but he was only kidding of course, because when he told Moses to hold his bosom again the leprosy disappeared. God did like his little joke, didn't he?

Turning a rod into a snake and then giving and curing Moses of leprosy were not really things that would have happened but, again, it showed the imagination of the writer of the story. How can a totally inanimate object suddenly move, breathe and live? In any reality it cannot, but why not, if dust can become a fully functioning human being, capable of thoughts and emotions?

The Lord told Moses to go. He said he would be his mouth and would tell him what to say so Moses agreed and went to seek permission of Jethro (or Reuel), his father-in-law, to leave. Jethro agreed and Moses took his wife and sons and left for Egypt.

Moses met with his brother Aaron and they returned to the Pharaoh. He asked him to set his slaves free but Pharaoh wasn't too keen. His slaves were working hard for him and he didn't want to lose all the work that was being done for no wages. The Pharaoh told his people to stop bringing straw to the brick makers. He said, in future, they should go and get it for themselves. Boy, he knew how to punish people. Get their own straw? Whatever would he think of next? The trouble was, though, that as the brick makers had to gather their own straw to make bricks, this slowed down the process dramatically. They couldn't gather straw and make bricks at the same time, but this riled the Egyptians and the slaves were beaten increasingly. In short, the Pharaoh had said, 'No', to freeing his slaves but that meant trouble was to be afoot.

Moses talked again to the Lord and said the Hebrews were still slaves and the Pharaoh would not listen to him who was of 'uncircumcised lips'.

The phrase 'uncircumcised lips' seems rather odd and it has puzzled both me and Bible scholars, but what it is thought to mean, and it seems logical, is that Moses was somehow tongue-tied. Not in a physical sense and needing an operation, but he felt whatever he said no one ever listened. He could have been of 'uncircumcised ears', meaning when someone else was talking he was incapable of listening, a common trait even today.

When Moses again spoke to the Pharaoh, he was four score years old and his brother Aaron was four score and three years.

If the Bible writers knew the actually ages of people they must have calculated them using some form of calendar and if they did this, then surely they must have known what year all this happened so why not give the year? I am sixty-four years old and I know this because I was born in 1953 but then again, since the year 1AD we have known what year it was. I don't suppose this could have worked for the years BC. We could only date those years in retrospect. Perhaps they just put a mark on a wall or somewhere every time another year had passed and they knew this by the seasons. In truth though, even if these people did exist, no one could have known their ages. Look again at our friend Noah. How could anyone possibly have known he was four hundred and eighty years old when he started to build the ark, he was six hundred years old when it floated and he was nine hundred and fifty years old when he died? Did Noah put a cross on a piece of paper each year and take it with him aboard the ship? I would think he would have had far more pressing things on his mind.

The Pharaoh was not to be talked into letting his slaves and his livelihood go, so Moses and Aaron did their trick with their rods. Aaron cast down his rod in the presence of the Pharaoh and his servants and it turned into a snake. All the other men cast down their rods but Aaron's rod swallowed up their rods. Of course it did. Why would anyone question it?

God told Moses and Aaron that when the Pharaoh went into the water, they should stand on the river bank and hold the rod which had turned into a serpent in their hand and command that all their people should be freed, and if the Pharaoh still said no, they should smite the rod in their hand upon the water and the water would turn to blood. This would make the fish in the river die and the water would stink so the Egyptians would have nothing to drink.

It didn't cross their minds, I suppose, that the Hebrews would go thirsty as well.

They did this to the river and also did it, it seems, to every stream, lake, pit and puddle, which made the Pharaoh cross, so he went indoors.

Then the Lord spoke to Moses again and told him to go to the Pharaoh and demand that his people were freed otherwise he would smite all his borders with frogs. He said the frogs would get everywhere. They would be in their houses, their bedchambers, under their beds, in their ovens and even in their kneading troughs.

The frogs came and this really got to the Pharaoh so he caved in and said if the frogs could be cleared, then the slaves would be freed. The frogs all died and they were gathered into heaps and they stank.

The frogs were gone and the naughty old Pharaoh hardened his heart again and changed his mind, so God instructed Aaron to cast his rod and smite the dust of the land so that it should turn into lice. After the lice came a swarm of flies, but still the Pharaoh relented only to harden his heart once more, so God laid his hand on the cattle of the Egyptians so that they died. He later sent a plague of locusts which not only covered Egypt, but actually covered the whole earth and darkened it.

So what good did this do? It may have deprived the Egyptians of food but it also deprived the whole of the earth's population of food. There would have had to have been countless trillions of them. Where did they all come from? And how could those in Egypt or the Bible writers ever have known that the locusts were upon the entire earth? These were ancient times. They would not have even known much of the world existed. Perhaps their entire world was just the Middle East. Thinking about it, perhaps it was because it is only this small area that is ever mentioned in the Bible.

There were ten plagues in all and Moses had forewarned of every one. He told the Pharaoh that each was sent from God.

I would think the Pharaoh was a bit miffed about the day he let his daughter bring Moses into the house in that soggy basket. It was obvious at that stage that he was a Hebrew but still the Pharaoh did nothing. He had power over everyone around him and held their very lives in his hands, but although he obviously knew who Moses was he still let him be. It seems Moses was totally unharmed, right from the time he asked for all the slaves to be freed, up until the end of the tenth plague. Why ten plagues? How do we know there were ten plagues? How do we know if this story holds any creditability at all?

Evidently, as the story tells us, the last plague was the worst and it killed the eldest son of every family, including Pharaoh's. This plague was so terrible that God instructed Moses to mark the doorposts of all Hebrew houses so that Hebrew boys would be safe. Pharaoh was so upset at losing his son that he relented and let all the Hebrews go free.

This is, in Bible terms, quite a quaint little story but once again, here we are, seeing everything being dealt with by extreme violence and megalomania. Why? God wanted the Hebrew slaves freed and he was the all-powerful, all-seeing and all-doing God. He could do anything. He had made all the animals on a Friday and had made Adam out of dust and had put many billions of stars in the sky. He was such an amazingly clever person. Why didn't he just wave his little finger and free the slaves in the first place? They would all have been free, ten plagues would not have descended upon Egypt and several young lives would have been saved. Why the lust for carnage and murder again?

Also, if God was all-seeing and all-knowing, then why did he have Moses paint all Hebrew doorposts? If God knew everything and could make the complete universe in six days, then surely he would have known a simple thing like where the Hebrews lived.

The Hebrews were freed. They were free men and women but for some reason, they felt they had to rush to leave. They had God and Moses on their side but left so quickly that they didn't even have time to let their bread rise. That would not have taken long but their hurry and worries were well founded because despite the ten plagues, the death of his son and giving his permission, the naughty old Pharaoh changed his mind yet again and sent an army after them.

They were chased as far as the banks of the Red Sea and their fate seemed doomed but, just in time, like the cavalry in an old western film, help was there. God performed a miracle. He told Moses to hold up his staff and as he did so the waters parted to give them a clear and dry path to cross. They crossed and reached the other side safely and then, as the army pursuing them came along the same path between the waves, Moses again raised his stick and the waters returned to normal and they were all drowned.

Once again, why the need for death? God could do anything. Why didn't he just teleport Moses and his gang across to the other side, leaving the chasing army just bemused rather than dead? And how do you just part water like that? In reality it cannot be done, surely?

Moses and his band of ex-slaves were free but the story does not end there. They were free but they were in the desert, which brought forth its own set of problems.

They wanted to find a land called Canaan, which God had promised them, but the journey was arduous because, as we all know, the desert isn't renowned for its abundance of water or fruitfulness so everyone became really hungry, but Moses had faith and he told everyone the Lord would provide. God did provide food the next day because all the ground became covered with a white food that tasted like honey. Moses told them it was manna from heaven. They all ate this and also partook of all the birds God sent them. To satisfy their thirst, Moses tapped his staff upon a rock and water issued forth.

This is how God fed and watered them all in the desert, but am I being too simplistic in saying, why did God cover the earth with the white honey-tasting stuff and why did he bring forth all the birds for them to eat and the water from the rocks? Why didn't he just make them not hungry or thirsty? Wouldn't that have been easier again?

The gang travelled on for week after week and eventually they came to the foot on Mount Sinai and God told Moses to meet him on the top of the mountain, where he gave him the Ten Commandments that the people were to live by. They were written on two tablets. No, not Solpadeine. These were tablets of rock.

Can you smell the irony here? Probably the most important of the Commandments is the one that says, 'Thou shalt not kill'. I'm sorry to have to be mean towards this god, but hadn't he been killing people with plagues recently? And wasn't it he who drowned an entire army that was chasing Moses? In earlier days, wasn't it he who killed every man, woman, child and newborn in the entire world apart from Noah and his family? Hadn't he killed off most of the animals with them as well? Looking at this from a logical perspective, was he quite the right person to be stating that killing was bad and therefore outlawed? Wasn't he being just a tiny bit hypocritical? It would be a bit like Hitler saying, 'Thou must never go to war', or Harold Shipman saying, 'Thou must be kind to old people'.

Moses was up on the mountain talking to God for quite a while and his people below became restless and agitated, so they decided to build a golden calf and worship that instead of God. When Moses came down from the mountain and saw his people dancing around the golden calf and worshipping it, he was not best pleased. He had the stone tablets with him that were given to him by God, so he smashed them to pieces. Temper, temper! It got the better of him again.

Sorry, but I wonder if they were dancing and singing the old Vera Lynn song, *Veal meat again*. That was awful, wasn't it? Sorry.

This almighty and all-powerful God had brought them out of slavery. He had vanquished their pursuers and he had also sent them manna from heaven. They owed him much but rather than trust and worship him who had proven himself to them, they decided to build a golden calf on a plinth and worship that instead, just because they had been waiting a while. And then, to top this off, Moses came down from the mountain holding things which, even today, are held in great esteem by many people, and decided, in his wrath, to smash them.

Going back to the golden calf which was, as they thought, their new God, how did they make it? Where did the materials and craftsmanship come from? I suppose it didn't have to be made of actual gold. The word 'golden' could just be describing its colour but even if this is so, it had to be painted gold, at least. Where did the paint come from? They were in the middle of the desert and were surviving on manna from heaven. Where were all the tools needed to build such an idol? Surely there wasn't a B&Q or similar nearby?

Luckily, God forgave the people for worshipping the calf and he just told Moses to set to and made a couple more Ten Commandment tablets. He promised God that the Hebrews would keep the Ten Commandments. In doing the tablets a second time, did Moses remember what was on the first tablets? Did God have to dictate the commandments again? Or did Moses do his best to remember what was on them but made a few slip-ups along the way? Perhaps it did originally say 'convert' thy neighbour's wife. I jest.

When we look at this story and the stories of Adam and Eve and Noah we have to, as I have said before, totally acknowledge that they are naive, to say the least, but they are also enchanting. I feel though, that what we must not do is take them seriously as true historical accounts. Some will and do and one of those people may well be you and if this is the way you think, then that is fine with me but adding logic into the mix, I'm sorry but I just cannot see it and certainly cannot agree.

Here we have a baby in a basket in the river who is adopted willy-nilly by a Pharaoh and his daughter. He has a life of luxury before losing his temper and murdering someone and then he has to run away and sit down a well. He is then found by seven daughters of a father who has two names. The father then gives him one of his daughters because he has looked after them and his sheep for an hour or so one morning, before he sees God talking to him from a burning bush. The story goes on to plagues of frogs, lice, flies and locusts before God parts the waves of the sea for them to cross, their pursuers are drowned and then they are given magic food in the desert. The freed slaves know who God is and know he has delivered them and has fed and watered them and yet they suddenly decide to worship a model of a baby cow instead. When Moses sees this, he smashes the Ten Commandments which the world is to be ruled by but God, who normally kills at the drop of a hat, says, 'Oh never mind, Moses. Just go and make some more.'"

Is it all true? Really?

Would God want to punish me for all eternity when all I have done is led a good and loving life? Is he this insecure and angry?

The Story of Jonah

The story of Moses is lovely, naive but lovely, but let's move on to the story of Jonah, which is also delightful. A little silly again, but delightful nonetheless.

Now the word of the Lord came unto Jonah, the son of Amittai, saying, 'Arise, go to Nineveh, that great city and cry against it; for their wickedness is come up before me'. But Jonah rose up to flee unto Tarshish from the presence of the Lord and went down to Joppa and he found a ship going to Tarshish. So he paid the fare thereof, and went down into it, to go with them unto Tarshish from the presence of the Lord.

Once again, the Lord had found a city full of wickedness. It seemed there was wickedness everywhere but, again, instead of just changing the ways of the people with a click of his fingers he told Jonah to go and, 'Cry against it'. This, I presume, didn't mean to weep but to shout at them to try and get them to stop it all.

Jonah's ship went to sea but the Lord sent out a great wind in the sea.

He could summon up a great wind just like that so, as I say, why couldn't he just stop the people from sinning in the same way?

Anyway, the wind blew and there was an almighty tempest which was likely to break up the ship and its mariners were afraid. They cried, 'Every man unto his God!' and then started to throw everything overboard to lighten the ship. Jonah, however, didn't seem too bothered by it all and had gone below decks to have a sleep.

Cool or what! All above him were panicking because of what seemed like imminent death through drowning in a tempest but did he worry? No. He felt tired so thought he would just go and sleep through it all. What a dude!

The ship's master realised Jonah was missing so went down to see where he was. He found him and said, 'What meanest thou, oh sleeper? Arise and call upon thy God, if so be that God will think upon us, that we perish not.'

The rest of the crew decided that the tempest was of someone's making so they decided to cast lots to find out who was responsible.

It seems no one really knows what the actual 'casting of lots' entailed but it had to be something like flipping a coin or drawing straws, but whatever it was it seemed to have worked because they soon found out from it that Jonah was responsible.

They said to him, 'Tell us, we pray thee, for whose cause this evil is upon us? What is thine occupation? And whence comest thou? What is thy country? And of what people art thou?'

They were in the middle of a raging sea and had thrown everything overboard in order to save themselves. The tempest meant their lives hung delicately in the balance. The situation was more than quite desperate. Surely they would have asked how their lives could have been saved but no, all they wanted to know was where Jonah came from and what he did for a living.

Jonah said unto them, 'I am a Hebrew and I fear the Lord, the God of heaven, which have made the sea and the dry land.'

Now, Jonah was a prophet so didn't he know what God was like when he was annoyed? If he knew and feared God so much then why did he disobey him in the first place? He should have known God wouldn't just sit back and have a cup of tea and a biscuit and let it all happen.

By now the crew were exceedingly afraid. They asked him why he had brought this upon them as they knew Jonah had fled from the presence of the Lord because he had told them so. They asked Jonah what they should do to him to stop the sea being wrought and tempestuous and he replied that they should chuck him in the sea. He was quite stoic, it seems. He said if they cast him into the sea the tempest would subside and all would be well, but the men could not bring themselves to do this so they rowed with all their might to reach dry land, but they could not because the tempest was against them. Then they cried unto the Lord and said, 'We beseech thee oh Lord. We beseech thee. Let us not perish for this man's life, and lay not upon us innocent blood. For thou O Lord, has done as it pleased thee.'

They then decided to change their minds and toss Jonah into the sea and the sea immediately quietened and the tempest abated. They feared the Lord exceedingly and offered a sacrifice to him and made vows.

Jonah had defied his master and had taken the ship to Tarshish and God thought he should suffer for disobeying him. Why did everyone have to jump for fear of their lives every time God spoke, and why were the entire crew, and everyone else at sea that day, so cruelly punished just because of Jonah when they had done nothing wrong? They hadn't aided Jonah to flee from God. He was just a passenger on their ship. They were all totally innocent people and yet they feared for their lives and also learned to fear God exceedingly. This puzzles me, the enigma that is God. He is supposed to be all loving and yet we are all supposed to fear him at the same time. It seems he loves us right up to the point we do the slightest thing wrong and then he hates us so much he suddenly wants to kill us. Am I being too flippant in suggesting, just maybe, he was slightly bipolar?

Jonah had been tossed overboard and the sea had settled, so let's move on with the story.

It seems the Lord didn't want to let Jonah die. He had foreseen what was going to happen so he had cunningly prepared a great fish to come and swallow Jonah whole in order to save his life. The fish did swallow him and he was in the belly of the fish for three days and three nights.

I'm sorry, but how likely is this? Are we supposed to take this as another true historical fact? How can a man live inside a fish for three days and nights? If we look at this with any kind of even semi-intelligent logic, we have to realise it was impossible. There are fish big enough to swallow humans, but where did Jonah get his air from? No human could ever live under water for even three hours, let alone three days inside a fish. The natural environment inside a fish is simply a method of swallowing food, breaking it down, absorbing the nutrients within it and then ejecting what is left over. This would have happened to Jonah. He wouldn't have been able to just sit there merrily by one of the fish's gills to breathe and take in the scenery around him, would he?

When, as an innocent child, I went to Sunday school, they taught the story of *Jonah and the Whale*. Even then, my teachers were rather naive about science. Obviously, a whale is a mammal and Jonah was swallowed by a fish. Am I splitting hairs here? Maybe I am, but it does show how little some religionists know of the world around them as they stick to their book and ignore reality.

Jonah sat in his fish and prayed to God for his safe deliverance. He uttered the following:

And said I cried by reason of mine affliction unto the Lord, and he heard me; out of the belly of hell cried I, and thou heardest my voice.

For thou hadst cast me into the deep, in the midst of the seas; and the floods compassed me about; all thy billows and thy waves passed over me.

Then I said, I am cast out of thy sight; yet I will look again to the holy temple.

The waters compassed me about, even to the soul; the depth closed me round about, the weeds were wrapped about my head.

I went down to the bottoms of the mountains; the earth with her bars was about me forever: Yet hast thou brought up my life from corruption, O Lord my God.

When my soul fainted within me I remembered the Lord: And my prayer come in unto thee, into thine holy temple.

They that observe lying vanities forsake their own mercies

But I will sacrifice unto thee with the voice of thanksgiving; I will pay that that I have vowed. Salvation is of the lord."

And the Lord spake unto the fish, and it vomited out Jonah upon the dry land.

I'm sorry to have to bring this up yet again, but here was Jonah sitting inside a fish and saying a prayer. If we think about it for even only a second, we have to realise there was no one with him and he was deep under water. How on earth, or at sea, do we know what he said? No one knows, do they? Can you say a prayer inside a fish? Maybe it is the best 'plaice' to do it. Sorry.

His prayer was long, laborious and, in places, almost unintelligible. Why didn't he just say, 'Okay, God, I've done wrong. I repent. Can you let me out of this fish?'

Another very charming but incredulous story that, somehow, we are supposed to take seriously. Or maybe it is all allegorical? Maybe it has some deep meaning that we have to interpret for ourselves but I fail to see what that meaning is. The only thing I can see is the fact if you upset God you are in for it, but that doesn't just come from this story, does it? It comes from the whole Bible.

Much of the Bible is the word of Co— (I'm talking about fish and genuinely nearly typed Cod there, sorry.) Much of the Bible is supposed to be the word of God which has been passed on to people in dreams. Maybe this is the case here. Maybe the particular writer of the piece did have a dream about a man being eaten by a fish and then naturally thought it was God who had planted that dream in his head. We all have very strange dreams but we had better not take them all too seriously.

Going back to Revelation.

4.14.

These are they which were not defiled with women; for they are virgins. These are they which follow the Lamb whithersoever he goeth.

These are they who will follow Jesus but why do they have to be virgins? What difference does this make? Perhaps there is something special about having virgin followers. Something that I cannot see. What I can see though is this obsession with sex yet again. Why doesn't it say those with blonde or ginger hair will be the followers of the lamb? Or maybe those with black sandals and not brown ones? Again, the onus is placed upon sex.

And what of those terrible women who have 'defiled' these men? Should they, once again, be stoned to death? Homosexuality is so hated in the Bible and here, even heterosexuality is being frowned upon with such loathing. So much sex is frowned upon and yet the Bible writers just love to include it whenever they possibly can.

Am I being too simplistic again in saying that we should all ignore this obsession with sexual rights and wrongs and just get on with our lives and enjoy them? So many take all this as being completely literal and therefore feel guilt every time they indulge in what is, after all, the most natural thing ever to evolve. Whether someone is having sex with another of the same sex, with someone of the opposite sex or even just on their own, in no way should any guilt ever come into it.

Enjoy!!

Robert Ingersoll

US Civil War veteran and political leader Robert (Bob) Ingersoll, 1833-99 was obviously a wise man and thinker. He was a man I would like to have met and talked to at length.

Known as the 'Great Agnostic', Robert Green Ingersoll popularised the criticism of the Bible and scientific rationalism. Before he served in the American Civil War he was a lawyer and became Illinois Attorney General. He was also a lecturer who was known for his wit as he exposed the orthodox superstitions of his time. His quotes have stood the test of time and are still very apt today.

A quote from him.

If God created the universe, there was a time when he commenced to create. Back of that commencement there must have been an eternity. In that eternity what was God doing?

He certainly did not think. There was nothing to think about. He did not remember. Nothing had ever happened. What did he do?

Can you imagine anything more absurd than an infinite intelligence in an infinite nothing wasting an eternity?

You can be religious and praise God all you like and you are very welcome to do so, but this kind of very straight and forthright logic gets me every time. If we give it a little thought and with an open mind, I'm sorry but we must see that Mr Ingersoll's thoughts are true.

Another of his quotes:

Justice is the only worship.
   Love is the only priest.
   Ignorance is the only slavery.
   Happiness is the only good.
   The time to be happy is now.
   The place to be happy is here.
   The way to be happy is to make others so.

One more quote:

A fact never went in partnership with a miracle. Truth does not need the assistance of miracle. A fact will fit every other fact in the universe, because it is the product of all other facts. A lie will fit nothing except another lie made for the express purpose of fitting it.

A quote from *The Writings of Robert G Ingersoll*:

Each nation has created a god, and the god has always resembled its creators. He hated and loved what they hated and loved, and he was invariably found on the side of those in power. Each god was intensely patriotic and detested all nations but his own. All these gods demanded praise, flattery, and worship. Most of them were pleased with sacrifice, and the smell of innocent blood has ever been considered a divine perfume. All these gods have insisted upon having a vast number of priests and the priests have always insisted upon being supported by people, and the principal business of these priests has been to boast about their god, to insist that he could easily vanquish all the other gods put together.'

Isn't he right? Each nation does have its own god. I would agree with Ingersoll and say we created those gods, while some will argue that it was those gods who created us. I would say that all these gods are equal in the fact that they were only created by us and, therefore, do not exist, where you will probably state strongly that one of them, your particular one, does exist and is the only one.

There have been thousands of gods and yet yours is the only real one.

Isn't it strange that if you were born in a particular area you would follow the god of that area? Why is it the one and only true god just happens to be of the area you were born in?

If you were born in England or America you will most probably follow the god of the Bible, whereas if you were born in Tibet you would worship Buddha and so on and so on. Why is it generally and strongly this way round and not the other?

Ingersoll's thinking seems way ahead of his time. Today we could see many such thinkers as we learn more about the world we live in but Ingersoll lived a century and a half ago and I would imagine his thinking was deemed almost as radical as that of Charles Darwin. He was an intelligent man but was also probably considered a heretic as well. As I said at the start of this little interlude, he was a man I would love to have met and talked to at length. He was also a man that I would love to have learned more from.

One more quote:

If hell were real, each occupant would be a shining reminder that God has failed.

When I was a child I spoke as a child, I understood as a child, I thought as a child; but when I became a man, I put away childish things.

Corinthians 13.11

I suppose you could read and take this in whichever way you chose. I would say I put away the Bible itself, while you could say nothing but the Bible makes sense so you put away everything but it.

Life After Death

During the last fifty-five years I have never kept it a secret that I have no belief whatsoever in any one of the thousands of gods that are supposed to be out there. I don't know too much about any of them apart from the one who is generally worshipped in the area where I was born. At first, I only had this niggle against religion which was set in my mind the day I was asked, as a child, to move from the front pew to make way for someone better and more important than me, but through the years my beliefs and disbeliefs have manifested themselves through thought and have brought me to where I am today. I now live in a world where I feel totally free and it is a world full of wonder. The only limits or borders I have, are the ones set in my brain through intelligence, thought, rationality and common sense. I have never needed the Ten Commandments to tell me it is wrong to murder or steal. Surely that is common sense, totally and utterly. I don't need the Bible to tell me to love thy neighbour. Isn't that common sense as well?

As I have no biblical beliefs you could be very quick to deduce that I have no belief either in life after death but, to some extent, you would be wrong.

I have studied the Bible and the Christian religion and can find no logic or real purpose in it. What I have read in it I can quickly dismiss in my own mind, but with life after death, I have seen some evidence and there are things in it that do make me question its validity. Please do not jump up and say I am a total believer in it. I am not, but I do feel there is something. Some things make sense and I cannot simply dismiss them. The story of creation was written some 3,500 years ago in a time of pre-science and, although the Bible seems to know exactly what happened during the creation and seems to know exactly what that god was supposed to have said to himself as he was doing it, they had no idea of the shape of the earth or sun or moon or even where the sun went at night. With life after death, though, it is still happening today. People are dying today and people say they are contacting the dead today. Does that make sense? It does to me to a small extent, although I am still very sceptical about it.

Many years ago, I had a couple of friends round for dinner and as we talked the subject of life after death was brought up. My mind immediately totally dismissed the subject as dross and I could have left it there, but that would have been flying directly in the face of my being. My mind is fascinated by anything and everything and although I dismissed it, my mind wanted proof. It would not just let me be dogmatic so I said to the person talking that if he was so sure of his subject, perhaps he could prove it. Really, I thought he would back down but no, he wanted to prove it and we then started on what was to become an interesting evening, to say the least.

We cleared away the dinner things from the dining table and then cut out squares of paper on which we wrote letters and numbers, plus the words 'yes' and 'no' and then we placed an old upturned wine glass in the middle. After another good mouthful of red wine, I joined the rest, my two friends and my wife, and placed my finger on the upturned glass. My friend went into what looked like a bit of a trance-like state (Nothing unusual for him) and then uttered the old and usual words, "Is there anyone there?" No, he didn't say 'Knock once for yes and twice for no.'

How he knew, I did not know, but he said there was somebody there and asked the person, or spirit or thing, to spell out its name. With no help from me, but probably from my friend, the glass moved and spelled out the word GERGE. We fumbled in our brains to think what the word meant but then the spirit was asked who a message was for and it spelled out DLLY. Again, we could not work out the name so we moved on with me still in total disbelief and wondering what the hell I was doing. Another slug of wine helped me join in more.

The next so-called contact was supposed to be someone called Peter and this spirit managed to point to the fact that he was an army officer and was killed in the First World War and was watching over me. Again, I did not believe and was becoming quite bored with the whole situation. I needed more wine and I needed proof, as nothing so far had given me the slightest evidence or encouragement so I decided to up the game and ask a question. I said that if all this was real then surely a simple question could be answered. I said I would become a believer if the glass moved to the number of the first house I had ever lived in. I took another mouthful of wine and readied myself to wallow in my smugness, but then the glass moved to the correct number but I tried to dismiss it as a fluke. My wife and friends berated me for not believing, as no one else in the room could possibly have known the number of the house but I saw it as just a coincidence. Perhaps a lucky guess. The answer was number three but is was not difficult to guess, was it? Either that or I just wanted to see it as a coincidence. It would have been more believable if I had been born in number 139. I felt I was not being dogmatic in my reactions but this, to me, was not enough proof on what was a very controversial and almost weird subject so I upped the odds again.

"Right," I said. "Now tell me, in order, the numbers of the rest of the houses I have lived in prior to this one."

There were four others and in no way did I think my question possible to answer, but it did happen, with only one house number missed out. Even that was not a mistake. The house in question had been built in between other, numbered ones and was only known by a name.

I was suddenly quite stunned and perplexed. Here I was, half drunk and in the middle of something that I had always thought of, in my words, as complete tosh but it had been proven that I was wrong. In no way could anyone have known the answers to my question. For once I fell silent.

A few days later I was with my mother and talked to her about it and mentioned the words or names, GERGE and DLLY. She shocked me again by saying she did once have relatives called George and Dolly and Dolly was still alive. Once more I was stunned.

As a man who is completely honest and open with his thoughts, please believe me when I say the whole of the above story is true. In no way would I make such a thing up. It would be easy for you to say that this is only written as a book filler but no. I can honestly swear to its genuineness.

Later, when married to Chrissy, my second and late wife, I asked her why I kept having this vision in my head of an elderly and plumpish lady wearing a grey coat and having grey hair and grey whiskers. She asked me to tell her more but there wasn't much more to say. I told her I simply knew she was something to do with her and the letter 'G' was relevant. Chrissy smiled and said her name was Mrs Gymer and she used to look after Chrissy sometimes as a child. She said they had a great love and respect for each other.

Mags, my wife now, (I've had a few) used to be into horses and had her own when younger and I have mentioned to her about the time her horse bolted for a gate and she fell off. I also told her about a man in the village who wore scruffy clothes and worn out boots. These too were true statements.

This is not something I have really delved into since and I still do not understand it in any real way but, as I say, I cannot dismiss it. I am not a true follower of it and do not think I ever will be but there is something there that cannot just be ignored.

I heard the late Colin Fry once said in an interview that (And I have said the same thing in my *Wonderment* chapter on the universe) all energy is the same now as it always has been and always will be.

Energy can morph from one form to another but it cannot just simply disappear. What Colin Fry implies is that thoughts are energy and therefore they are always there. This ties in with what I saw someone once term as *Anima Mundi* which is a connection between all living things on the planet. The person I saw talking about *Anima Mundi* actually went a step further and said that it included the fact that every thought ever thought still existed somewhere in the cosmos and could be tapped into as you would a library or the Interweb. I do admit that this seems highly unlikely, as does talking to the dead, but I have seen some proof. Personally, I have no belief in souls but am I wrong again? Are there souls floating about out there? Are there souls which do have a loving and caring need to contact their families, if only to tell them all is well? Perhaps, rather than talk about souls, I should talk about spirits. Perhaps the spirit inside someone and of someone is the energy that lives on after them. I cannot see a soul that was planted inside someone by a god but I can see the spirit of them being the energy that person generates and gives off. Again, I cannot prove or disprove this theory so I keep an open mind to it. No one can actually disprove the existence of any god 100% but it is practical to say it is so highly unlikely that we can almost count on the fact. We can't totally disprove the fact there are ten-legged, blue and white striped men with three noses who live on Pluto but, in reality, we can assume it, as it is so unlikely. Life after death is different to me though.

Yes, I have seen evidence for life after death, but in no way does this invoke any ties with religion. There may be something in it, something we do not totally understand or even cannot begin to comprehend but, to my mind, it cannot have anything to do with the Bible or that particular god or any of other thousands of gods who have been invented.

Whether this contact with the dead comes from the dead or we are just tapping into energy, I do not know and I honestly do not think we will ever understand. We can see the universe but we do not fully understand it. We cannot see spirits, souls or the energy of the dead, so what chance have we of fully understanding them?

Perhaps though, one day, there will be a huge Eureka moment and someone will give a simple answer to everything, but will that possibly come before we destroy the world we live in? I have forecast the crashing of our population due to major wars within it and then we will lose the science we rely upon today. We will be living much simpler lives and there will not be the time left for proper science, only thoughts. Again, I am very open to being proven wrong and I sincerely hope I am.

Will we ever know what truly happens when we die? My mind discounts heaven and hell but it cannot discount something being there. I suppose the biggest thing we can do is live the life we have to its fullest today, while we have it.

'We can live today with a dreadful fear of hell or we cannot worry about hell and live today.'

That was me and I think it makes sense.

Colin Fry also used to explain that people made contact through him not only to comfort the living recipient, but also to tell that person that life is for the living and they must get on with their lives instead of worrying about those who have passed over. We all lose people we love and we all need comfort of some kind, perhaps any kind, but then, in the end, we do all have to move on and forge a new life for ourselves. I can vividly remember holding my Chrissie as she drew her last breath and then laying her back on the bed with no life at all left in her tired little frame. She still looked like my wife but she was gone. I kissed her on the forehead, said goodbye and knew I would miss her dreadfully but I also knew, even at that point, that from then on I had to make another life for myself. They were hard, painful, tearful and almost pitiful times but slowly they passed and slowly I managed to rebuild my life into the great one it is today. Luckily, I am a strong person and although I did really struggle sometimes, I did have myself to rely upon, but there is nothing wrong with needing support, whether that support is from friends, relations, a medium and the afterlife or a group such as the Samaritans.

Whatever support you seek, though, has to be non-permanent. Even a medium can be good for you but, in the end, you must grow and learn to slowly support yourself. I used to work with the Samaritans and I remember its founder, Chad Varah, talking in a seminar at York University. He stated just this: he said we were there for those who needed us but that need should never become a permanent thing. An emotional injury should be treated just the same as a physical one. The injury is there and when you receive the injury you need all the treatment you can get, but eventually that injury must heal because if it doesn't, your life can be ruined. Yes, it is fine to seek a medium but, in the end, you must eventually move on. It may be a hard thing to say but the dead are dead and life is, as I have said, for the living. We can lean on anything for a while but must move on with, eventually, only ourselves as the best support available.

In summary to this chapter I will say that I have seen some evidence of something after death. It is not something I would yell about from the rooftops or something I would or have ever delved into wholeheartedly since, but I do believe there is something there. People do become so interested in it that, as with religion, they live totally by it instead of living their own real lives. I do not. All I can say is it is a very interesting thought.

In a television interview Colin Fry was once told he shouldn't be trying to help people think for themselves. The person added that it was the church's responsibility to tell people what to believe. A damning statement or what?

Just as with myself and my books, all this man was trying to do was teach people to think for and help themselves and the person he was talking to had stated very openly that this was not what was wanted in the church. The statement made by him was very damning. Damning to his church and his religion and those who followed it. It was damning to any thought ever of free thinking and free will.

As I am writing this, my wife has just had a sad telephone call to say her uncle was found, this morning, dead in his bed. This gentleman led a good life and has always been there through my wife's life and my life over the last fifteen years. We were not excessively close but I held a large respect for him and his warmth and kindness. Ron has been on this earth for a good number of years and, quite suddenly, he has gone. In a way, you can easily understand why so many people hang on to heaven and an eternal existence in heaven. Despite the fact that our Ron has been a big part of my wife's life for so many years, he is gone. Just like that, he has ceased to exist and no one will ever see him, touch him or speak to him again. That is it and if we do not believe in religion or any other properties of life after death, it is the end and, very suddenly, final. How easy, and comforting, it must be to believe that, one day, Ron's family will see him and speak to him once more when they too die.

Colin Fry was never a man I followed just for his apparent ability to talk to the dead and he was never a man I followed because of his beliefs in anything. He was just a good man with a sound logic, a logic that he had thought through for himself. He believed in God and I do not but that means nothing. At least he believed in his god after thinking about it. If we had ever met we would have had views that differed somewhat but if we had ever met, I'm sure we would have had plenty to say to each other. Sadly, though, we will never meet in this life because Colin was taken from his life by cancer and died, at the time of writing, earlier this year.

Colin Fry 1962-2015. RIP

PHILOSOPHY is like being in a darkened room looking for a cat.

METAPHYSICS is like being in a darkened room looking for a black cat that isn't there.

THEOLOGY is like being in a darkened room looking for a black cat that isn't there but then shouting, "I've found it!"

SCIENCE is like being in a darkened room looking for a black cat but turning the light on first.

Prayer

What is prayer? How do we pray? What do we pray for? Why do we pray? Do we even really know who we are praying to?

Is prayer a huge benefit to us? Is it beneficial at all? Do those who do not pray miss out terribly on life?

Do we deserve the receipt of what we pray for and does prayer give us an undeserved advantage over others? If this is the case are we being self-centred in our prayers?

If we are at war and we pray to win, how does any god decide which side to be on?

If we pray for an ill person to live and yet they die, is it your god's fault?

Millions have prayed and many still pray. Some pray constantly. Let's look at it all in detail.

There are seven billion people living on our small planet and can we possibly say that every one of us has a right to pray and that prayer will be listened to by a god? Can we say that any god could possibly listen to seven billion people at the same time? Can we say that with all these people praying and him having to listen, he has the time to judge every single prayer and come up with a solution to each one individually? Surely all this relies purely upon the supernatural and no amount of real reasoning and logic can provide evidence for it.

Many would tell you, though, that there is real evidence and many would rejoice in it. I was talking to a man a few weeks ago who said he had complete evidence that prayers were listened to and answered. I settled to listen carefully and intently to his words because I always yearn for evidence and to learn, but what he said was he had once been to an interview for a job and when he returned home he sat in his kitchen and prayed to Jesus that the job should be given to him. The following day he received a telephone call to say the job was his. Of course, Jesus had listened and had made the appointment his. Praise the Lord and crack open the Champagne!

A simple mind could well accept this and pray for everything but any logical and enquiring mind would see the gaping flaws in the man's argument.

The man had been for his interview. Was he:

1. The only interviewee?

2. Capable of giving a good interview whilst others were not?

3. Of a good general appearance whilst the others were scruffy?

4. More qualified educationally than the others?

5. More experienced?

6. All round the best person for the job?

He could well have been any or most of the above and therefore got the job. Why did he think, automatically, that it was his prayer that had worked? Surely, if he had to pray in the first place, he had little confidence in his own abilities and his suitability for the post. The other thing that bothers me here is the fact that this Christian gentleman actually relied upon his prayer and God to give him an unfair advantage over other candidates. Surely cheating in this way should be against his religious beliefs? And what of those employing him? What if he had no qualifications or experience and others had plenty? What if he was not a good person but others were? What if they had realised he had lied and bluffed all through his interview? Weren't the employers more than a little confused as to why they had given this man the job when others were infinitely more suited? Going back to the interviewees, what if all of them had prayed to God to be given the job? How would God have made up his mind? Perhaps he would have let the person get the job who was best suited in the first place, thus annulling all prayers said to him. In this incident and many others, the person praying is doing so either as an undeserved advantage (cheating) or because they do not have confidence in themselves. Surely we should be relying upon ourselves rather than upon the supernatural?

As a child, I was taught to pray. I was told to say my prayers to God each night and for a while, through complete ignorance and innocence, I did as I was told. I would put the palms of my hands together, close my eyes and ask God to look after me and my family before getting into my bed, safe in the knowledge that God would do as I asked.

This was all so sweet and innocent and I really do believe it helped me settle down for the night, but, as I grew older and started to really think for myself, it became obvious to me that I was praying to thin air and nothing and no one was ever listening. I realised that I was praying to the Christian God when others were praying to other gods and there were many of them. Surely they could not all exist and listen? Why was mine supposed to be so special in the area where I lived? Then the penny dropped. The god of the area where I lived was just that. It just happened that I was born in that area. If I had been born in a different area, I would have been praying to a different god. The only thing that made my god so special was being in the area where I lived. I was born in England so it was quite natural that the god I was taught to pray to was the God of the Bible. It would have been the same for the language I spoke or the clothes I wore or the food I ate. If I was born in India, I would have been eating curry and onion bhajis rather than roast beef and veg and if I was born in Italy I would not have been praying in English but in Italian. If I was born in Germany, I may have been wearing lederhosen rather than jeans. The penny had dropped. It seemed there were as many, if not more gods than there were countries or areas, so why was mine the one and only?

I'd had the seeds of atheism planted in me as a youngster but my thoughts (quite deep for a child) began to multiply and germinate within my little brain. Just what was I praying for and who was I praying to? If I didn't pray for my mother on one particular night, would she still be alive and well the following night? Of course she would. If I didn't pray to do well in my maths at school, the following day would I suddenly forget that a quarter of sixteen is four? My maths, in those days, was brilliant. By the age of eight I had learned long multiplication, long division, decimals and fractions. I could recite all my tables without giving them a single thought. Why did I need to pray to be good? You could say that it was God who gave me my mathematical ability but I would strongly reject this. I was just lucky that I was born with this ability, just as some are lucky in that they can pick up a guitar or violin and play it. Some people are born with the wonderful ability to sing and I am completely envious of them and opposite to them. I feel my natural ability is to be able to deal with life and reality, but would I trade that with the ability to sing and play musical instruments? I would have to answer, 'No', to this but to sing and play would be good. There have been times in my life, such as sitting around a camp fire in Africa, when I would have loved the ability to play a guitar and sing to entertain my fellow travellers but I do feel my ability to look up at the universe and try and grasp its reality does outweigh the other urges.

Going back to me being comforted, as a child, by prayer, I can easily see that many are comforted still today. Children probably do still jump in bed, safe in their knowledge that God is looking over and after them and what harm can that cause? The harm it can cause is the fact that, like me, they are indoctrinated into a religion before their little minds have a single chance of grasping the actual reality that I love and that I live for. They are taught to believe in the supernatural when they have no conception of what it is. Thinking realistically about it, wouldn't it be better to just jump into bed and snuggle down for the night knowing your family are downstairs and they love you dearly with all their hearts? That they love you, provide for you and are there to protect you?

In no way am I stupid enough to think that all parents are like this. I just use my grandchildren as illustrations. Parents can and should be a child's world, but I realise some are not and their children cannot snuggle down, warm in the thought that they are loved and cared for. How many abused children have gone to bed with bruises or worse and with a great need to pray for something better? This is understandable but in the morning, after praying their little innocent hearts out, has the abuse disappeared? Are the bruises still there? Of course they are.

We do live in a world where pressure seems to fall upon normal lives. Our world is complicated and demanding and the problems caused by just ordinary everyday living can easily leave most people feeling they need a crutch to lean on. Some then turn to God and religion and we then see grown adults kneeling and saying their prayers each night just as the children do. Are these people really believing in what they are doing or are they just clutching at straws because they live in a world they simply cannot understand or cope with? I'm sorry but, to my mind, reality is all we have and no amount of praying will ever change that fact.

I said earlier that if I did not pray one night for my mother's health, would she suddenly suffer before the next night's prayers are said? This, I suppose, could bring forth a problem. What if my mother was not prayed for one night and then, the next day, she had a horrible accident? Can you imagine the guilt I would have felt? I was a child and my child's mind would have told me my mother had suffered because I hadn't cared enough to pray for her. This fear could, and probably does, instil a drastic need to pray just in case. But if we look at this in a realistic way we could say that she suffered through my lack of praying but we could also say she had suffered through God's sheer hatred of not being prayed to and being worshipped upon high. Had God deliberately harmed my mother simply because he had a thoroughly nasty side and I had not talked to him and worshipped him enough the night before?

Writing this piece about me praying as a small child has inspired me to look on the Interweb for other examples of children praying. I have come across the following:

The first thing it says is that this person (the author) was raised by 'God-fearing' parents. I'm sorry but I do have serious problems with this. It has been said to me that 'God is love and there can be no love without him', and then here we are with someone saying they were 'God-fearing' parents. Which one do they want? Surely they cannot have both. If this god is the highest and most loving thing in the entire universe, why should we fear him? And if he has to be feared to such an extent that we must praise and worship him so vehemently, just to appease him and stop him harming us, then how can he possibly be this all-loving thing? Surely this is just one huge contradiction again?

The article proceeded to say that this person was taught, as was I, to pray from an early age and the person's parents would read passages from a children's Bible to them and after the reading they would discuss the story.

It is a good job it was a children's Bible. I suppose much of the content of the adult one had been censored out. It would be a little awkward, to say the least, if the parents had to explain Ezekiel to under tens. And, if all the sex and violence had been edited out, would it then just be a pamphlet as Mrs Brown had said?

The person who wrote the article went on to say that teaching young children to pray is a good thing which brought, 'Heartfelt Reverence – belief that God could and would do what he had promised'.

This brings up certain questions.

'Belief that God could and would do what he had promised'.

So, we have a child who is so young it has absolutely no understanding of life at all and he or she is told that they can pray to God and he could or would do what he had promised. So if they prayed for something simple the next day, such as a new bicycle and they do not get it, then do they feel their parent's god had let them down? If they are children of abusive parents do they hate this god when the abuse doesn't stop the next day? Children are told that God watches everything they do. It is totally horrible to talk about, I know, but what if a child is being sexually abused and they pray to God for this disgusting torment to stop? Not only does the abuse not stop but they are also saddled with the knowledge that God was watching as it happened and still he did nothing about it. That child could grow up having every right to not believe in any god and you couldn't possibly blame them, as they had been so terribly let down, but this then makes them an atheist and they are then told they will burn in hell for all eternity while the child's abuser repents, goes to heaven and has a life of luxury. Is this what we should be teaching our children?

I heard a story of a child who once prayed for a new bicycle but knew he wouldn't get one so he stole one instead, but promised to immediately repent his sins so that no harm would come to him.

My way would be to teach children from this same very early age that they have great worth. We should show them that they are loved and respected and hold a great position within our families. We should chastise when they do wrong but boy, should we praise when they do right. Although they are only children we should treat them all as equals and they should wallow in unbounded love and joy and this unbounded love and joy need, in no way, to come from any religious superstition. If we can teach children to grow to respect themselves fully for the people they are and also respect those who respect them, then they will grow without the need for superstition at all. They will grow with the strength inside them to live their lives with reality and common sense being their only boundary.

What I would say in conclusion about children praying is it is my strong opinion that no child should be indoctrinated into any religion. As Richard Dawkins has so rightly said in the past, there is no such thing as a Christian or Muslim child. We can only have children of Christian or Muslim parents.

Total reality is, to me, a far greater thing than any religion or superstition and I do live my life by it, but I know many people need to either believe in religion or cling on to it for support or through fear and this has to be everyone's prerogative, but I do feel strongly that anyone entering into religion should do so freely and at an age when they can understand and make up their own minds. Children should learn to see life through their own eyes and work it out for themselves. In no way should they be bombarded while still being innocent beings who should only have to think about playing and being loved by their parents. The love, comfort, security and protection given by good parents has to be of far greater value than praying and relying on something that no one can provide even an ounce of real empirical evidence for.

Saying grace:

In the past, I have seen families sitting round a table and holding hands or putting their hands together to say grace and, thereby, thank God for the food that is about to be eaten.

A question here quickly strikes into my mind. I have been to an American Thanksgiving where we were all encouraged to start eating at three p.m. The kitchen and living room of the house were in no way small and almost every surface, apart from the chairs on which we were eventually to sit, was covered with all manner of things from turkey to ham to apple pie, pumpkin pie and lashings of bread and butter, cakes, biscuits and whatever other comestibles you could possibly think of. Wine, beer and spirits were in abundance too.

Getting back to the question. Here we were with far, far more food than we could ever need or even eat and after we had eaten buffet style for a couple of hours, we were sat down at a large table ready to have the 'real' meal. I was already quite stuffed at this point and looked at everything set out so finely before me, that I honestly felt I didn't need, when the gentleman of the house suddenly said, very seriously, "Let us pray."

I was an English atheist in a house full of God-fearing Americans and I suddenly felt quite uncomfortable. Luckily, everyone closed their eyes as they prayed and, in doing so, they couldn't see me just sitting there and looking around, wondering what the hell was going on.

They said grace and thanked God for providing the food they were about to eat. What about the stack of food we had already eaten? I thought. Why didn't we praise God for that? Perhaps he hadn't supplied that part.

Why did they think their God had provided all that was before us? Surely it was our hosts who had worked hard, earned money, saved and then gone to the shops who had provided everything? They had worked hard all morning to prepare the food as well. They hadn't simply popped out that morning for a walk in the park, only to return to the house and find it overflowing with goodies of every kind, supplied by God, had they?

You would be quite right to say you could guess what is coming next but here we go:

There we were, sitting amongst this almost obscene amount of food and thanking the god of these people for it, when there were starving people throughout the world who had nothing. We were about to start round two of an eating binge with our stomachs already bulging while millions of others around the world suffered acute malnutrition. How could we be so blessed with so much from this god when others were so hungry? Once again, here were these people who thanked God for it all when they had no thought whatsoever for others. What arrogance was it to think they deserved so much when so many had so little? The injustice of it all never even entered their minds. Here again were people who were highly religious and believed every word of it and yet, in reality, they really didn't give a toss or concern for anyone else. Their own 'self' was all that mattered. They had obviously prayed to God when all the starving folk in the world had obviously not bothered. Do you honestly think a starving person would not bother? I would think any starving person would pray to any god for any amount of food. Perhaps they just hadn't prayed to the right god, as my hosts had done. Everyone tucked in with gusto while I ate tentatively with them, knowing full well that there was no real need. We finally finished eating at ten p.m. and still there was food left over. What happened to a couple of loaves and a few small fishes? Is it any wonder that half the population are overweight and obesity is seen today as an epidemic?

In my books, I do talk about my Lucy. She is my young granddaughter and we totally adore each other. I was sitting next to her at the dinner table a few weeks ago when dinner was being served, so I held her hand and said we should pray to God for providing our food. The look on her sweet little face was brilliant.

"Don't be stupid, Granddad," she said mockingly. "You know all that stuff is rubbish!"

I have told Lucy of my beliefs and non-beliefs but have never done so in any persuasive way. I have told her she must live her life by listening to both sides of any argument before making up her own mind. It seems she certainly had made up her mind on this subject. Okay, so it happened she agreed with me but even if she hadn't, I would have respected her views in the same way because, whichever way she thought, those thoughts were of her own making and not those that had been drummed into her. She is a child who is actively encouraged to think for herself and live knowing she is of value and is truly loved by those around her. I think her life will be sound.

If you were really ill with pneumonia and you had enough strength to visit just one place, would it be:

1.A church where you could pray for help from religion?

2.A doctors' surgery where you could seek help from science?

Continuing with the chapter:

As I said earlier, my family used to pray as children. We had no real formal teachings in the art of praying and just used to put our hands together and utter what it was we wanted to say. We might pray for our health or our parents or even scrambled eggs for tea, but pray we did. We did it all in a quite ad hoc manner but evidently there is an actual art to praying, as we shall see as I put down things I have learnt.

It seems we should all find time to pray, even in our busy lives. It is suggested that we pray, probably when we wake and when we go to bed, as these are times when we are not so busy and have time to concentrate. It also says there is no set time for prayer as God is ready to listen at any time.

Many people pray during hard, stressful or emotional times when their need is the greatest and some can stay in a constant state of prayer throughout the day. Observant Jews can pray three times each day and Muslims pray five times each day. I suppose those in terrible torment for whatever reason may pray much more often than this.

The next thing they say is to find a good spot for praying. Usually, it seems, this is kneeling beside your bed but they also suggest you pray somewhere that is evocative, such as beside a river or before a natural view. Although I never pray today I can understand this to a certain extent, as you do get a strong inner feeling in such places. My feeling is one of wonderment at the natural world before me but if you believe in God, then I can see why such a place invokes the same feelings but they are interpreted in a different way.

I am told that prayer can be used as part of rituals where the burning of sacrifices takes place as offerings to God and yet it can simply be a talk with God.

Looking back again to my earlier days when I prayed, at no time did any God ever talk back to me. Was he busy with more important issues? Was he busy with more important people? Was it my fault for not being sincere enough? Was I not worthy of God's attention? Others hear God's voice and word so why was I different? Well, it had to either be one of the former reasons or the fact that those who hear God's voice and word are only imagining it. Are they deluded by their needs and beliefs so much that in their desperation they actually believe they are hearing what they are clearly not? Are they hearing only what they want and desperately need to hear?

Going back a couple of paragraphs, it says that prayer can be offered during the burning of a sacrifice. Perhaps that prayer should be offered not to God but to the poor thing that is being burned for no real reason.

We normally see people praying by their bedside or in church or at the dinner table but apparently, prayer can be offered from anywhere at any time. Articles I have learned from say:

Prayers can be offered during song and dance.

Some Christians pray while exercising their body.

You can even shout prayers at the top of your voice and run for the tops of mountains if it makes you appreciate God.

Evidently you can pray wherever you are and during whatever it is you are doing as long as that prayer is heartfelt. God will always listen.

My life is full of wonder and I almost explode at the beauty of everything around me. It all points to nature and natural selection but to those who do not share my viewpoint, it all points to God. The difference here is that in my view there is no God, but that then gives me nothing to lean on and pray to for better things, so you can see the need for religion. To be religious does give you something to lean on and pray to and you do not have to be so strong. Many people are not strong but those who can be are free. We do not have to scream at the top of our voices or dart to the hilltops to appreciate, wonder and be thankful. We have it all because we have ourselves and that it all we need.

The articles I have read go on to teach how to get in a 'prayer position', how to 'prepare for praying', how to 'begin praying', how to 'make the request' and then how to 'end the prayer'. Out of respect for the person involved I would never interrupt their prayers and I would never tell them they are totally stupid for praying in the first place but I would suggest that life is so much easier without all this wishing and hoping and fearing something that only exists within the Bible. In making the last statement, 'only exists within the Bible' I am not being cruel or flippant. It simply is a fact. The only evidence for God is the Bible and the person who comes up with anything more concrete at all will probably be hailed as the next Messiah.

Someone once said to me that, through prayer, God shows his love.

I don't fully understand this. I understand that religious folk can thank God for them being born but is his love shown in that simple act and the fact they carry on breathing? Is his love shown by filling your table with food? Does he convey his love by the fact your family are left alive?

I can see plenty of reasons why religionists can thank God but what of me? I have no God in my life and yet I was born, I breathe, I eat and my family are alive. What is so special about this particular God's love? Could it be that people are frightened not to love him? Is it like a school bully who takes your sweets? It is better to hand over the sweets rather than suffer the wrath of the bully.

In my sixty-odd years I have been lucky enough to have never gone hungry but plenty of religious people have. Does this mean that God, in this case, actually favours the atheist in me? I have lost people dear to me and it has been hard but this has not happened just to me. Has it not happened to all religious people as well? We cannot keep all those who are nearest and dearest forever just because we pray, can we? If we did, we would end up with relatives who are as old as Noah was. Some religious folk yearn for love and they seek it in their god. I am lucky as I have found it in abundance without any faith at all. I have never prayed to any god to be well fed or loved. They have both come by just living in our world and doing as best I can.

To sum up this chapter, it seems religious people will pray to their particular god for almost anything and if what they pray for comes true, then their particular god must be true as well. If their prayers come true, then God is on their side and if their prayers do not come true it must just mean that God was busy that day. You can imagine someone, like my daughter, who is pregnant and prays to God for the child to be a boy. If it is a boy then it's, 'All praise to God!' but if it is a girl then that is the way God wanted it. It was his will so, 'All praise to God!'. He can't lose, can he? When you think about it, there are seven billion people on our little planet and every one of them stood a fifty-fifty chance of being a boy.

So why do people pray?

They pray for a few reasons:

1.For some assurance that everything will be okay in their lives because they do not have the courage of their own convictions

2.They pray for things they want and are not strong enough to get for themselves.

3.They pray for things they are too lazy to get for themselves.

4.They pray for God to change the course of their lives so that they do not have to bother themselves.

5.They pray so as to get an unfair advantage over others.

6.They pray simply because they cannot cope with life.

7.They pray out of a pure selfish attitude towards their fellow humans.

8.They pray because they are simply frightened not to.

Before I end this chapter, I would like to go back to the beginning of it and comment again on the man who prayed to be given a job and, therefore, was given it.

As I said, he prayed so as to get an unfair advantage over other applicants so, in his religious righteousness, he didn't give a damn about the feelings of others. It didn't worry him if the other applicants were more qualified or far better suited or even more caring and thoughtful people. All he wanted was to please himself in his 'self-society'. He may have been the best candidate for the position and if that was the case he would have been given the job anyway, but he didn't care either way. He prayed for the job and he got it. That was all that mattered.

They say the whole world and everything in it is God's plan. Everything we do is governed by this all-powerful being or spirit and we all have to live by his rules and plan. He knows everything and everything is mapped out for us. From what I have learned, this is the way of things. God is love and God is everything. We are nothing without God and without God there is nothing else. We must pray to and worship him constantly and be fearful of his every step and whim and yet we can simply ask him to give us a job and he will say, '*Yep, That's fine. In no way are you the best candidate and in no way are you the nicest person but you've prayed to me, so sod the others.*'

This is not really likely, is it? If it is, it means neither the person who prays or even God really gives a toss about humanity.

A much bigger thing explodes in my brain as well. Let's say this man's prayers were answered after God had already made his plan for him, the world and the universe we live in. This means that this simple act of prayer offered by a simple man, on a simple issue, has just changed the course of history.

Eric the Penguin.

I have seen this a few times and it has been posted on a Facebook page recently. I thought I would share it with you.

God can't exist because of Eric, the God-eating magic penguin. Since Eric is God-eating by definition, he has no choice but to eat God. So if God exists, he automatically ceases to exist as a result of being eaten.

So, unless you can prove that Eric doesn't exist, God doesn't exist. Even if you can prove that Eric doesn't exist, that same proof will also be applicable to God.

There are only two possibilities. Either you can prove that Eric doesn't exist or you can't. In both cases, it logically follows that God doesn't exist.

You see, this proves that God does not exist and could you possibly argue with it?

Suicide, Assisted Dying and Euthanasia

We all know now, and I know I have stated it more than a few times, that our earth contains seven billion human beings. This is a number which, in my opinion, cannot be sustained and something has to be done. Someone has to, very quickly, stand up and say that enough is enough. I'm doing it now but will anyone listen? We are living on a tiny planet and it cannot provide enough resources for us all. In my younger days, most of us had our 'three score years and ten' and then we died, possibly making way for someone else. Today, though, that average age has risen from the said 70 years to something like 85. Medical advances have been a huge boon to humans and human civilisation but every advance in medical knowledge has, today, to be tempered with a tinge of worry and real concern. Of course it is right to try and help our own race but this 'help' has also to be seen as a hindrance, as we cannot support all these people to this great age. Where is all this increase in age going? How long will it be before we are all living to be 100 years and, in the UK, long enough to receive that telegram from the Queen?

What is the answer to all this? Do we stop medical research? Do we stop intensive care for the elderly? Do we even have to, in the end, consider the wholly unthinkable act of euthanasia? How do we ever say that if you reach a certain age you are automatically going to be legally murdered? Can there ever be such a thing as legal murder? How would we do it and, indeed, who would do it? Certainly not me.

Our nursing homes are filling up rapidly with residents who are suffering from dementia. How many homes will be needed in the future to cope with everyone as our bodies live far longer than our brains, and how much will all this cost in both cash and human resources? How can we all afford it? With the numbers increasing all the time we, quite simply, cannot afford it.

It is a sad fact too that dementia is not limited to the aged alone. It doesn't limit itself to the over eighties and can strike anyone at any time. Even people in their fifties are suffering, but why? It does seem that the vast majority of dementia comes from age but why are these younger people suffering? I feel it is because of our never-ending and wanton exploitation of our planet and every chemical it holds.

All of the other animals on our small planet live natural lives with nature being their ruler. In good times they breed and multiply but when things are hard, their numbers decline. They are fully dependent upon the seasons and weather and the ecosystems in which they live and their numbers can only ever be as great as that ecosystem is able to sustain. We are different though. Remember what I said so many times in *Wonderment*. We are the ones with the huge brains and intellect and are the only ones who have enough intelligence to destroy the world we live in, rely upon and call home.

We are defying nature at every opportunity but, in time, nature must win through and always will. We think we are winning when, in the end, all we are doing is putting off the inevitable when, deep down, we know that the inevitable is chaos. We cannot smoke and we cannot drink and we cannot take drugs without nature eventually taking control and telling us quite bluntly that we have done wrong and we are going to lose, so why do we think we can carry on burning fossil fuels and using harmful chemicals without there being any repercussions? We can't.

Can I here convey something from the Interweb? Believe me when I do quote it, that I do know I am just as responsible and guilty as anyone else around me. Also, please believe me when I say I know this is supposed to be a book on my views of religion but we will come to that I promise, as suicide, assisted dying and euthanasia are often controlled by religion. Sorry, I digress again.

When crude oil is burned, either accidentally or as a spill control measure, it emits chemicals that affect human health. These chemicals include carbon dioxide, carbon monoxide, lead, nitrogen oxide, particulate matter, polycyclic aromatics, hydrocarbons, sulphur dioxide and volatile organic compounds.

We use huge amounts of other chemicals in a huge number of ways in a huge variety of products. All these, if we think about it, must cause harm but if we even totally ignore all these, we must see that even the use of crude oil alone is poisoning us and our planet. We only have to sit in a traffic jam and open our minds and we should immediately be aware of what is going on around us and how many harmful chemicals our vehicles are giving out and how many we are breathing in. We all do it and are all to blame. Is it any wonder our brains are being ruined? We must open our minds but, probably, close our windows.

To talk about any particular person in a particular way without their permission would be wrong, but I do know one lady who sums up dementia so well that I have asked her family's permission to include her here. To protect her, I'll call her Gloria.

Gloria's husband was elderly and not in good health and was, therefore, cared for full time in a nursing home. She and her family were, and are, lovely, warm, kind and caring people and, as she didn't drive, Gloria was always brought in by one of her sons to visit. Her husband was cared for well and so was Gloria when she visited. She was always warmly welcomed and became a friend to everyone who worked in the home.

This carried on for quite a few years and Gloria and her family became almost an integral part of the home but then, in a short time which seemed like overnight, things started to change. Dear Gloria went rapidly, and almost pitifully, from being an ordinary, bubbly and loving lady to become someone who, at first, spoke almost unintelligibly at times, to then quickly degenerating to such an extent she was admitted into the same home as her husband but into its dementia wing. At the time of writing, Gloria seems unable to hold much of a conversation at all and I am not really sure if she really knows where she is or who she is. Her family would know more than I do.

In homes throughout the country, and world, there are people (Many younger than myself) who have dementia and/or other illnesses that are so bad and debilitating that they have no quality of life whatsoever. What kind of life is it to either not know who you are, or have to spend 24 hours every single day of the year lying in bed knowing full well who you are and what your life should be like, but are condemned to lie staring at the ceiling? Can you imagine the enormity of what must go through their tormented minds? Gloria is still regularly visited by her family and I do hope she knows who they are, but what sort of life is it when the only people some others see are those who come to either feed them or change their soiled pads? Every single aspect of these people's lives is totally under the control of others. Can you even imagine the simplest of things in life, like having a terrible itch but not being able to scratch it? Imagine the frustration when you haven't even the ability to ask someone else to do it for you.

('Gloria' passed away shortly before the publication of this book. RIP 'Gloria'. A wonderful lady.)

Many carers are truly dedicated to their work and offer a completely first-class service for those in their care. They make life as bearable as possible but what sort of life is it when you cannot even do the most basic of tasks for yourself? What sort of life is it when you cannot live? How can staring at a ceiling all day be called living? How often can you wonder at the same small crack or paint blemish above you? It's an old cliché perhaps but if these people were dogs or cats or pigs or horses, we would be advised to have them put down or possibly risk the chance of being prosecuted if we didn't.

Here we come to the crunch. Why can't these poor people be thought of with the full compassion they deserve? Why can't they be treated with as much compassion and reality as other animals? Why are these people not allowed to die with the dignity and self-respect they fully deserve? Why must they suffer terrible torment, total lack of dignity and the loss of all self-respect that other animals rightly deserve and get. Why is all this happening? Again, much of it is down to religion. Religion says that the Lord giveth and the Lord taketh away and it is His will whether we live or die. Religion says this and its followers do 'follow' it all, word for word, with no thought or compassion at all for those who suffer. I feel this is being inconsiderate, to say the least. Thinking about it, how absolutely arrogant must someone be to think they have the right to choose whether someone else lives or dies or suffers? Do they think of themselves as gods? How could you possibly put yourself on such an elevated pedestal?

In our British government, a certain number of places are kept for religious people (twenty-six bishops of the Church of England sit in the House of Lords) and, even after many, many years, these people still hold a strong sway over our laws. But why? The Bible was written three thousand five hundred years ago when little was known and people died very much younger than they do today. Yes, it is right that no one can totally disprove the existence of God, but it is all highly unlikely and even if it is all true, why should these unelected religious people in power sit and judge how much a person must suffer and how much loss of dignity and self-respect they must endure before dying? How can anyone, religious or not, possibly ever say that another person should live whilst suffering terrible pain, anguish, torment and torture? I have seen it so many times, both professionally and personally and maybe those holding this power should see it too. They should see it not just for a few minutes but, somehow, over a period of weeks, months or even years. Have they ever heard people scream in agony and hear them beg sincerely, long and hard and eloquently, to be allowed to die? I have heard prayer being offered to God that the end should come and the suffering should cease but, no. Their god either didn't listen, wasn't interested or actually enjoyed seeing the scene being played out before him. My conclusion has to be that he either does not exist or does not care.

A couple of years ago a friend of mine, (I'll call him Bill), lost an eye to cancer. He had an operation and then had his lost eye replaced with an amazing-looking false one. It really was difficult to tell the difference. His favourite sport was shooting, but the loss of his eye meant his aim was not as good as it had been previously. This was upsetting for him but he was still a far better shot with one eye than I will ever be with two. This fact wouldn't have cheered his soul, though, as he had partially lost something quite huge in his life.

After a time, Bill's life was just returning to something like normal when he started to suffer from pains in his abdomen and these pains rapidly became worse and worse. He had nursed his late wife through cancer and strongly suspected this was what he was now suffering from again himself, but doctors failed to diagnose it. Despite visiting surgeries and hospitals, cancer was not diagnosed but his condition deteriorated rapidly. He was sure in his own mind that cancer was what he was suffering from and he feared dreadfully the thought of going through what he had witnessed his wife dying from so, as his condition worsened, he realised that, to his mind, there was only one way out. One Saturday morning, he took one of his beloved guns out to his shed and used it to end his life and torment. I don't know to this day if Bill was indeed suffering from cancer but he was certainly suffering. Suffering to such a huge extent that he felt blasting his own head apart was his only release.

I know this is a terrible story but it is a true one. The story is terrible and graphic but how else can you talk about a terrible death other than in a terrible way? Yes, some do just go to sleep and do not wake up again but for many, the process is abject torture. Bill decided, very bravely in my mind, to seek and find the courage to do something about his situation, but others either do not have this strength and courage or they lack the ability to do it through disability, illness or frailty.

Bill had no one to help him with the process of dying and was forced to do it alone on the floor of his shed and in a brutal way, but others are receiving help these days in the form of assisted dying in Switzerland. These dear folk are taken there and are treated with the absolute utmost of respect and dignity and are allowed to die as good a death as is possible. We all have to die but how it happens should not be judged by others, religious or not. Those who go to Switzerland are exercising choice and I strongly feel we should all have this right if we are terminally ill and have had enough. Surely our lives are our lives only and no one else should ever have a say in how they end? And we certainly should not be judged by others when our lives are nothing to do with them. Those who make the law do not even know us, so why should they be allowed to judge us?

As it was suicide, Bill's death would be classed as a sin in the minds of those who are religious, but how can any person of any faith ever try to condemn a man for ending his life due to awful pain and anguish? Is he now burning in hell for ending all the anguish that God had bestowed upon him? Is this just a little ironic? Or, maybe, it is just a little stupid. Was God testing Bill and, in committing suicide, did he fail that test? Was he not a true Christian because he could not bear the unbearable? What sort of all-loving God could inflict torture of this magnitude on as kind a man as anyone could ever meet? If this god does exist then what is wrong with him? What sort of dreadful psychotic illness is he suffering from?

Chrissy, my dear late wife, told me sincerely one day, whilst dying from cancer, that she'd had enough and she wanted to die. She was quite stoical and almost calmly asked me to do something about it. I cried inside as I told her I couldn't, but why couldn't something have been done? Not by me, perhaps, but why couldn't a doctor or hospital have given her something to have helped her along her way in peace, dignity and comfort? That wonderful woman had suffered enough and she knew it. She was to suffer far far more in the weeks to come and, in the end, the end came just as we knew it would and just as it would have done those weeks before, had she been granted her dearest wish at the time. Had her wish been granted, she would still have died but would have done it her way and not in a way others demanded and legislated for. How can someone's death be governed by people who think in their own minds that they know better? How can you possibly judge and condone the suffering of others, just because of some lines you have read in an ancient black book?

What does religion say about suicide? Let's take a look.

Basically, the act of suicide is classed in the Bible as breaking the Sixth Commandment 'Thou shalt not kill'. For some reason, suicide is classed as murder. This means that poor old Bill, who was suffering too much to bear, felt his only release was to end his life but, at the same time, was committing murder. It is very unlikely that he would have missed with his shotgun but if he had, would he have been put on trial for attempted murder?

What puzzles me a little here is the fact that, although it is seen as a sin, some believe suicide is not an automatic way into hell. Some say it is and others say both suicide and real murder are 'pardonable sins' and the only sins that are unforgivable are rejecting Christ and blaspheming the holy spirit. Does this mean that Hitler is sitting in heaven while many of those he had tortured and killed are roasting in hell for not believing? Are we talking another giant religious contradiction here?

Things I have been told:

Others are quick to judge and condemn those who take their own lives.

My first response to the above was, WHAT! How can anyone judge and condemn others when they are obviously in a totally dark and horrifying place? My life is very good and I am totally happy but many are not in this privileged position. Many are living on the edge of a giant precipice and the only way they can see is down. How could I, sitting on totally level ground, possibly judge that person standing on the edge? Religion does judge but in reality you cannot possibly do it.

People who contemplate suicide have often been struggling with serious problems, such as depression, alcoholism or other forms of drug abuse.

'Struggling with serious problems'. Of course they have been struggling with serious problems. How serious do these problems have to be to even contemplate ending your life? No one walks down the street without a care in the world and then suddenly decide to jump under a bus, do they? I feel the above statement trivialises the whole issue. This statement seems to want to quickly put across a point, but I feel that point is far too serious and justifies far more thought than this.

Bill's life was good but his illness took over and dragged him to the edge of that precipice. We have to think long, hard and deeply to even get the tiniest of feeling of what was going through his mind as he awoke that morning, knowing that this would be the last time he was to ever be in a bed and awake.

We have to imagine him taking out and loading his gun, knowing that what was to come out of the barrel this time was not going to kill a pheasant or rabbit, but was going to viciously end his own life. We also have to see him walking to his shed, sitting on the floor, placing the gun in the correct position and then finding the immense courage needed to pull the trigger. That man did not just have 'serious problems'. He had an insurmountable tragedy in his head and had to find a solution and if that solution had to be suicide then who, religious or otherwise, could possibly even think to judge or condemn? Believe me, no one dies by their own hand on a simple whim. Choosing death over life is not like choosing one biscuit over another or one holiday destination over another. It is a horrendous decision to make and some feel, either through physical or mental anguish, that the decision has to be made. We should all be in unison with our thoughts and condemn no one. Maybe we should all stop being judgmental and help them all we can while they are still alive.

They say: *God has a great plan for life. God has created us in his own image. He created us for a purpose. God has a specific plan for everyone.*

Can I see another huge contradiction here? If God has a 'specific plan for everyone', then surely Bill's suicide was all part of that plan. How can you plan someone's life and death and then blame that person for their actions? It is like being created as a homosexual and then being vilified for what you are.

They also say: *God's plan is for life and not death.*

If this is the case, then why did he make Bill choose the latter? Why did he make his life so unbearable that, in the end, death was his only option? Also, if his plan is life and not death, then why does he often take the lives of young children before they reach an age where they can even understand the concept of taking their own lives?

Another: *Life belongs to God. It is never our place to take our own life or someone else's life.*

If we truly believe our lives are the property of a god, then what is life all about? Our lives should never be the property of anyone. Our lives are ours and we have the right to do whatever we want with them without the interference and judgement of any supposed god or any of his followers.

Also: *The solution to despair and hopelessness is not suicide but faith in God.*

Wouldn't it be good to be able to ask someone who is so wracked with pain that death seems their only option, if this is what they should believe and follow? Do we honestly think that if they put their faith in God, enough of their troubles would melt for them to then carry on with a normal life? I don't somehow think it would happen, do you? People put their full faith in God but has no religionist ever contemplated suicide? Do all people who follow God wallow in luxury and utter contentment? Of course they don't. Life can be hugely difficult for all of us at times, whether we follow the Bible or not and reading the Bible is never going to alleviate the suffering of cancer. I think I can confidently make the assumption that Bill's suffering would have been just the same if he was an atheist or theist.

Another lovely statement which I think is priceless:

No matter what you feel or what happens, God does exist and he deeply loves you.

Do you think Bill thought this right up until the time he pulled the trigger?

RIP 'Bill'. A truly lovely man.

Assisted Dying:

As I have said, assisted dying is illegal in the UK but in some states of America, such as Washington, California and Vermont, it is legal but is called Physician Aid in Dying or PAD. The difference between the two is who it is who actually administers the lethal dose of medication. Euthanasia requires the lethal dose to be administered by a physician or other third party whilst PAD dictates that it must be the patient that does it and who determines when and where it should be done. Of course, a physician doesn't actually administer the dosage but has to be consulted and has to be part of the plan in order to prescribe the drug necessary. The physician is assisting the suicide but is not actually involved at the end.

If we look at this all without thinking too deeply about it, we would come to either one of two decisions:

1. It is the life of the person wishing to commit suicide that is in question and we should not question that person's wishes.

2. All life belongs to God and, therefore, no one should ever take their own life whether that suicide is by their own hands or assisted by someone else.

We could simply follow No 1 or No 2 but, in reality, there are many questions that lie in between. We can stand on whichever side of the fence we wish but, in truth, we must all look at the fence itself.

Let me make up a story to illustrate my point:

Elsie is well into her eighties and is basically sound of mind, despite having some loss of short term memory. She can remember the war and what happened then and before and she can even almost fully remember her childhood, but sometimes she cannot remember if she has eaten breakfast or has made her bed.

Elsie lives alone in the large house that she and her late husband purchased many years ago and which was the home in which she gave birth to and brought up her son and daughter. The house is full of memories and within its walls she feels comforted and secure. Her home is full of gifts that have been bought for her by her family and friends and each one of them holds a special warm memory. Her chair is hers, as is her bath and her bed. Her every happening over the years has stemmed from that house.

Problems have arisen for Elsie because, added to her loss of short term memory, is the fact that she is really struggling physically and has fallen a few times within her home, with no one being there to pick her up. Her family realise that residential care is probably the best way forward but Elsie is totally reluctant to leave her home and lose her independence, while her family realise the many hundreds of pounds, care would cost each week would soon see the funds from selling the much-loved family home disappear. They don't like to think too much about this but it is a fact. It is a fact to consider but the guilt of thinking about it hurts.

In her heart, Elsie does feel she cannot manage but wants to end her life in the home she loves, but she does realise that any form of euthanasia is out of the question. Through old age and illness, she is put into a very dark corner and the only people she can speak to, as her friends have long since passed away, are her son and daughter who are also in the same dark corner themselves. They have worked hard in looking after their mother as best they can whilst leading busy lives themselves and are coming to the end of their strength and perseverance. They do want what is best for their mother, but what is best for her? Is the best thing for her to be forced from her home and into somewhere that she desperately does not want to go? Is the best thing for her to be left in her own home but see her life degrade into one where she just cannot manage and suffers neglect through her own inabilities? Or is it best for her to be assisted to die while she still has the ability and state of mind to make that choice?

Elsie's son and daughter talk to her at length and, eventually, Elsie tells her GP that yes, she has had enough and wants to die. We are assuming here that euthanasia has been made legal and her GP agrees. Elsie is assisted with her request to die.

Elsie has had a good life and has decided to end it but certain questions have to be asked. Originally, she felt she could not really live but, on the other hand, she felt she could not contemplate suicide or assisted dying but, after talks with her family, she decides this is the best way through. Maybe it was. She did not lose her dignity, pride and self-respect and she did not have to leave her beloved and precious home but, in talking to her family, she was swayed into making her decision.

Did her family help her to come to this decision through the sheer and utter love they held for her or did they have an ulterior motive? Beneath all the show of love did they really want her out of the way so that the house would not be lost? Were their future plans based on the hundreds of thousands of pounds the house could realise or did they do it all with just their dear mother's welfare in mind? In the end, were they sad or satisfied? We will never know.

This is the problem we face. Any form of euthanasia would have to be the decision of the person involved but it would also have to be investigated very intensely, just who had influenced that decision and why.

Does this mean we should never introduce assisted dying in the UK? I think we should, providing we can put in place strict enough safeguards to make sure we are doing truly what the individual wants and needs. Life does belong to us all and surely it has to be our choice if we want to end it.

Elsie's story does put assisted dying in a very controversial place and euthanasia of the elderly just because they are elderly will always be controversial, but what of those who are terminally ill and want to leave this earth while they do still have the cognitive ability to decide for themselves? Why should they have to suffer to the end, when the end could be brought forward for them and they could die without the suffering? Why shouldn't a person be brought to a dignified end instead of worrying just who is going to judge and condemn them? Especially in the name of religion.

Recently, there have been these cases of people travelling from the UK to Switzerland, to be helped to die as they realised there was no future life for them. They probably also realised that God was not about to turn around and heal them so death was their answer. Through a great amount of love and understanding, the families of these people have helped them to get to where they want to go and how brave and dedicated an act this is. The problem is, though, that the families are then questioned by the law of their country for assisting death.

Should this happen or should they actually be congratulated for demonstrating their open love and dedication?

All this is a dark and deep subject but I do feel we have to, one day, all grow up and face reality and that reality must be that it is our lives and our choice as to what we want to do with them.

As Frank Sinatra once sang,

I would certainly like to do it 'My Way'.

Religious people discriminate against lesbians, gays, bisexuals and transgender people.

Why?

When I was young, people used to discriminate against those with ginger hair or freckles, but it was then realised that this was pathetic. Many ginger-haired people these days are seen as, and are, gorgeous. When will religious people see that if they have a grudge against anyone who is slightly different to them in any way then the problem is all theirs and no one else's?

How arrogant it is to think you are so wonderful that you can judge others? Not only is this arrogant but it is also so very, very sad.

Love, Character and Us

I was having a conversation on Facebook a few weeks back, talking to two or three different people and the conversation turned to love. I said that, to me, love is the greatest thing ever. It is a word that only has four letters but is the biggest word ever invented.

I felt this was a perfectly simple, true and plain thing to say but to my surprise, someone came back at me in a rather cross way and said quite bluntly that I had no idea what love was. This seemed strange as I had never met the person who had made this statement and, to my knowledge, I had never even spoken to her on Facebook, so I asked her why she felt so strongly that I knew nothing of love. She replied that I could not possibly know the first thing about love because I am an atheist. Pardon?

My mind worked overtime for a few seconds but I could not see her reasoning, so I kindly asked her to explain. She came back at me with no small amount of fury and said I knew nothing of love because God is love, he is the only love and without God it was impossible to give or receive love. It was that plain to see so why could I not see it? She sincerely thought I was some kind of idiot. Maybe I am. Oh dear!

The problem was, of course, that I could not see it and why not? Why, because her argument was totally illogical, totally baseless, totally futile and totally wrong. Why should it only be religious people who can give and receive love? I can give and receive it by the ton but she could not see it and I think this shows a huge problem with religion. This lady's mind had been set by either her book or by her Bible teachers and she did not have the ability to see beyond that. To live just inside your own brain is a dark, dangerous and sad place to be. If she could have opened her mind and eyes for just a few seconds she would have realised love is everywhere, it is free, it is beautiful and we are all entitled to a good, hearty and generous slice of it.

I later posted an article on Facebook which asked the following:

It has been said that there is no other love than God's love. How do you know God loves you, how does he show that love, how do you benefit from that love and how does this affect you in your day to day life?

I added that I had written the post, not out of any hate or even dislike for religion but because I was genuinely interested. I waited and waited but once again, no replies.

It is a little sad really when religionists talk about everything to do with their particular religion and god but when you ask for details they are not forthcoming. They say they are going to heaven and you are going to hell, but when you ask where they are, what they are like and what happens when we get there, they cannot provide even a modicum of an answer. You ask them to explain their god's love and the same thing happens.

I was told that God's love is real but you cannot prove it, just like you cannot prove someone alive loves you. The reply had to be that the person alive is there to tell me. I do not have to imagine it. My wife can stand before me and tell me she loves me. She is there, I can see her, I can see her lips move and I can hear her voice. I can also see the sentiment on her face. I know her love is real. You cannot see God's face (Does he have one?). You cannot see the expression on his face and you cannot literally hear what he says (Can he speak?).

God made man in his own image. God walked in the Garden of Eden. He spoke, he listened and he breathed and yet God is supposed to be just a spirit with no bodily form at all. I was strongly berated by someone once for attributing human traits to God. It wasn't me who did this. It was the Bible. I still cannot quite understand this but just have to accept it as another of the Bible's little contradictions.

It is my true and realistic belief that we all have love and we all need it. It cannot just be given and received by those who have belief in a certain god. The statement must be ludicrous, to say the least.

I have known strong Bible believers who have had great love for their fellow human beings. I have also known strong Bible believers who have tried hard to portray great love for others but that love has come from just a sheer sense of duty and is not real. There are also, quite plainly, many religious people who have a vile hatred in their brains and no love at all. As I have said, atheists and theists are all entitled to as much love as they warrant and deserve but the same can be said for atheists and theists alike when it comes to anger, as they can both exhibit just as much anger and hatred. Love, or indeed hate, does not come from any god. It comes from the person.

There are supposed to be thousands of gods out there and even if you believed in every single one of them you would not be entitled to any more love than an atheist and, believe me, yes, hate is there for everyone as well. Love is far more rewarding though, isn't it? It is a great deal easier to live with.

Through Facebook I have been involved in many discussions while the US were bringing in the law regarding homosexual marriage. Little love was shown here by religious people. The motion was vehemently opposed by many and hatred was thrown around, quite appropriately perhaps, in 'gay abandonment'. Where was this 'God's love' while this was happening? Okay, we know the Bible is supposed to be against homosexuality but doesn't the Bible also say that God made us and we are all part of his plan? They say we follow the path set out by God, so how can we hate someone who was made homosexual by God and then made to follow a path set out by him as well? It is partly because of these huge contradictions that I find I cannot believe. Well, these plus any slight shred of evidence, I suppose.

I was born heterosexual but some are born homosexual. Some are born bisexual and others have no real idea what they are at all, but we were all born as we are and what the hell is wrong with that? I have known people of all these different persuasions and they are all just normal people who try their best and do their best for themselves and the society they live in. What is better? To be a homosexual or to be the one who hates so much, they kill or want to kill them for their beliefs? Once again, on Facebook, I have seen pictures of homosexuals being whipped and even being thrown to their deaths from the tops of tall buildings. There is no way of corroborating these pictures but I have no reason to suggest they are fake. So much for God and religion being the only love in the world, when these people are supposed to be followers of religion and yet they can kill just because of someone's sexual orientation. Of course, as I have already said, it is not just religious people who have hatred inside them. Atheists do, too. The difference here is that you would not see a gang of atheists throwing innocent people off tall buildings. If the atheists were there they would probably be thrown off together with the homosexuals. Some atheists do hate but is this as bad as those who hate in the name of religion? Can you throw people off the top of a building and possibly think your particular god would be pleased with your actions? Is homosexuality a bigger sin than murder? I have not seen the former in the Ten Commandments; 'Thou shalt not fall for other men'.

According to the Bible there must be sinners everywhere. Homosexuality is one of the sins and these people are hated for being themselves but what of other sins? Why don't we see people being hounded and persecuted for masturbation or fornication? Why? The answer is obvious to me but this is only 'my' answer. Those who commit these 'abominable sins' are not persecuted because, unlike homosexuality, most of us either do it, have done it or will do it in the future. I'm sorry, but what can possibly be wrong with masturbation and sex before marriage? Nothing, I say, but then again, they are obviously nowhere near such hateful crimes as homosexuality. Isn't this persecution of your fellow human beings also showing a great amount of arrogance when religion is supposed to teach one to be humble? How can you be religious and humble and yet put yourself so highly above others that you feel you not only have to look down upon them, but you also have to persecute or even murder them?

If someone commits a murder or steals from an elderly lady or abuses a child or commits rape then yes, they must be caught and be punished because these are crimes against humanity and people suffer, but we cannot go around condemning people just because of so-called sins committed against a black book which was written thousands of years ago. This is purely showing hatred, hatred that should have no place in today's world. The trouble is that this is a hatred which is not abating. It is growing rapidly as our population explodes.

To truly love someone or even something and have that love returned is by far the biggest thing that could ever come into anyone's life. We ruin our lives if we let even the smallest amount of hatred or anger come into them. It would be easy to say that as I am an atheist, I must hate religion and religious people, but anyone who thinks or says this would be totally wrong. Believe me, I hate no one and I cannot hate anyone because I have no hate in me at all. All hate does is eat away at your core and very being until it ruins the life you are trying to lead. If I hated you, the reader, it would not affect you and it certainly would not ruin your life in any way, but it would ruin mine. My thoughts would be consumed with that hate and, sometimes, to such a great extent that it would eat away at any or all of the love inside me. Many people, especially today, are consumed with hate and that must be a very dark and dingy place to reside.

In reality, love does not come from the heart, as a heart is only an organ that pumps blood around our bodies, but if I enter a room where my family are it does seem my heart is suddenly filled with a warmth and joy. We do feel it in our heart, although the feeling stems from our brain, as that is where our consciousness lies; but perhaps we feel it in our heart because our brain has stimulated a certain chemical which then enters our blood-stream and affects our heart. Whatever happens, we do feel it in our heart.

Even in just talking to my grandchildren I fill, almost to overflowing, with love and when one of them tells me they love me I almost explode. A few days ago, my wife was talking to our Lucy and she said something derogatory about me to her. What she said was only mentioned as a very light-hearted joke but Lucy took exception to it and came back with the fact that Nanny was wrong and she really, really loved her granddad. That little girl, at nine years old, already has more love inside her than do many adults, whether they are theists or atheists.

As I said in detail in *Wonderment* and have also said previously in this book, love is not just confined to the love of people. Just look at the wonderful world we live in. It is full of things to love and marvel at. It is all there for us to enjoy and it is all free, providing we can see beyond our own noses and understand what it is we are looking for and at. Through the window of my home I can see a large tree. To many it is just a lump of wood with green leaves on it, but open your eyes and mind and then think again, and what is it?

It is a giant plant that has evolved over hundreds of millions of years. It takes in carbon dioxide and gives out oxygen so is, therefore, providing some of the life I need in order to write this book. That huge tree came, originally, from just a small seed. The seed weighed probably only a few grams but now, many years later, the tree it spawned must weigh something in the region of five to six tons. Where has all that growth come from? Those tons of growth have come purely from the rain it has received and the chemicals in the ground that it has used and absorbed. Then turn that all around and look at you or me. We are the same. We have grown from a single sperm meeting a single egg and through the chemical nourishment we have received from the earth we are what we are today. Whether we are a tree or human being or rock or even an unnatural thing such as a car, we all started out as simple chemicals. Life is a wondrous thing if we look at it with love, true passion and an open mind.

In our world, there are some who cannot seem to find a way into society and they therefore feel on the edge of it and are somewhat lost. Some have a distressing feeling of inadequacy, either because of a lack of intelligence or a feeling of self-loathing which has, more than likely, been instilled gradually by others. I would add that the feelings of these people are simply within their own minds and they are as valuable as are the rest of us. Many such people turn to animals for love as they feel all the animals can do is give love in return. An animal doesn't throw that love in your face or make fun of how you look or behave, so people can often feel safer with this type of love and why not? Maybe they can only give and receive love from animals but even this is infinitely better than living their lives being consumed by hate.

I do feel that those with hate inside them then throw that hate in whichever direction they can. Homosexuals are hated, coloured people are hated, religious people are hated and so are atheists, but this is not because they are what they are. It is simply the fact that this hatred is in the mind of the hater and it has to be thrown at something. A man is a homosexual and therefore he has to be hated. Someone is black and therefore they have to be hated. Someone is a Muslim and therefore they have to be hated. 'All Muslims are terrible people'. Of course they are not and in no way are they! The problem is that this is precisely the way some people, religious or otherwise, think and they are totally wrong.

How can one person, who has probably never even talked to a single Muslim person, possibly know that all Muslims are bad? And this question must be said of all groups whether they are Muslims, Christians, Hindus, Asians, blacks, tall, short, fat, thin or hairy. No one person can ever be anything different to us. Just because they do not think in the same way, or look the same as us, doesn't make them wrong. I know of one person in particular, who shall remain anonymous, who thinks everyone is wrong on all subjects apart from him. In fact, he doesn't think it. In his own tiny, tightly closed and feeble little mind he actually knows it. To him, anyone who acts slightly differently to him has, naturally, to be wrong and despised and yet this person leads a totally dull, uninteresting, boring and dogmatic lifestyle that no one else would ever possibly wish upon themselves or others. To him, his life is what life is all about but I think I and thousands of others would consider it a sentence too hard to bear.

In my writing, I do criticise the God of the Bible, the Bible itself and those who strictly live their lives by it. I do this with no hatred in me whatsoever. I do it simply because I do not understand it all. You will have noticed that I do not pull apart to any great extent what the Koran says. This is not out of fear or any bias towards Muslims or any particular dislike of Christians. The only difference is the fact I have not read the Koran and do not know much of what is inside it. I'm sure if I studied it I would find inaccuracies and contradictions there as I do in the Bible but until I do study it I must, largely, leave it alone.

With the Muslim terror activity, we have suffered and the advent of so-called Islamic State we have seen (wrong but inevitable to some extent in our society) a rise in hatred shown towards all Muslims, but again, we must not let a few radicals cloud our minds and judgement. I feel there ought to be far more Muslims standing up in unison and denouncing all forms of terrorism but, on the other hand, in no way are all Muslims bad people in any way.

In my time, I have watched much television, sometimes for pure entertainment but mainly as a learning tool. To my mind though, television is dumbing down along with today's society and there are less and less programmes broadcast that anyone can actually learn from. I could be wrong but I do feel continuous soaps and soppy programmes with soppy celebrities doing soppy things just to fill the screen have become a sad and all-too-prevalent expression of today's society. Okay, let the masses have their shows but why have hour after hour of the above when we could – please – cut it down a little and give us something to learn from? What has happened to good, what I would call, 'wholesome' entertainment, or science programmes? They have all been swept away, together with true reality and the desire to learn and improve oneself.

Having had my little rant and tantrum I will get on with the book. Television, to me, is nothing like what it used to be and there are only three or four programmes each week that I actually look forward to watching and one of them has to be the series, *The Great British Bake Off*. I love the programme. Never is there a contestant who I cannot like and it is always a shame when, each week, some fantastic baker and person has to leave the show. Where do they find such wonderful contestants?

This year was especially good as the cross-section of bakers included many people who had obviously originated from different parts of the world. To be a baker of a high enough standard to reach the tent takes quite a lot of intelligence. It is not hard to see that an uneducated person who lives on burgers and chips, pizzas and cola and crisps will never even be considered. So what does this say?

To me it plainly says that, no matter where these contestants originate from, they are there of their own fruition, merit and intelligence and they are all there purely on their brains and abilities while many are sitting at home swilling their cola and saying they hope a certain person loses because they are black, Asian or a Muslim. Racial hatred does not spur from the race itself, it comes from the feeble minds of those who are uneducated, unthinking and judgemental for no, even small, logical reason.

I cannot swear to the fact but there probably were people watching who did actually want the Muslim girl to fail in 2015, but she didn't fail, did she? Nadiya Hussain won through and received the highest accolade she could ever have dreamed of. Nadiya went into the competition as a very polite and humble lady who honestly thought she could give it her all but had no chance of winning. Through it all, she really did struggle for confidence but gradually her talent shone through and her skills became plain for all to see. In the final she was up against two lovely men, both of whom were fantastic bakers but Nadiya had the edge and was announced champion in front of a large crowd which included her delighted and delightful family.

I am not just waffling here about my favourite television programme. What I am trying to portray is the fact that hate only comes from the hater. It is only in their mind and never the problem of the person who is hated for no real reason. We probably did have the person sitting at home swilling cola and eating ten packets of crisps while watching, looking at the screen over their well-filled belly but we also had the winner and her family. Nadiya was not only a very worthy winner but was a total joy to watch as she came across as a beautiful and modest but intelligent human being and every one of her family seemed the same. If I had to choose between her and her family, or the Coke-guzzling viewer, I know who I would rather live next door to. Nadiya showed something that is not in all of us and yet it should be, and that is passion. She was not just a brilliant baker and a lovely person but she showed passion in what she did. Is it a coincidence that those who show hatred only seem to show passion in that one thing? If their only passion is hatred, then their lives must be totally unbearable and totally unfulfilled and unworthy. Nadiya showed a passion for life and her baking but does it matter what we show passion in? We can show it in our work, our homes, our family, our hobbies or even in our religion but, as with love, passion has to be a huge part of our lives if we are to live them to the full. This and true emotion is what won Nadiya through. Well done.

Please believe me when I say that love certainly does not just come from any god, and you never will have to worship and believe in order to have it. It comes from intelligence and simple common sense and we could have an ample share of both if only we could open our minds (and hearts) to it.

Below is a view I have seen expressed in religious teachings for children. I've seen it expressed, without thought, on quite a few occasions:

What is easier to believe:

1. That all paintings in an art gallery came from an explosion at a paint factory?

Or;

2. That each one was planned and painted by a master artist?

What the users of this little piece are trying to say, of course, is that if a painting has to be planned and painted then the universe must have been planned by God.

This is how they are trying to convince gullible young minds that God exists and should be followed. The problem here is that many children are gullible and their minds are reasonably easy to mould.

In reality, though, how can you possibly compare a painting with the universe or even our planet? We could use the same analogy for everything that has ever been made. Back to the Victoria sponge mentioned in my last book. If you put all the ingredients of it on the floor would they suddenly turn into sponge? Again, the analogy is pathetic.

Those using this silly little piece would obviously know their analogy was wrong, but it has deliberately been phrased this way to fool children into believing, and what a start to a relationship with God this is when the first contact is formed on a lie.

Once again, it is purely my own opinion, but I do not think these people are showing too much intelligence in their work and teachings but, then again, some may say the same about me and I would say they are totally welcome to their opinion.

Bible Basis and Beginning

So much of the Bible has to be supposition but I do not mean that in a nasty or mocking way. What I mean here is the fact that none of us were around when it was written so if we are to believe it, we have to hold a certain amount of faith in when it was written and who actually wrote it. None of us were around during the early life of Queen Victoria but we know all about her because of a vast array of documented history and photographs. Do we have evidence of who wrote the Bible and when? Let's explore.

As I was not there when it happened I shall be looking at various sources and quoting from them.

My first source tells me that the Bible was not written in one specific year or in one specific location. It was not written by one specific person either. It is a collection of writings and the first of these was laid down approximately 3,500 years ago. The first five books of the Bible are called the Pentateuch or Torah and are attributed to Moses, who lived somewhere between 1,500 and 1,300 BC.

I suppose here we have to take Moses as living in 1,500 BC, because if he was only born in1,300 BC we could not attribute these pieces to him, as they were supposedly written

3,500 years ago. If Moses was born in 1,300BC he would have been 200 years too late.

It also says that the first five books were 'attributed' to Moses. Attributed to and written by are two totally different phrases. If a painting is attributed to Constable it is straight away saying its authenticity is uncertain.

Another thing here bothers me and that is, even if young earth creationists are totally correct and the earth is only 6,000 years old, there is still a two thousand five hundred year gap between everything coming into existence and the first writings of the Bible. This says the earth was almost halfway to where it is today already, before anyone thought about writing this 'historical' account of its creation. If it was written so long after the creation, then how do we know what actually happened? God said, 'Let there be light' and there was light. How can we possibly know what he said and if he said it? And, thinking about it, why would he have said it anyway? Who was he saying it to? He was the only thing in existence at the time. I know Christians are going to say to me that I am stupid and that this is what God told Moses and if that is what they wish to believe, then that's good for them. I would question, though, what someone who really was not alive told someone who only may have existed three thousand five hundred years ago. Perhaps I am wrong in applying too much logic again.

It is said that God dictated the Pentateuch to Moses in 40 days on Mount Sinai. Let's say Moses did write the first five parts of the Bible and God gave him all the info. If this happened, then it happened three thousand five hundred years ago. It would be easy to say that Moses, in 1,500 BC, would not have been able to write. I have delved back into my family history and this was the fact for some of my ancestors only perhaps a hundred and fifty years ago, let alone three thousand five hundred years ago, but this assumption would be wrong.

There was writing at this time and an alphabet had been invented.

In the early days of man there was no need to write or record as their lives were simple. They were hunter gatherers and the only recording they did was to, much later, paint on rock walls. Beautiful paintings that still exist today were a kind of record of the animals they hunted. I am no expert on them but could they even have been painted to please some god or other? Painted as a kind of prayer to tell their particular god what they wished to kill in order to survive? The oldest of these dates back some 40,000 years. They could be seen as paintings or messages or wishes, but not writings.

As early civilisations grew, life became more complicated and people then had more to remember. It became a natural step forward to put down somehow what it was they needed to keep in their minds. Even in these busying times most people were still living quite simple lives and had no need to record their activities, but those in business or scholarship developed a need to record so as not to lose money, or to teach others.

Moses would have used a writing system called cuneiform, which was a method of making various marks scratched into a clay tablet, using a reed or stylus. Many of these tablets, not relating to the Bible, have been found but what of the tablets that Moses produced? I can find no record of these particular ones being found.

I can only speak from my own mind here and please forgive me if I am totally wrong again. I am writing this book on a 13-inch laptop and on it I have stored eight books, hundreds of emails, a string of family photographs and a vast amount of other various data. Just how much would Moses have been able to store on a clay tablet? The first five books of the Bible are quite epic stories. Just how many tablets would have had to be created and stored? On my laptop, I can quite easily get four hundred words written clearly and legibly on a single page. I wonder how many could be squeezed onto a tablet? We will delve into that in a while.

In my King James version of the Bible, the first five books, Genesis, Exodus, Leviticus, Numbers and Deuteronomy take up two hundred and twenty-six pages with an average number of approximately fifty-four lines and seventeen words on each line, a sum that gives a total of two hundred and seven thousand, four hundred and sixty-eight words. I wonder just how many tablets that would have taken? Either Moses had a vast warehouse in which to store his work or his writing was later translated and much added. Writing in cuneiform was a long and highly laborious task and it is said there would have actually been seventy-nine thousand eight hundred different Hebrew words and over five million different characters. I am no expert in cuneiform but could he have managed all this from God's dictation, in the middle of a desert, in just forty days? Repeating myself here a little, they were in the desert. Where did all the clay come from to make the tablets? Were they not sitting on the top of a mountain at the time with all their followers down below singing and dancing around, worshipping a calf? Another thought is that, again, we have this god, who is capable of doing anything that pleases his heart's desire so, if he needed the pentateuch written down on tablets of clay why didn't he just magic it, as he had done making the whole universe and every single thing in it in just six days? Why did he spend forty days dictating it to Moses when he could have done it in a flicker an eyelid? Why did he wait another three thousand five hundred years to reveal his plan for computers when he needed one so desperately then?

One more thing to contemplate here is the fact you can only write on wet or damp clay. To make the writing permanent that clay had to be fired. Again, they were on top of a mountain.

Where were the firing kilns? Wouldn't the tablets have just crumbled if they were left to dry in the sun?

I have come across some of my favourite things here, figures. It says that each cuneiform tablet would obviously have to be handled so it would not measure more than one metre square and each tablet would have taken approximately just three hundred words. In this case two hundred and sixty-six tablets would have been needed. The thickness of each tablet to survive being fired would have to be somewhere in the region of 6 inches or150mm which would give an approximate weight per tablet of 102 pounds. This gives the weight of the whole pentateuch as something around twenty-seven thousand pounds or thirteen tons. We, again, have to remember these had to be transported from the top of a mountain and then around the desert.

It seems the tablets survived long enough to be translated but, as I say, where are they now? What a boon for religion it would be if someone could show them to us but they can't, can they? As with everything else, there is no proof.

Apart from his mention in the Bible, there is no record of Moses' existence and if he did write the Pentateuch, he wrote about what had happened long before he was born and did it on many, many tablets which have not actually been found. In my heart, I do actually feel a little callous here in saying all this, but if the Bible is to be believed and adhered to as a true historical record, the Pentateuch is the very foundation and cornerstone of our existence and there should therefore be substantiating proof. Surely we should be in no doubt as to what happened. Many of you will, once again, say I am wrong and no doubt you will have prepared your arguments. I may be wrong but despite trying, I cannot see this logic my brain craves. Is it me again?

Some who have studied the Pentateuch now think the style of writing varies enough between the different books, to suggest there may well have been four different writers and this is the trouble. We don't really know. Really, we can have no idea.

I have read that the Bible was written over a period of 1,500 years and by 40 different authors and in looking for evidence of these authors all I have found is, 'It says so in the Bible', as it mentions their names within the text. Again, I am sorry, but this does not seem proof to me. My books say they are written by me. It says so on the cover. We don't know the authorship just because my name is mentioned somewhere in the story.

I feel I am trying desperately to understand all this but I am knocking my head against a brick wall and just cannot find a way through. I just cannot seem to get my head around it. We have a book, the origin of which was an absolute minimum of two thousand five hundred years after what it is talking about, and it was written on tablets which have never been found. Even in the New Testament the story of Jesus Christ gave word-for-word accounts of what he said, but was supposedly written sixty years later. Again, was it made up? Was it all put into the writer's mind by God or were they words that Jesus, 'May well have said'? I think I remember writing in *Wonderment* about the rabbi who admitted that the latter was probably the true fact.

The only evidence we have for what is written in the Bible is what is written in the Bible, but there must have been a reason for it to come about. My personal idea is that these people who, we have to remember, were living in the Bronze Age, had no knowledge of science whatsoever and yet their brains still wondered, as we do today. Just because they lived in times of little or no understanding didn't mean they didn't want and need to understand. No civilisation ever has lived without the need for understanding and exploration, because if we didn't have a wish to understand and therefore move on, we would all still be living in Africa and hunting with our bare hands.

You can imagine the people of the Bronze Age sitting around a fire at night having a chin-wag and looking up at the multitude of stars above them. They watched as each star made its way through the cosmos and then, if they stayed there long enough, they would see the sky gradually brighten once more and daylight return. They would have witnessed comets and meteors and lightning, all of which would have thrilled (and frightened) their imaginations. During the day the sun had been shining and then it had disappeared, only to return the following morning. They loved the sun and even felt its warmth doing them good, but despite puzzling with their still somewhat primitive brains, they could not fathom out where the sun had gone and why it would certainly return. You can almost feel the wonder in their minds as they stared, as the sky turned blue once more and warmth came back to their land. We look up and see countless billions of stars. We also know there are countless billions of galaxies but they knew nothing of them and yet they yearned for answers. They never had scientists, telescopes, satellites in space or any of the other aids we have today. To their minds, they were sitting on a constant and non-varying earth which was light sometimes and dark at other times. It was warm sometimes and cold at others. They were also sitting on a world which, to them, was flat. But as I say, they were inquisitive and needed answers so what did they do? They started to think and make up their own explanations, and why not? Their imaginations needed satisfying so they came up with what they thought was a wholly plausible explanation. It was plausible to them and had no need to be anything greater. Never did it demand a burden of proof.

They imagined, quite logically for them, that someone or something must have made it all and so, eventually, they invented God and what could possibly have been wrong with that? To them, it made perfect sense. God had made their world and the sky above and if he had done this he must have made them as well. If he had made them then he must be their master and they must behave in a manner that pleased him. It also made sense to them that if they did behave they would be rewarded and if they didn't they would, quite rightly, be punished. But how would they be rewarded or punished? This is where heaven and hell came into existence. How simple and yet how sensible to Bronze Age man this all was. God made you and you obeyed him or else. They learned to fear this thing they had invented, as it was 'It' that determined and controlled their lives and so they worshipped 'It' more and more.

The advent of God also gave them a new concept, something to pray to for better things. Times were hard and every little molecule of help was very gratefully received.

There have been countless gods worshipped in the past and even today, in no way am I saying the God of the Bible was the first or even the most significant, but this course of action does seem a logical one in my mind, but this is all from only my mind. It is by no means a totally factual answer.

If we look back to Chapter 2, Revelation, we see that stars fall to the earth from the sky. We also see God with stars in his hands. I pay everyone the courtesy of being intelligent enough to know just how big stars are and everyone must know that God could never have held even one in his hand. We do see what we may call 'shooting stars' which are small rocks or even just grains of material entering the earth's atmosphere and burning up. What we all know is the simple fact that stars can never, in any way, simply 'fall to earth'. We know this, but those who lived at the time of the writing of the Bible did not have this knowledge or science behind them and the stars they watched traversing the night sky were just simple specks of light, twinkling enchantingly above them. We know that our earth is tiny compared with all stars but how were they to know this? They never knew, but we do. Stars to them looked small so why shouldn't they fall to earth and why shouldn't God hold them in his hand? As science has progressed we have all learned about the size of the stars and through this learning, we have to accept that this part of the Bible, at least, is simply not true.

At the time of the Bible being written, the Bible was science and the only science available was the Bible. It was all they had and all they knew but humans have a highly inquisitive nature and gradually and over millennia, piece by tiny piece, they learned more until we have reached where we are today.

Over time, science has progressed by huge degrees while, obviously, the Bible has stayed the same. For many, many years the Bible and science were compatible but, probably since Galileo, and certainly since Darwin, a great divide or rift has appeared and gradually opened up, which has torn the once Bible cum science book apart. It is only natural, I suppose, that some have moved on with science whilst some have stuck steadfastly with the Bible.

I look at it as a kind of marriage analogy. Two people fall in love, or think they have. They get married and then one person studies life and living and wants to move on while the other is quite content to live their life for the next sixty years just as they have done in the past. A divide or rift appears and divorce is just around the corner. The problem with both religion and marriage is that rarely can the split happen with everyone staying amicable, kind and passive.

Today, a Facebook friend of mine has posted the following. His thoughts are very similar to mine and, although he puts his in a slightly different way, they do come up with much the same conclusion. Let's see what he says:

Let me try to explain the origin of religion in brief.

Millions of years back, humans evolved from four-legged primates. The main purpose of evolution was to survive in the changing environment of the surrounding. Around 350,000 - 600,000 years back, the Neanderthals appeared on earth. The ability to communicate and discuss had improved with evolution. The reason why four-legged apes evolved to two-legged humans was for survival benefit. By evolving from four-legged apes to two-legged humans our ancestors could throw stones and spears even while running, which gave them a huge advantage over other animals. A four-legged animal like a lion can kill its prey only after a physical fight/contact. Two-legged humans can kill bigger, stronger and poisonous animals for food or protein by using two hands to throw stones/spears from a safe distance. So to increase the chance of survival humans evolved from a particular species of apes.

The origin of religion.

Early humans used to live together in a group, like in a village. One day a small child died suddenly. The parents cried uncontrollably. The villagers came together and tried to find out the reason why the child died suddenly. Nobody could find a reason. They analysed what the child did before he died. One villager saw the child cutting the tree behind his house before the child got ill and died. Since nobody knew the exact reason why the child died they thought probably the child died because of cutting the tree. They started thinking that the tree had supernatural power and started worshipping the tree so that no child died suddenly.

For those villagers, this particular tree became their god. In another part of the earth, some people saw a child beating a cow before she got ill and died so they thought the child died because of beating the cow and started worshipping the cow as God in that village. Similarly, in many other parts of the earth a stone became God, a snake became God etc. Thus, humans created gods from their imaginations. God did not create anyone or anything. Moreover, since the early humans didn't know science they thought rain was because Almighty God, who stays in the sky above them, sprinkled water on them. That's why all religions refer to God as the one who stays above us (Uper Wala; father in heaven etc).

Today we know that rain happens because of evaporation and condensation. Similarly, many things people did not know earlier are now known with the help of science. Of course there are many more things which science does not know but will be known soon. God did not create humans. Humans are still evolving. Our brains are becoming sharper because evolution is still going on.

During the time of Krishna/Jesus/Mohammed there was no TV or mobile phones, but today humans can even clone humans. Humans are even staying in space. Today there are various man-made satellites through which audio, visual and other types of data are transmitted. Today we have the Interweb, through which we can be in touch instantly.

Danger of religion.

When religions originated, as explained above, the purpose was to protect loved ones from danger, to discipline humans and society, to increase agricultural production and out of fear of getting into trouble etc. The purpose of all religions everywhere was for the betterment of own societies.

As the practice of religious rituals passed on from generation to generation for thousands of years with firm belief, it is natural for a child to follow what his parents/society have practised. In the true sense, religion is just a tradition passed on from early humans evolved from various parts of the earth. Just as army/air force/navy from different countries have different traditions, similarly humans who evolved from different parts of the earth created different religions.

Since we cannot say that others' traditions are wrong, we also cannot say that others' religions are wrong. Sadly, today *everyone claims that his religion is the only true and best religion and others are false and bad. Everyone claims that the god he worships is the only true god and the god others worship is wrong. Religion has created hatred, groupism, intolerance, killing etc. Today, religions kill more humans than cancers do.*

Religion cannot explain anything.

If God created humans why would he create some with black skin and some with white skin and some with yellow skin, that hatch racism? Only evolution can explain why some humans are white-skinned while some are negroid or mongoloid. If God in omnipresent, what was God was doing when a girl was being raped? Was God enjoying the rape scene? The truth is that everything comes from physical and chemical reactions of atoms and molecules available in the earth.

Conclusion.

All religions are just a product of the imaginations of our ancestors while looking for the reasons for deaths, calamities and miseries. All religions started to protect loved ones from danger, to discipline humans, society etc. There is no reason why we should fight in the name of religion. Let us all consider religion as a tradition and respect each other's religion as we respect each other's traditions. We the educated people must speak out against religious intolerance and violence/killing in the name of religion. Let us all be good human beings and respect one another, love one another and spread humanity, not hatred, for the betterment of our children or else our children will live in insecurity and fear throughout their lives.

This is the view of a gentleman based in India. He calls himself 'Humanist Citizen' (Probably not his real name), and obviously he has his own way of putting things. He does it very well and I thank him sincerely for giving me permission to include his thoughts.

What do others say about the Bible?

The first thing I found when looking for a reason why the Bible was written was a simple statement. It read, 'That ye might believe'. I don't think we need to go into that one too much.

Here are some other ideas as to why the Bible was written, why it has to be real, why it has to be fake and why people believe and do not believe in it. These are points of view from the minds of others:

'The apostles could not have written the Bible because they were only poor people and the poor could not write. What would be the point of writing the Bible in those days anyway, when very few could read?'

'The Holy Spirit was just that and was not, therefore, capable of writing so he passed his word on to men so that they could record his thoughts and wishes.'

'The Bible was not meant for those who could not read. It was meant for religious officials who could read it and pass it on to others.'

'A common reason for writing the Bible was to relay the writer's personal relationship with God.'

'The Bible was written to maintain a history of how everything came about.'

'The Bible is the total word of God and it shows just how he wants us to live the lives he has given us.'

'It is simply there to control the masses.'

'Jesus' own words prove the Bible is wrong. He says he will return in the lifetime of his audience.'

'The Bible tells me all atheists are evil and corrupt. I know from personal experience that this is not true.'

'The book was written by humans in an age which was ignorant, superstitious and cruel.'

'The Bible is the true word of our Lord and that is that.'

'It could never be a true record of history because none of it makes sense.' 'Every word in the Bible is true but then again, they are just words.'

We could go on and on talking about it and finding other people's views but, in the end, we can only have our own. I have mine and you have yours and, in the end, I suppose we will never all agree on which is correct and isn't that what makes our world so great? We can disagree and by doing so, most of us can reach some common ground and learn. The problem arises when dogma is the basis of an argument and that then leads to hostility. The worst we should do is agree to disagree. My father was never wrong, even when he was a hundred percent wrong and his dogma led to hostility. It is sad to see so much war and hostility being caused today through the same emotion. I see it on Facebook so måny times, where people at both sides of the argument become aggressive and a mini war breaks out between them over what was really nothing to start with.

Why am I saying this in this way? I don't really know. Perhaps, deep down, it is an act of self-preservation. I know my views are strong but they are just that, my views. Yes, it could be an act of self-preservation as I know my views do upset people, but it is also an act of kindness in as much as I do like to put my views across but, at the same time, I do not like upsetting others. We all have our views and I am lucky to be able to put mine into book form, which gives me great satisfaction and a platform to speak from.

I love the following sayings and anecdotes.

My favourite parts of the Bible are when Jesus was talking to God (himself) and someone who wasn't there was writing about it.

Another

No one can reason with a fool because fools are unreasonable.

(Is that you, or me, or both of us?)

Tell them God is real, they believe you. Tell them paint is wet, then they have to touch it to make sure.

Another:

I have as much authority as the Pope. I just don't have as many people who believe it.

And another: (I love this one.)

America prays to God to destroy our enemies: Our enemies pray to God to destroy us. Someone's gonna be disappointed. Someone's wasting their time. Could it be everyone?

I feel this one says so much.

Morality

How many times have I heard someone say that if you are not religious and fear God, then you can have no morality because, if you do not get your morality from God, religion and the Bible then you cannot possibly have any morality at all? Very sadly, I have even been asked, if I am an atheist why do I not have sex with children? They then say, without any thought or foundation, that all atheists are completely evil and must therefore be devil worshippers. You can see why, in their minds, I suppose. You cannot get your morals from anywhere else but the Bible. You do not believe in the Bible so therefore you have no morals and if you have no morals, then you must truly be a terrible person who even has sex with children. It then follows that if you are as terrible a person you must be like the devil and you must, then, worship him. It all makes sense, apart from the fact that it makes no single atom of sense whatsoever.

I do find this is a big affliction that many religionists suffer from. If they wish to be religious then that is totally up to them and in no way would I say they are bad people in any way. In no way would I say I am better than them because I think the way I do. I could put myself above them because I feel my thoughts are rational and theirs are not, but they could also put themselves above me because they feel it is my thoughts that are unfounded and bear no relationship to their reality, a reality based upon their love (and often need) for God, Jesus and their book. The problem arises when they are so lost in that book that anything outside it becomes clouded and obscured. It then becomes difficult to separate an atheist who is just trying to do his/her best in life, from someone who must be a worshipper of Satan, Lucifer, the devil, Apollyon, Abaddon or Son of Perdition or whatever name they want to call this thing.

In *Wonderment* I mentioned that if God created everything from nothing then, surely, it follows that he must have created the devil. The Bible seems adamant that there was no other creator than God and, I may be wrong, but if this were true, then God could have created the devil just so that he had something or someone to blame all the bad things on. It also follows that if God was supposed to have created the devil, then the devil is only a part of the whole Bible/religion story and if an atheist doesn't believe in the Bible or God, then why should he believe in and, indeed, worship, the devil? Surely the two go together and if you do not believe in one, then how can you possibly believe in the other?

Now, in reality, an atheist is simply a person who believes that God does not exist and perhaps the whole concept of religion is wrong. It may be because it is truly wrong or it may be that they think it is wrong simply because they cannot grasp the truth of it. Whatever it is, atheists loving and worshipping Satan is no more true that atheists eating babies. What? No, we really don't, you know. Well, not all of us anyway.

Absolute morality in the Bible.

Isaiah 5:20.*Woe to those who call evil good, and good evil; who put darkness for light and light for darkness; who put bitter for sweet, and sweet for bitter!*

The Bible teaches that right is right and wrong is wrong. These and good and evil are absolutes that are set by God, are defined by him and also policed by him. This is where the Ten Commandments come in. God has set out his laws and woe will come to any who do not adhere to his word. It is said that these absolutes are placed in everyone's hearts as the consciousness of good, bad and evil and this conscience guides us as to which path to follow; hopefully, the path to God.

The phrase, 'We have conscience in our hearts, placed there by God', is a bit confusing. Firstly, no conscience is in our hearts, it is in our heads, and why should we get our conscience from God? Isn't it something that is in our heads and is developing there as the years pass? A child has a conscience, but that conscience must be taught and affirmed by those around it. Providing a child is taught basic right and wrong, is praised for the former and chastised for the latter, it will grow up to learn and do good. Absolute morality is not placed in a child's head or heart from the time it was born, although any normal child will have a basic instinct to realise for itself the simple ethos of right and wrong. If a child is never taught of God then will that child always rob, murder, pillage and plunder? Of course not. Come to think of it; if a child is never taught of God then will he or she ever feel the need for him at all?

How easy is it to say that right is right and wrong is wrong but can it all be this clear cut? Not according to the Bible. Looking at a woman other than your wife is deemed a sin under God's rules. How clear cut is this and how can we all stop ourselves from becoming sinners? I love my wife totally and utterly and I am also rapidly becoming an old man, but still I can't help myself looking lustfully at another woman and if my wife never looked lustfully at another man again, then I would worry she was losing her relationship with reality. What can be wrong with looking? Why is this classed as a terrible sin? If it is and I am to be punished for it, can he that judgeth over me please take another three and a half million cases into consideration?

I have said it before but if people, especially youngsters, do not masturbate from time to time they would probably explode and yet this is seen as a sin. What makes it worse is the fact that as God watches everything we do, then is he watching you as you do this? If he is, then why? Are we not allowed any privacy at all? Even if we are sinners then surely he could show just a little decorum and look away politely. Surely there are a few billion more important things for him to watch over rather than a teenager relieving the huge sexual urges that were installed by his or her creator in the first place? When you think about it, I wonder how many teenagers do actually struggle with this; with the thought of being watched by God as they do it. Surely masturbation is a 100% natural thing for us all to do and we should all do it without the slightest feeling of guilt, remorse or the awful feeling that we are being looked at.

If we read the Bible we see that people should be stoned for adultery or for breaking the Sabbath. According to the Bible, the very fact that we are here at all relies upon incest. People are killed for little or nothing. Lot's wife was turned to a pillar of salt just for looking back.

Adam and Eve had sons, Cain and Abel, and later went on to have more children but after Cain murdered Abel, he married and had children. The only other people alive at that time were his mother and father so it figures that he must have married his own mother, as did his own son, Enoch. So we ended up with Adam and Eve, Cain and Eve and Enoch and Eve. Incest has always been frowned upon but the Bible certainly did its best to promote it.

Also, we have to realise that working on the Sabbath in biblical times (and for many, many years after) was seen as a terrible thing to do and the punishment for this was death. We have to look back to the man who was stoned to death for picking up sticks for his fire on the Sabbath. Haven't vicars, parsons and priests always worked on the Sabbath?

Can you see what I am saying? The Bible promotes incest and stoning for little or no reason and yet just looking lustfully at a woman who is not your wife, or masturbating, is seen as being totally wrong and probably punishable by spending an eternity in the pits of fire that we call hell. I cannot really see any reasoning, reality or correlation. The Bible also condones slavery and tells just how hard you can beat your slave. Is this morality?

So if we are to get our morality from the Bible then we either have to think very hard or we have to cherry-pick. It seems okay to stone people or have sex with a close relative and yet the law of today says no. It seems wrong to have homosexual sex and yet the law today says yes, it's fine. I'm afraid if we got our morals from the Bible alone we would all be stumped as to know what to do at all. If we decided to stone someone for working on a Sunday, then would we be able to quote the Bible in court and say that God had condoned it? Mind you, if we were in court giving evidence then I suppose we would have already sworn on the Bible anyway. We would be tried for committing a crime that the Bible says is fine, and then the authorities would use the very book we were following and being tried for following, to assert that we were telling the truth in what we said.

God's morality is absolute and that would make you think that no one who follows God's word could ever stray from those words, but has no one ever suffered because of religion and religious people? Of course they have. We have talked earlier in the book about priests abusing and raping those in their charge. They did this whilst hiding behind religion, but what of religion itself? Priests only hid behind religion but what of suffering actually caused in the name of religion?

The Crusades.

I will not go into this in too much detail as it all happened so long ago and was not suffering that was actually caused in the 'name' of religion but 'because' of religion. People did not purposely go out and kill those of a different religion or set out to torture in order to convert others to their particular faith, but it was because of religion that it all happened.

As we know, the Bible and its stories all centre around the Middle East. The story of Noah says that all the animals of the world went into the ark but, in the time of this story being written, the Middle East was the only known area. No one could have had any inkling of other lands such as South and North America and Australia. The Middle East and Jerusalem in particular was the home of religion and as religion played a huge part in the daily lives of most, Jerusalem was deemed as being highly important.

In the Middle Ages, Jerusalem fell out of the control of Christians and became ruled by Arab invaders and then by the Turks. Under the Turks, in the 11th century, Christianity and

Judaism were frowned upon and persecuted and Jerusalem was no longer the religious centre for these people. Of course, the church could not accept this and felt a duty to respond and the only way it felt it could respond was through war. I have no idea how fervent they were at responding but if they were anything like the leaders we have today, I would think they were quite excited about it. European leaders were encouraged to go and take back the city and hence the first Crusade started, in 1096. Some joined the Crusades to gain wealth and some did go because they felt it their religious duty, but others went simply because of the adventure.

In all, there were nine Crusades which spanned almost two hundred years and many, many people died but, ultimately, all the Crusades were unsuccessful. They did, however, bring about contact with the East and its people and the West did gain from that in many ways, but was this worth any of the deaths caused?

I have read several differing figures as to just how many died during the Crusades and, as they vary so wildly, I am not going to even hazard a guess and try to put down my own figure. All I will say is that as they were fighting on and off for almost two hundred years. It doesn't take a genius to work out that the death toll must have been horrendous.

It also amazes me to think of the sheer logistics of getting men to fight in these wars. We can deploy soldiers by air anywhere in the world today, within just a few days. We can fly to the other side of the world in a day but these people had to group, to march or sail to a land that few knew anything of. Even on the field of battle, today, we have fully qualified and highly trained paramedics and hospital facilities, with highly professional operating staff. What did these soldiers have when they were badly wounded? They had nothing.

The methods of war have changed dramatically since the Crusades but the eagerness has not. These wars were fought primarily because of religion and we are still fighting for the same reason today. If we took religion out of the equation in Jerusalem at the time of the Crusades, would the wars have happened? If we took religion out of the equation today would wars still happen? I do believe they would but one huge factor would have been taken out and the number of wars would have to lessen.

In this book, I am concentrating on the Christian religion that I was once baptised into and drew away from, but if we look at terrorism around the world and now conflicts including the so-called Islamic State or IS, we see that horrible and disgusting things are being done to innocent people in wars that are carried out in the name of religion. I have no bounds whatsoever in my grief for all the poor Jewish people who were persecuted so grotesquely in WWII, but why were they persecuted? It was because of their religious beliefs. I'm sorry but my mind says, if we take away religion we also take away much hatred, persecution and suffering.

If we were to publish depictions of the prophet Mohammed there would be hatred and complete uproar, as this would violate what Muslim people would say is their right. What I would like to see is the same throng of people standing up and totally denouncing all violence perpetrated in the name of their religion. It is, of course, utterly and completely true to say that not all Muslims are terrorists but would I not be somewhere near the truth if I said that many terrorists are Muslims? I fervently believe that we are all equal and no person or race or religion should ever be discriminated against. Neither do I have any problem with people going to other countries to live. Here, what I would like to see is real integration. How about some of these people standing up and shouting, 'Look at me! I am now American or English or German or French and I am proud! I still have my religious beliefs but I appreciate others have theirs and I love and will serve my new country!'

Wouldn't this make us welcome them more wholeheartedly?

The Inquisition.

I know the Crusades happened many years ago, as did the Inquisition but, as with the Crusades, the Inquisition does have certain reflections today.

The Catholic Church, in the Middle Ages, was worried about people losing their faith in that church and, instead of talking to those concerned and trying to reconvert them, as would any sensible person or group, it was decided that anyone who was against the Catholic Church would be rounded up as heretics, tortured, found guilty and then possibly burned to death. Once again, here we are not seeing the kindness and love of God and religion spread even-handedly among God's people. Once again, we are seeing the eagerness to harm others. 'There is no other love but God', they say. Again, where is that love?

The Inquisition was made up of priests who were given the authority to arrest and imprison these heretics. Heretics, who I may add, whose only real crime was to use their own brains to think for themselves. This thinking, like today, was not encouraged as it gave them freedom and with freedom they could not be controlled. We see the same today with the Catholic Church being against family planning. They seem to think people should be controlled at every possible opportunity. Even at the level of sex again.

During the Inquisition, those accused stood little chance as they were cruelly and horribly tortured until they confessed. (More religious love.) If they confessed before torture they were not tortured and if they were tortured, then they confessed. It was as simple as that and to the priests in charge, everyone was a winner. The Catholic Church was the ultimate power during these times and it made sure through fair means or foul that it stayed that way.

Anyone who attempts to construe a personal view of God which conflicts with Church dogma must be burned without pity.
Pope Innocent III.

In this piece, I have deliberately not delved too far into actual torture and torture devices and methods. I will leave the pain and suffering of those tortured and the joy and glee of their torturers to your own imaginations. What amazes me is how anyone could actually torture another human being, let alone get a sheer thrill out of doing so and yet you still see it today if you study those who do the same thing. It is a hugely sad fact that the human psyche still has not changed, even after hundreds or even thousands of years. Of course, not all hate comes from religion but much is still held by religious people and in the name of religion. I do not and never will hate anyone. I argue against religion but, in my mind, there is never one tiny spark of hate. A huge lack of understanding maybe but never any hatred. I do debate the subject of religion but I do it in a kind way, but it amazes me how many, on both sides, still revel in hatred as did those during the Inquisition.

We from the West have warred in Afghanistan for many years. We went in and fought the Taliban but, eventually we had to leave. A few of us are still there but, in our leaving, did we honestly think the Taliban would stay lying down? We went into the war with the usual human gusto but went in without a properly-thought-out exit strategy, so when the time came to leave we could not do so with any confidence. It didn't take an Albert Einstein or Stephen Hawking to work out that the Taliban would, once again, fight wholeheartedly for what they believed in once their adversaries had left.

Who and what are the Taliban?

They emerged in the 1990s in Northern Pakistan, following the withdrawal of troops by the Soviets from Afghanistan. Their promise was to restore peace and security to the region and to impose their own austere version of Sharia Law once in power.

In Pakistan and Afghanistan, they soon introduced Islamic punishments such as public executions for murderers and adulterers and the amputation of limbs of those found guilty of stealing. Men were required to grow beards and women were forced to wear burkas. They banned television, music and cinema and disapproved of girls over the age of ten years going to school. We have the famous case of a fourteen-year-old girl, Malala Yousafzai, who, whilst sitting on a bus in the grounds of her school, was shot in the head by a gunman who quickly professed that he was a member of the Taliban and he did the shooting. Something to be proud of, I'm sure.

The Taliban in Afghanistan were accused of providing a safe haven for Osama Bin Laden and al-Qaeda, who were blamed for the attacks of 9/11 and this brought about the invasion by the West.

I know I am talking about Islam here and not the Christianity that this book is about, but if we think about it, here we have so-called Christian countries delighting in going to war with Islamic ones. I am well aware that I say it all the time but why do we, as a human race, love war so much? Why can't we live in peace as do other animals? Why do different religions have such different ideals that we must go to war over them? If God is love, then shouldn't we all love each other? If religions are peaceful then shouldn't religious extremists be extremely peaceful?

The Taliban and other groups have used hundreds, if not thousands of people as suicide bombers, but how do they persuade someone to blow themselves to pieces in order to take others with them? Once again, the answer is simple and it relies, again, upon religion. Not everyone has a hugely great or successful life here on earth, so what if you can convince them that this life may be rubbish but a far better one awaits them on the other side? It isn't hard to do, is it, because millions of religious people already think this. What if you could tell them that if they were to blow themselves up they would go to a much higher place and a far better life? Then you have to add on the fact that as they had died for their religion, their particular god would see them as heroes and their salvation and eternal life would then be one of a prince, with all the trappings this would bring. Only the briefest of moments of fear and pain endured would bring wonder beyond their wildest dreams for a whole eternity. Can you see why they would go for it? No, it is not just because they are stupid.

The problem is that it is not real, is it? These people would sacrifice their own lives for even a promise of something better, but how likely is it all? Killing others, or even killing yourself for no real reason, can have no place in any realistic society. We need change. We need people to get a grip on life, abandon all hatred and live together in what is, due to overpopulation, becoming a very demanding time for us all.

As you can see by what I have written, morality is not just found in the Bible. In fact, in many cases religion just flouts morality totally. In no way would I be stupid enough to say that morality is only the domain of atheists, as I know there are equally as many bad atheists as there are bad theists but the fact is that immorality is deeply embedded in all walks of life, society and human nature and this does need to change. Hatred, in whatever form it takes, must be cast out as it is only through love, understanding and reality that we can save the world we live in if we want to carry on living in anywhere near the same way we do today.

I once remember someone asking Richard Dawkins why, if he had no belief in religion, he didn't go out and commit crimes. The questioner seemed to honestly think, in his own mind, that without religion you must be capable of anything. Richard Dawkins gave his answer in his usual educated and intellectual way. My answer to this would have been told in a little story.

The story would go something like this:

If I was walking along a street and I saw an elderly lady walking towards me and I knew she had been to the post office to collect her pension I would approach her and take her arm. I would then walk her home to make sure she was safe. She would thank me for my kindness, not because I was religious but because I had acted as a gentleman.

I would then explain to the person who had posed the question that, as I am an atheist, I would not have carried out this act of kindness through any religious obligation or hopeful gratitude of God. I would have done it through a common sense of decency and civility. I would also have done the deed just in case the questioner was around and had suddenly lost his faith.

If we are only going to get our morals from a fear of a god and the Bible, what kind of morality is that? Surely morality should come from our own minds in the sense of knowing what is right and what is wrong. Should Bible morality include stoning people for adultery, death for apostates and death for breaking the Sabbath? Should daughters seduce their fathers in order to become pregnant and should women be turned to pillars of salt just for looking back? No, these are stories from a Bronze Age book. We should all get our morality from intelligence and common sense. These things alone should teach us to love one another, understand one another and live together as decent people should. The past has seen huge crimes and misdemeanours carried out in the name of religion and atheists who, although they do not commit crimes, 'In the name of atheism', have also caused much strife in the world. We have to remember that this small world is the only one we have and we all have to live on it as best we can.

If we look back to the Crusades or the Inquisition, we cannot forget what happened but we can see they happened in times of little understanding. We have a big problem on our hands today in as much as we are still doing similar things although, over these many years, we should and must understand that what we are doing is totally wrong. I know I harp on and on about living together and loving each other and looking after the beautiful world we live in but, unless we do, we will never escape from the Middle Age mentality that our minds seem set in. This is not the 11th or 12th century. This is the 21st century and we really must start thinking. I've said the following so many times before but I am going to repeat myself here again. In the end, reality is all we have and is all we need. We can only hurt ourselves and those around us if we try to search for anything else.

In depictions of the earth which are said to illustrate how the earth was thought to have looked in Bible-writing times, I've seen vast pillars under a flat earth which has a dome over the top.

The pillars of the earth are obviously there to support it, the earth is flat and the globe above houses the stars and moon.

In my wildest thoughts, I cannot possibly see that anyone alive today actually believes this is what the earth and the universe look like. If the earth has pillars to support it then what is supporting the pillars? We know the earth is not flat, and we know the universe cannot possibly he housed in some dome above us. What could this dome be made of? Glass perhaps?

The illustration makes us look like something that we would find in a museum or Victorian household. Something precious that is protected by its glass dome or a snow scene perhaps.

We all know that the earth is a sphere, as is the moon, the sun and all the other stars out there and we all know that we are held in place by gravity. We revolve around the sun and the sun revolves eventually around the centre of our galaxy.

Once again, this illustration shows us at the centre of everything and it also shows that the rest of the universe is just a small area above our heads, making us the most important thing in it. Again, we now know this to be not the case. Science has moved on and its thoughts and findings have totally changed. Isn't it about time we all moved along with it?

The Love of and Need of God

In an earlier chapter, I talked about love and why we should all show it and, hopefully, receive it. Here I want to talk more about love, but this time about the 'Love from God', the love that is supposed to be the true and only love.

If we listen to people talking or see them debating on Facebook, we will quickly see that they constantly talk about the 'Great love of God' and then add that God is love and there cannot possibly be any love, of any kind, for anyone without him in their lives. Fair enough, if that is what they think but I thought I would explore this a little further and asked in a particular Facebook group just what love they received from God and how it manifested itself. I posted it and waited a few days but, again, as always, didn't receive a single reply so then I posted the same question on a different religious site. Guess what? No reply again. I have just read a question from someone which was very simple. All it asked (of a man who constantly talks about religion and his great belief and involvement in it) was, 'How far up is heaven'? The man had to admit that he did not know. Even the simplest of questions cannot be answered. In debates, they go on and on about biogenesis and abiogenesis or macroevolution and microevolution. They try to make out they understand these and can prove through them that evolution didn't happen. They can understand every little argument that is fabricated against natural sciences and natural selection as if they are all professors with huge intellects, as big as the Empire State Building, and yet when you ask the simplest of factual questions regarding the religious beliefs they fight for, they cannot give an answer at all.

Biogenesis – Attributed to Louis Pasteur and meaning that living things only come from other living things; e.g. a chicken from an egg.

Abiogenesis – The process by which life arises naturally from non-living material.

Scientists speculate that life may have risen as a result of random chemical processes happening to produce self-replicating molecules.

Macroevolution is evolution on a scale of separated gene pools.

Macroevolutionary studies focus on changes that occur at or above the level of species, as opposed to 'microevolution', which focusses upon smaller evolutionary changes within a species or population.

Although I am happy and completely contented with my life, I do think deeply about it. This thinking has brought great wonder into my life but the above, relating to God's love, has brought an uncomfortable thought into my mind.

People profess strongly about the love that God gives them and they profess to live their lives by that love. They do this but do not understand one iota just what form this love takes and what it does for them. How can we decipher this? My only conclusion is the worrying one, that they are praying and worshipping their God when, in reality, they do not really know what they are doing, who they are praying to, what they are praying for and what, in the end, they are receiving in return?

You can't convince a believer of anything; for their belief is not based on evidence, it's based on a deep seated need to believe.

It is hugely and upsettingly sad to think that there are actually people out there who have such empty lives and low esteem that religion is the only entity they feel they can use to try and gain a foot-hold and fill their otherwise deep and dark void. Also, to think in this way must mean that their lives are so unfulfilled that they must, actively, look forward to going to the heaven they dream of. How can death be the only thing in life that is left to look forward to? This is a horrendous way to be and I do, genuinely, really feel greatly for anyone who has found themselves to be at that point, but life is a great gift and surely we must do something more with it than this? Could you even imagine having a bad day, (we all do), and your only conclusion to it is, 'Well, that one's over and at least it is another day closer to death, heaven and God.'

Does it happen? I think so.

Let's say you are deeply religious, but have a good life with your friends and family and enjoy greatly the world around you.

Let's say you have a good understanding of what your life is all about and a full knowledge of your religion.

Let's say you also have a good understanding of what your heaven and hell are like and you honestly feel the love of your god.

Let's say you have even seen heaven and hell, where they are and what happens when you get there.

Let's say you have a good understanding of just who, what and where your god is and how his love comes to you and transforms your life while you are here.

If you are and have all of the above then, to you, your life must feel complete as is mine, but it has to be an awful fact that many do hang onto religion as would a drowning man hold on to a floating leaf on the top of the water in order to try, desperately but inevitably in vain, to save his life.

I am not blind enough or stupid enough to believe that this awful 'lostness', if that is a word, is confined only to people of a religious nature as there must be many atheists who are in the same situation. Out of the two, though, who are the better equipped?

Is it?

A. The religious person who does not have a true and fulfilled life but does have someone or something to lean on.

or

B. The atheist who does not have a true and fulfilled life, has nothing to lean on but is still strong enough to rely upon himself to get through.

Which is more comforting, the thought of God helping or the thought you do still, after all, have some amount of inner strength to help see you through? I suppose the fact you pray to and worship God every day but are still, in the end, in the same low and depressed position does say something. Does it say that either that God is not listening, not interested or possibly, even, he isn't there at all?

Can we say; 'They do it because they cannot do without it?'

Why does God love us?

In researching this I have come across an article which explains it in what the author sees and believes as true details. I will not copy it all out but will try and do my best to summarise it.

It seems that God doesn't love us for our deeds and goodness. He simply loves us for what we are. He doesn't love us because we are lovable. He loves us because we all deserve his love.

The state of mankind since 'the fall' is one of rebellion and disobedience and the heart is deceitful and desperately wicked. Our innermost beings are so corrupted by sin that we don't even realise the extent to which we are tainted. No one is righteous and no one understands.

It goes on to say what has been said to me before and that is, God doesn't just love, He 'is' love and that love is not a love of the soppy, romantic and sentimental kind. His love is of the 'agape' kind, the love of self-sacrifice and this brings us to what everyone says is God's greatest show of his love for us, the sacrifice of his son, Jesus Christ, on the cross.

Let's look at why this came about.

Firstly, to make it easier to understand later, I shall accept for a while again that the earth is only six thousand years old.

Science tells us that the universe came from nothing and people of a religious persuasion will mock this and say it could not have happened and yet, they also believe that the earth came from nothing; but their nothing came from the hand of God, who had already existed for an eternity when there was nothing. Whatever anyone else believes, the Bible says God made the universe and everything in it in just six miraculous days. He made millions of animal species on a Friday and then made man (Adam) the following day. Adam was made from dust and it has to be assumed, I suppose, that all the other animals were made from it as well.

Science believes we evolved over millions upon millions of years and are made of chemicals such as hydrogen, oxygen, carbon and so on, whereas the Bible says we are all made from dust. If we were to experiment and do a breakdown of our body's components, what would we find? Would we find the chemicals I have mentioned or would we just find dust?

Anyway, Adam was made from dust and so were all the millions of animals before him, so why didn't God grab hold of a few handfuls of dust and make Eve? God had made a slight error and had almost forgotten that Adam would need a woman to mate with and populate the earth and then he realised his mistake and took one of Adam's ribs out and fashioned it into a woman. Why? Surely there was plenty of dust still lying around? He had made elephants and whales in split seconds. How long did it take to fashion a complete woman out of a rib bone?

Sorry, I digress.

Adam and Eve were given everything they needed and we are told they 'had dominion over it all'. They could eat of every tree in the Garden of Eden but had strict instructions not to eat of the fruit of the tree of the knowledge of good and evil. They had plenty, an absolute cornucopia of food, and the world was theirs but, with the help of a talking snake, they did partake of the fruit of that tree, which was seen by God as a terrible sin and it seems that sin was still in the heads of people at the time of Jesus' crucifixion.

This raises a few points in my mind.

If the eating of the fruit of the tree of knowledge of good and evil was such a bad thing, then why did God create the tree in the first place? What place did it hold in the ecosystem of the Garden of Eden? What was the point of its existence at all? If it was there, surely some animal would have eaten the fruits and then we may have had an all-knowing aardvark or a tainted tiger or a pheasant philosopher.

1. If we had this tree then, where is it now? Has it 'evolved' into another form of tree?

2. Where did the talking snake come from? And why a talking snake? Why not a talking parrot or mynah bird or budgerigar? That would be a little more likely. The snake seemed to know more than the people. Had he already eaten of the fruits of the tree perhaps?

3. Why was this such a terrible sin when, in reality, all they had done was a bit of scrumping?

4. How would or could the eating of any fruit possibly suddenly give you knowledge of everything? Far-fetched, you must agree. No?

5. Adam and Eve consumed the fruit and their sin was deemed terrible, but didn't God later destroy every human apart from Noah and his family, in order to right this wrong? Nearly all people had become sinners and Noah was thought to be the most righteous of men, but it seems there was awful sin even inside his head or heart, a sin inherited in us all from Adam and Eve and their little hissing friend.

6. Taking the earth as being six thousand years old and Jesus being born two thousand years ago, this question arises. Adam and Eve's sin was the original sin and was deemed as being terrible. God had tried to eradicate it by flooding the planet but that hadn't worked. Why did he then wait another two thousand years or whatever to do something about it? He was omni this and omni that and omni the other, so why didn't

he just wave a little finger and banish all sin, in all people, in an instant?

7. Jesus was said to be the Son of God and he was also said to be God himself. Why would God either put himself or his son through this dreadful torment just to forgive everyone their sins? If my wife committed a sin I wouldn't have myself or my son severely tortured and then crucified in order to forgive her, would I? What would be the point? She had done wrong, so why would I make myself suffer so horribly? As I have said, this god was the great God and he could do anything. He could make the whole expanding universe out of nothing in a few short hours and he could make millions of animals in one day. Surely, bearing all this in mind, he had the ability to simply forgive us without all the hassle?

8. If the Bible is right and Jesus was crucified to forgive us our sins, then why do we praise God so vehemently for it when we are now living two thousand years later? Surely Jesus could not have died two thousand years ago to forgive the sins of people who would not be born for many, many years to come?

9. If we look at our world as I did in *Wonderment*, we will find it is falling deeper and deeper into sin. Wars and murders and tortures are rife, as is mental and physical abuse, corruption and every other sin imaginable. Religionists praise God on high for his sending Jesus (or himself) to the cross and forgiving all sins but, again, his plan hasn't worked, has it? Jesus rose from the dead shortly after being crucified and yet he hasn't been seen for two thousand years and when was God last seen? Maybe, if the Bible is true, it is about time they appeared once again to show their great love and help us through what is rapidly becoming a hugely demanding and distressing time.

Having Jesus crucified to forgive our sins seems to be the greatest show of love ever made by anyone but, in reality, it wasn't one of God's better ideas, was it?

Personal love from God.

It seems that God's love is personal and he loves everyone at the same time. You can find these kind of statements on many different Interweb sites but, again, there are seven billion people on our little planet. Can God love us all personally and at the same time? It has even been said that God's love is so great that it puts Christianity above all other religions. Isn't this being a tiny bit arrogant when there are so many other religions out there? Mind you, I suppose most of them do claim to be the best. God seems to love us all totally and unconditionally, with a love that nothing else can stand a chance of matching and how do we know that? The question is always answered with the same sets of three words: 'God is Love', or, 'It is written'.

In some way I can understand to a certain extent the love shown by God in crucifying his own son or self. It is a huge sacrifice, said to be for us. I do not believe it happened for one moment. I can possibly understand why some others may believe it but I am trying hard and cannot see yet what this 'personal love' from God is and how it manifests itself. Is his love tangible or is it just a feeling inside and if it is just a feeling inside, how can we know that feeling is real?

Is God's love given to us in the form of answered prayers? If so, and he loves us so much, then why are all our prayers not answered? If we pray for a sunny day tomorrow and it happens, is this God's love? If we pray for a sick person to recover and she does, is this God's love? If we pray to have a huge win at bingo and it does not happen, then does that mean that God doesn't love us quite as much as we thought?

Maybe it would naturally have been a sunny day tomorrow and maybe the sick person would have recovered and maybe I just did not have the correct numbers on my bingo card. Maybe it was all down to natural occurrences and nothing to do with God after all.

If we look at a true believer in religion, as opposed to another human being, we should see that the true believer has a great need for God's love but that love is all they wish for. They do not see that love as a way to God's heart and his wallet as well. If this was the case, then some of my questions would then be answered. They would not be in this loving relationship purely for their own material gains or needs. They would be in it for the sheer love and contentment it brings, for God's love is personal to everyone and is a huge reward in itself.

The above is fair enough and if that is what they seek and is all they want and desire, then few could argue with it, but it does make me wonder how God can love us all individually when there are so many of us. Still, we are only talking here of the God of the Bible, when there are plenty of other gods having personal relationships with plenty of other people. Half the world is made up of atheists so that half do not even have to be considered, but is it possible for God to know us individually and then love us all in the same way?

They say that God's love shows the distinctiveness of us all and that love is tailored to that distinctiveness. We are all distinctive and there are so many of us. Could God have possibly made us all so distinctive and could he possibly love each one of us in a different manner? It is also said that this love from God helps us deal with our distinctiveness, but surely we should just be happy and even rejoice in being ourselves. We are all different and wouldn't it be bloody boring if we weren't?

I have been told that God's love helps us in the way he controls and models us and nurtures and matures our lives. I know some are weak and do feel they need nurturing, controlling and modelling but isn't this sad again? Shouldn't we all be our own modellers, nurturers and controllers? Shouldn't we be seeking our own lives and destinies, rather than wallowing in this love of God and sitting back to wait for it all to happen? Even if you do feel the need for God's love and do love receiving it, I would strongly suggest you still pursue your own life. If you sincerely believe you are part of God's love, and therefore part of his plan, it is far too easy to go along with it all and waste your life waiting for something to happen. What happens if you want to be a world-renowned opera singer and honestly feel you have the capabilities to achieve your dream, when God is pushing you to clean the male toilets in a multi-storey car park? Do you simply swish your mop around the urine-soaked floors and entertain others with something from *Carmen* or *Rigoletto* while you are doing it? Would you be satisfied with God's love and plan or would you rather follow your own dreams and desires?

When it comes to describing God's unfathomable love, even the Bible admits defeat.

I wonder why.

When the Missionaries arrived, the Africans had the land and the Missionaries had the Bible. They taught us to pray with our eyes closed. When we opened them, they had the land and we had the Bible.

Jomo Kenyata

What Is the World Coming to?

As I am putting the finishing touches to this book, the world is going through the horrendous violence of terrorist attacks committed mostly by Muslim extremists. We are also seeing bombings, shootings, people being mown down by trucks and aeroplanes being blasted out of the sky. All this is indeed horrendous, but what I see as even more horrendous and worrying is the fact that some of those who are being blown up or gunned down by the Muslim extremists are actually Muslims themselves. Why is religion leading to this and why are the worst of these religious people perpetrating these heinous crimes even against their own? Why is religion even pitting its own kind against each other? Aren't there enough problems in the world and aren't there enough problems being caused by religion already?

If they are murdering those who support the same religion, then surely they cannot really be committing these crimes in the name of that religion. I am an atheist through and through and if I decided I wanted to murder in the name of atheism then surely I would not go out and shoot or bomb other atheists. Mind you, has anyone ever heard of a radicalised atheist? Some of us are noisy maybe, but not radicalised murderers.

Muslims are in no way the only religious group to radicalise their followers to such an extent that they think it totally correct to murder. People of many religions have, over time, eagerly gone forth and persecuted others. It has been happening for thousands of years and even the Bible seems to promote and condone it. What makes one person hate others so much that they can gun down dozens of innocents with no thought for them or those they are leaving behind? What makes one person think he or she is so far above others that they have the right to gun down those whom they consider inferior to them or their beliefs? In no way can arrogance of this magnitude be tolerated. We are told we must tolerate and show respect to those of any religious persuasion but at which point does this respect turn into a lack of understanding and then dislike, through to disrespect and finally on to hatred? 'But hang on,' I can hear you say, 'Has no atheist ever murdered?'

You may say it and, of course, you would be totally correct in doing so.

I have seen the following lines and think they are very apt.

If a Muslim shoots they say his entire religion is guilty.

If a black man shoots they say his entire race is guilty.

If a white man shoots, then the poor man has psychological problems and is a lone wolf.

True enough.

Our tiny world is absolutely stuffed full of people and hatred abounds from every corner. Deaths are occurring for no reason other than hatred and temper and, yes, there are atheists who commit these crimes just as eagerly as religionists. In no way is being an atheist any kind of guarantee of being pure of heart and mind.

To give a simple illustration of this hatred, a few days ago I had to overtake three parked cars which were left on my side of the road on a slight bend in my village but, just as I had pulled out and committed myself to pass them, a lady in a car came the other way. The parked cars are usually there and when I am coming the other way and have to stop, despite it being my right of way, I do so calmly with a wave and with a smile on my face. This lady had no smile on her face at all. She looked like a bulldog that had swallowed a whole nest full of wasps and my wife and I were quite shocked by the absolute hate which was written clearly and in abundance, all across her face.

What makes a person hate this much and for no reason? All I wanted was to pop into the shops. I did not wish to steal all her savings, murder her family or enter World War III. I carried on driving with her glaring at me, but how much hatred would she have thrown at me had I stopped and got out of my car to talk to her? I know some have been stabbed to death for less. She was not a happy bunny and she could have been religious, an agnostic or even a noisy atheist like me, but whatever she was, she was probably not the best type of person to have as an enemy or even as a friend.

With a simple instance such as this arousing so much anger, it is not difficult to see why the world is fighting, killing and breeding hatred in every corner. It is very difficult to understand but not difficult to see. How difficult must it be to live with?

If I look back to my childhood years, yes, there were wars and yes, governments did seem only too willing to go to them and join in, but I never used to witness anger on the streets or terrorism in our cities. A murder was something that happened only occasionally and was the big thing on the national news if it happened. We did have people who murdered innocents but that was rare. Many of the murders we heard about were gangland murders where the person killed was well known to the murderers and the surrounding area whereas, today, we have people gunning down complete strangers for absolutely no personal reason. Some of the attacks are attacks on the country in which the crime is perpetrated, but have any of those who have been killed ever had any say in the policies of that country? Of course they haven't. The same goes for bombing and bringing down an aeroplane. Had any of those holidaymakers returning home to their country after a couple of weeks in the sun ever voted on their country becoming embroiled in the affairs of another? No. And did any of the murdered children in that aeroplane even know what these affairs were?

Let's say I have a massive grievance against the British, French or US governments (I haven't, of course) and let's say that, in my own mind, I feel that grievance is so great that I can justify committing murder in its cause. (I can't, of course.) Do I go out and murder those responsible, (those in government), or do I go to a rock concert and gun down, or blow up dozens of totally innocent people who, most probably, have no idea at all about, or any interest whatsoever in, my grievance? What's more, do I not care that some of those who share my grievance could well be in my line of fire as I pull the trigger? I do feel this has all gone beyond anger and those who have fallen this low are all quite insane. The trouble is that yes, we know they are insane, but they do not know this at all, do they? As with Adolf Hitler, they think they are completely sane and completely right, right up until the time they pull the trigger. The difference here is that the trigger Hitler pulled belonged to a gun which was, in the end, pointing at his own head. If these terrorists are so disillusioned by the world they live in and those that share it with them, then perhaps they should be insane enough to kill themselves, as did Hitler. Oh yes, many do, don't they? They strap explosives to themselves and then detonate them. They die and so does anyone else in the immediate vicinity. Many die and many more are horribly injured.

How insane must someone be to do this? How insane must they be to be talked into it? What of the person who does the talking and radicalising? If it is such a good idea, then why do they not do it themselves?

A quote from a famous comedian.

*Suicide f****** bombing. Now there's a bright idea.*

Every time there's a bang, the world's a wanker short.

Crude, I know, but very apt.

He then goes on to say: *Never trust a person who only has one book.*

How do you think they are going to turn out?

Apt again?

If we look back to the November 2015 attacks on Paris, to which I have obviously mostly been alluding, we will remember that, straight away, the French government ordered retaliatory air strikes on Syria. This didn't happen after holding crisis meetings over the following couple of weeks or months, did it? This happened immediately and with very little thought apart from reprisals and a knee-jerk reaction towards joining in with the hatred of the world. Isn't this acting almost as insanely as those per perpetrated the crime in the first place?

IS claimed responsibility for the Paris attacks and their reason was that France was attacking them in the Middle East. In their minds, France was intervening in their affairs and had no right to do so. France was attacking them and so were other countries, but why? Did IS think they could do whatever they wished to whoever they wished and the rest of the world should stand by and applaud? It is like a school bully terrorising children in the playground while their teachers stand and watch out of the windows. IS are a barbaric bunch of ideologists who feel they must bully others in order to gain the respect of their god, but is beheading children of a different religion ever a justifiable thing to do? It happens, but could their god ever actually condone it? How insane would this be? They say they are murdering in the name of Allah but is it likely that Allah would be pleased with their actions? I don't think so. Would the god of the Bible be pleased with such actions? In the end, don't they worship the same god anyway? I shall leave you to make up your own minds on these thoughts.

Our population has seen many hundreds of wars and atrocities in the past but why are we seeing them now? And why are the numbers proliferating at such an astonishing rate? Why have we never learned a simple and single thing from any of them? With the wars and strife everywhere that we see today, I see our little planet sliding into oblivion, but it doesn't have to, does it? To keep it anywhere near what it is today, we need to all think long and hard and very deeply about its future. Quite a few years ago I predicted a huge slide into oblivion by the human race. It is happening and today it does not take much of a thinker to see it, but, then again, wouldn't it be wonderful if I could be proved wrong? Wouldn't it be wonderful if everyone could turn around and say I was totally stupid in my thoughts and I worried about nothing? Wouldn't it be wonderful if all hate and other world problems simply disappeared rather than proliferated? The world is heading for serious trouble and the trouble is I am not alone in my thinking. Even the great Stephen Hawking agrees with me and has voiced his concerns.

I have quite a few grandchildren and, although I am quite a happy-go-lucky person, I do worry greatly for them and their future. I have only about another twenty to twenty-five years left to live but they all have almost a whole lifetime. In the time it takes for me to reach my grave, I do horribly see huge strife taking over. Wars, terrorism and general hatred will lead to deeper and deeper anarchy and divisions and this, coupled with vast fraud and corruption, will leave even old codgers like me struggling to live out what are supposed to be our normal lives and halcyon days.

In *Wonderment* I talked about my *Mr and Mrs X Syndrome*, which is based upon too many people living on a planet with too few resources. This is biting hard and has already started to cripple us. We are at war with ourselves and unless WE ALL STOP NOW, we are seeing the end of civilisation as we know it. More and more wars will proliferate and then we will see those who are left fighting for the last few crumbs that are left on the table. We see this already in the vast amount of fraud that is taking place. It is a little like a hard winter approaching and those who can are stocking up with as much food as they can to see them through.

In the time I have remaining to live on this planet, (on this beautiful and wondrous planet) some of my grandchildren will only just be thinking of settling down to produce their own families. They all will have the right to live in this wonderful world as I have done, but will there be a wonderful world left for them to live in?

Religion is taught to all at a very young age and children are well and truly indoctrinated into the religion of their country or family, before they even have enough understanding to question a single word of it. In the Christian religion, I have seen (more than once) a baby screaming blue murder as the vicar pours water over its head and indoctrinates it into his faith. What does that poor innocent being think is happening to it? It is being held by a complete stranger and that stranger could well be trying to drown it. The vicar expects the family to bring the child up as a follower of God and Jesus and he gets the child's family to swear that they will see that he or she does. Why do they go through this when a vast majority of parents who put their children through this ceremony have no intention of doing any of it? How many of them are actually even listening to the vicar's instructions anyway? How many of them are only there in that ancient building, performing an ancient ritual which was written down in an ancient book by ancient people, simply because, 'It is what you do'. I have heard this before and the statement dumbfounds me. The indoctrination of a child into any religion is a huge step and, if it is to be done, it should be done with much thought and understanding. Never should it be said that it is 'what you do'. This shows no thought or understanding of religion at all and anyone who says this obviously has no real thought about life either.

I say forget this indoctrination. I say forget all the tradition and superstitions and fear of God or gods. I say, yes, teach what religion is all about once the child is old enough to understand it because, at this stage, they will be able to form opinions of their own and will be able to form their own thoughts which are

301

based on objective reasoning and logic. I say let's, from a very early age, substitute this inane thought and reliance upon religion and go completely down the path of teaching our children the true meaning of life, love and living together. Let's teach them the absolute need for love and caring, both for each other and our planet, which is suffering so cruelly at our hands. Let's teach them that the only thing we really need to rely upon is ourselves and our children will be able to do this if they are loved, cherished, respected and taught they are of great worth.

We have to all be honest now. We do not all have to be honest in a few years' time. Every one of us needs to stand up now and scream, 'ENOUGH!'

We have closed our eyes for far too long and that 'Hungry lion' has come far too close.

(If you do not yet fully understand the *Mr and Mrs X Syndrome* or the *Hungry Lion* analogy, please read the *Wonderment* chapter, *The Wonder of Future Dilemmas*.)

Our world is on the brink of catastrophe and we need a miracle. Not a miracle in as much as we need Jesus to come back to life with his loaves and fishes, or turning water into wine or someone parting waves, but we need a miracle of the magnitude of actual world leaders standing up and actually saying what is happening and telling us what we must do about it. We need strong people offering us strong voices and we need to be strong and listen. We do not need religious leaders standing up and swearing it is all in God's hands and he will sort it with a second coming. We need total and utter reality from total and utter realists. We need to hear our leaders say that $2x2=4$ and we all need to listen and learn from what they say. We do not need to hear them say $2x2=3$ which is nearly four. We need the truth, we need it in abundance and we need it now, and we need it said plainly and simply and in a manner that every one of our seven billion people can understand. Harsh words must be uttered and harsh decisions have to be made if we are to save ourselves and we must all listen and act. We don't need God or Jesus to save us from the fiery furnaces of Hades, we need to save ourselves from ourselves. We do not need to save ourselves from the sins of the Bible but we all need to save ourselves from living the totally unrealistic and almost hedonistic lifestyles we have awarded ourselves and have become accustomed to in the past. Carrying on the way we are now is insane and we must all see that. We must all see it whether we are Church of England, Muslims, Buddhists, Atheists, Jews, Catholics, Sikhs, Hindus or followers of Hare Krishna or even the great Flying Spaghetti Monster.

We need to stop everything and totally re-evaluate our whole world and our systems of living. We all need to totally re-evaluate our relationships with each other and realise that we are all in it together. We need to learn about and from each other and understand just what makes others tick and accept it. The world does, in no way, revolve around us personally and neither can it ever revolve simply around our own, 'one and only' religion or God. We can neither rule the world by our thoughts alone or by the doctrine of our particular faith. We need, now, to ditch all the hatred and judgement that religion brings and we need to swiftly move on, with total reality being our only guide.

You may be sitting there saying, 'Oh, he does go on about it all.'

Yes, and you may well be right in saying it, but this is one thing I cannot leave as the magnitude of it can never be talked about too much, too openly or too strongly. If you think I have talked about it too much before, both in this book and *Wonderment*, then please feel free to abandon this chapter and move on but I do feel, in reality, if you are a thinking person as I am then you will, more than likely, read on and I thank you for it.

The 2012 Olympics in Great Britain were held as a great success but again, as I mentioned in *Wonderment*, how many true sportsmen and women, despite giving their absolute utmost to their sport, actually lost out on a medal because the person who had finished higher than them had, in fact, taken drugs to enhance their performance? I suspected it at the time and there is now a huge enquiry because yes, it did happen. They are investigating just how this came about and just how many did lose out. It seems one entire country, in particular, is being held suspect and it typifies the dreadful world in which we live. How can a person driving show so much hatred for another fellow road user, just because she has had to slow down and how can anyone cheat to win at their sport and then take all the accolades for winning? The cheat hasn't won, has he? In what sort of mind can it register that they are winners? It is obviously the mind of someone who does not give a tinker's toss about anyone or anything else. We are back to this terrible 'Self Society' again. The trouble is that if you cannot show respect for others then in no way, in the end, can you hold true respect for even yourself and if you cannot respect yourself, in the end, you will not respect the world you live in and which sustains you.

We see this in sport, which is supposed to be 'sporting'. We see cheating raise its ugly head in every aspect of our lives. If we don't care about winning a sport cleanly and fairly then how will we ever feel it wrong to cheat at life in general and to hurt others by it? We are, so rapidly, becoming a society which does not care at all and look where it is leading us. It is leading us down a path to destruction. This path has always been long and winding but, believe me, we are travelling fast now and a precipice sits waiting for us when we reach its end. We have the plain choice of reaching the end of that path and tumbling over like lemmings, or we can firmly and quickly apply the brakes now and stop. Are we going so fast though, that in applying the brakes, we will still skid, lose control and tumble over anyway? Let's hope not.

The big problem, to my mind, is that we cannot rescue ourselves from this precipice on our own. We need strong and honest people in our governments to help and guide us firmly through. But where are these people? Are they those who hold power in our countries already? I doubt it very much. They may argue over silly little things, as would primary school children, but surely, in their minds, they must realise what is happening. I feel perhaps they do realise but simply do not have the answers so they just go from day to day, waffling on about nothing while the hungry lion gets ready to pounce. I know they have their meetings to discuss war and climate change and immigration but all they do is talk. We need actions and answers.

This takes my mind back again to the film, *The Life of Brian*.

Brian has been arrested and is about to be crucified and Judith barges in on Reg and the others, who are having a meeting. She, very emotionally, tells them the news so what do they do? They vote and decide that the situation needs discussing. Obviously, Judith is not too happy.

We are in the same situation. All our politicians are doing is talking. Certain token gestures are being made, but nothing whatsoever is being done in any concrete manner. It is rather like borrowing from a payday loan company and putting off the repayments. All you are doing is putting off the inevitable and when you do come to pay off the loan, you find you can't afford to because the thousands of percent interest that have been added has then made the amount owed way out of your ability of settling it. The situation becomes untenable.

Wake up, politicians! We need you!

In the UK, as with much of the rest of the world, we have been through a huge credit crunch and many of our population have been surviving on annual pay increases of well under two percent. So what did the British government do? They do think sometimes. Rather than vote for their own pay rises as has been done previously, they formed an 'independent' committee to say what pay rise they should receive. This made it all far fairer to those who had voted them in and we could have all seen it as an advance in politics but no, it wasn't. This committee which, remember, was formed by the politicians themselves, then said that they were very underpaid and deserved a large rise. If my memory serves me correctly, I think they received something in the region of 11% while most of us suffered. Their actual pay increase would probably have been as much as some have to manage on totally. If they got their huge pay rise, then surely they should work to deserve it.

Are people such as this truly going to stand up straight and tall and say our world as we know it is coming to an end? I don't think so. I think they are, like others, just feathering their own nests for when the time comes. They are like hamsters, busy filling their little cheeks while they can.

IS are ravaging certain countries and are terrorising others and western countries are bombing them but it has already been said, quite rightly, by some that bombing alone can never beat them. The only other option is to put troops on the ground and then, if we do, the whole scenario will be played out again as it has so many times before. We will enter into yet another full war from which we have no realistic chance of forming any exit strategy before we enter.

We will try and think about that later, once we are all fighting and then it will be too late.

We will go in so willingly, because man has always loved war, and we will willingly kill the enemy. In doing so, though, we will also be willingly killing innocent people, as did those who attacked France and Manchester. These attackers didn't care about the innocent and neither will we. We have done it so many times before. We will call it collateral damage and will justify it all. Children will be maimed and killed but that is just a condition of war. Like shit, it happens.

Man will fight man and the innocent will suffer yet again but man will not care because man has the need, for some totally and utterly insane reason, to fight man. They fight for land and they fight for greed. They even fight because they think their god is the best. Our graveyards are full of soldiers who thought their particular god was on their side.

Why?

Nothing can be gained from war. Nothing ever has been gained and nothing ever will be. If my wife and I ever have a problem, we talk about it. We talk about it, make a decision and then put a plan into action. The problem is dealt with, is sorted and nobody gets hurt. What is wrong with this? Is it too dull and boring? Do we need strife in order to entertain ourselves?

Largely because of the world's credit crunch, many countries are struggling to get back onto their economic feet.

Because of this, services are being cut willy-nilly. Our police, fire and ambulance services have seen huge cuts and so have our councils. We have little money for anything and yet we can, all too willingly, find millions or even billions to fund war. It is a bit like a family having to starve themselves and their children every day and yet they smoke forty cigarettes a day each, which does them no good whatsoever but they still find the money for it. Cigarettes are not needed and neither is war. Let's all find a few brain cells from somewhere and banish all war and hatred and concentrate on what is needed, a fresh start and a new beginning.

Can we do it? Can we abandon all hatred and can we find politicians with the brains and backbones to lead us through? Can they manage to put the brakes on before we tip over the precipice that is before us? Can we all learn to drop anger? Can we all learn to love, understand and respect others? Can we find it within ourselves to ditch all judging of others and live and let live? Can we find a way of halting the growth of or even reducing our population to a level that that can be sustained by the planet we call home? Can we ever see that we do not necessarily need religion but if we do, that one religion is no better or greater than any other? Can we ever see that, if we do need a god, then that god is only one of thousands and cannot be called, 'The one and only god'? Can we ever stop being so arrogant that we think our own personal lives, views and wishes are all that matter? Can we ever ditch our love of war and need for it? In the end can we ever save ourselves, not from hell, but from ourselves?

Can we? Can we? Can we? Can we?

Can we? I don't know but sincerely hope so.

Joshua 10

Then spake Joshua to the Lord in the day when the Lord delivered up the Amorites before the children of Israel, and he said in the sight of Israel, Sun stand thou still upon Gibeon; and thou, moon, in the valley of Ajalon.

And the sun stood still, and the moon stayed, until the people had avenged themselves upon their enemies. Is not this written in the book of Jasher? So the sun stood still in the midst of heaven, and hasted not to go down about a whole day.

Again, this is a quote from the Bible, the factual account of history.

Is it really possible to make the sun stand still?

In the minds of the authors it was the sun that was moving when, as we know today, the sun appears to cross the sky because it is our planet which is spinning. They obviously did not know this, otherwise they would have commanded the earth to stand still and not the sun.

Either way, it is not possible but these authors had no science to lean on.

The question has to be, we know they had little knowledge of the world or universe, so should we be believing today what they said thousands of years ago? Shouldn't we be moving on with time, science and knowledge? Shouldn't we be using some amount of sense and thought?

My Conclusion

Having read this book, you will have noticed I am not a great fan of God, religion and the Bible. I did make that quite clear in my book *Wonderment,* I suppose. If you have read *Wonderment* you will get the gist by now. You may, as I have said before, see me as being dogmatic in every way. You may also see me as someone who is trying to destroy religion with a hatred all of my own but I can honestly say here that this is not, and has never been, the case at all, not in the slightest. I was baptised as a baby and was brought up with a general sense of Christianity in the background, although my parents and the rest of my family never actually practised their particular religion or ever really thought too much about their god, or even understood anything about what it all meant. My parents and family, then, never really thought at all, not too deeply anyway.

I was a child who questioned everything and even as a man, now striding viciously towards old age, I still do. I never, ever had the concept of just believing anything without analysing it first. To my mind, everything had to have a reason and there had to be logic behind it. I was always taught to respect my elders and betters but even as a seven-year-old I could see those older than me did deserve respect, but how could anyone ever be 'better' that anyone else? Why should one person be held on some sort of pedestal for others to worship just because they had money or owned a big house or held some kind of social rank within the local or greater community? Even as this small child, my brain told me that if I was to respect these people so highly then they had to do something to earn and deserve that respect. I also realised the fact was the same if reversed.

In the same way, I looked at the god I was being told of and taught about and I thought deeply about that too. Here was someone or something that I was supposed to worship and pray to and sing to, but why? What had he done and what kind of person was he to deserve the highest respect and praise ever given? I am no expert at all, even these days, on different gods from different countries and regions and religions and times, but even as that child I had heard of a few Roman and Greek gods and wondered why we didn't sing to, praise to and worship them on high as well.

My first doubts about religion came that time when I went to church with my cousin one Sunday morning, when I was about eight years old and he was ten. We were little, so we sat in the front pew so we could see what was going on and, as I was marvelling at the beauty of the building we were about to worship in, we were asked by the vicar to move as that pew was reserved for the rich family in the village. We moved to the back the church because we were only children and were not there to challenge the vicar's authority, but this small instance immediately placed a huge question mark in my brain. 'In God's eyes everyone is born equal', I had been told, so why were these people being chosen and given precedence over us? If we were all equal then why were we being moved when all we wanted was a good view to see and learn from what was happening? Years later, at college, we read *Animal Farm* and the quote, 'All animals are equal but some are more equal than others', really brought home this childhood experience to me. God was supposed to deserve my ultimate praise and worship and yet here, in his own house, prejudice and discrimination was openly taking place. It is only since I have started as an author that I realise just what a profound influence this small, and yet wholly significant, experience had upon me.

So why was this god above all gods supposed to desire and warrant such high standing? I went to church on occasion and went to Sunday school for a while and this is where I learned my favourite story Noah's Ark. It was the colourful and vibrant pictures of the animals that fascinated me but as the years passed I began to analyse and question the story more fully. Yes, there were lovely pictures of animals going into the ark two by two, but that was only the glossy part. What had been glossed over was the fact that God had asked Noah to build the ark to save himself, his family and two of all the animals so that he could destroy the rest of the animals on the entire earth, plus all its other human inhabitants. 'Hang on a minute here', my young brain told me. 'If this story is true then it isn't really a story but an actual fact, an actual true and historical incident'. If we were to believe in the Bible then we had to believe it as fact, and the fact was that God had murdered every man, woman, child and baby on the planet except Noah and his family. This God, who we were supposed to respect and revere so highly and who was so full of love and supposed compassion, was actually a mass murderer. If his creations had become such corrupt sinners, then why did he not just change them? He could do anything and everything, so why not just turn them into good people? Jesus later walked on water and then turned water into wine. With just a little thought he could heal the sick in mind and body. He could feed thousands with just a couple of loaves and a few fishes and he was just God's son (or himself), so why couldn't God have spared all these poor people from drowning by simply altering their behaviour, rather than drown them all? In God's eyes there were sinners amongst them but how many newborn babies and totally innocent children did he murder for absolutely no reason? No reason, that is, apart from his all-too-apparent lust for death. Can you imagine the torture, torment and utter terror of children who were swept away from their parents' arms to die a horrible and lonely death in the cold maelstrom that was the flood? As a growing child, I did imagine it and it wasn't pleasant, believe me. Wars today are still the same. We fight and have no care or concern for the children who are being torn or blasted to pieces.

Another little thought here: Noah and his family and the animals were saved because he had a boat. Was it the only boat in existence?

These thoughts were running through the mind of what was, by then, becoming a youth. A youth who had little idea about life or what he was going to do with it but at least he had his thoughts. Perhaps that mind and the one he still has today demanded and still demands too much logic and rationality, but to that mind rationality and logic is all we had and still have. If I look at my hands and feet, I see I have five fingers and five toes on each. It is fact and in no way can I convince myself there are four or six. The number is a fact that is plain to see. If I look at the night sky I see an almost infinite number of stars that are there in their own right and not just there to provide light in the earth's darkness, as is quoted in Genesis. If I look towards the horizon I see the earth sloping away from me, which is proof that we live on a sphere, when at the time of the writing of the Bible people thought the earth was flat. My brain asked and still asks the question, how did they know exactly what God did in creating the earth and universe and even know exactly what he said whilst doing it, and yet they didn't even know the earth was not flat or where the sun went at bedtime?

They seemed to know which day God created this and which day he created that, and they even knew he created a woman out of one of Adam's ribs and yet this was a time of pre-science when, in fact, they knew very little at all about the earth, its animals, its humans, its plants, its mountains and oceans, or anything at all about the universe beyond it.

They were in this time of pre-science and no one could blame them for thinking the way they did, as they had very little to go on. At this time, the Bible made complete sense and did so for many a long year after, but today we have science and science refutes the Bible in so many ways. We, of course, have the choice to refute that science if that is our wish but, once again, my logical mind, which craves rationality, tells me that science has found out so much and today's modern scientists have such fantastic brains and resources that surely we have to give them credit. Science is not just there to quash the truth of the Bible. Science is there to promote the understanding of the universe and us and our place in it. Science has already proven so much that, to my mind, holding on to the contents of a little black book which was written by people who really knew nothing is being futile, to say the least.

I have sincerely studied God and the Bible and have done so with an open and enquiring mind, but I cannot understand its significance in today's modern world. What I do understand though is the fact that many, many people still hold onto it as something historical and if they do believe it, need it, or are somehow comforted by it, then that is their right entirely. I do hope there are not too many people who hold onto Bible beliefs simply because they are frightened not to. What sort of god should ever make us fearful of him?

As I have said before, I do know people who hold onto religion simply because they are fearful of death and what happens after. I do genuinely feel sorry for these people, as they are living in constant fear of dying and that is ruining the lives they are living. Our lives are all unique and are all a wonderful gift (from our parents and nature, may I add). We should be so thankful that we have the chance of life and we should live it to the full. All our lives are special and we are all special. I cannot feel we are just pawns in any god's plan. We are all worth far, far more than that and we should realise it. Bible believers say that their god is all-loving and there is no love in the world without him. Having read the Bible, it seems to me that he is all-loving right up until the time he kills you for no particular or apparent reason apart from his own megalomania. Look again at Lot's wife, bless her; all she did was look back to her home city as it was being destroyed and suddenly she was turned into a pillar of salt. Then there was that poor man who was collecting sticks on the Sabbath. All he was doing was trying to provide fuel for his family and he was put to death by stoning. I can see why many people are frightened into believing, but fear breeds superstition and superstition wrecks lives.

As you will have noticed through my writing, I do abhor the practice of circumcision. Children, both male and female, are mutilated and this is largely through religion.

Isn't it through religion that people are flogged publicly while others stand and enjoy the savagery? I have seen footage of men laughing while a lady is flogged in the street and her only crime was to wear trousers under her traditional dress.

Isn't it through religion that people are still stoned to death for trivial things and isn't this practice promoted by the Bible?

Isn't it through religion that many women are so cruelly oppressed when we should all live totally as equals? Even from the start of the Bible, it seems to promote this.

So many were murdered in the Bible and yet probably the biggest of all the commandments says, 'Thou shalt not kill'.

I am not going to go on about my youth yet again, but when we were young and did wrong we were punished for it with either a caning at school or a smack from our father. This seems barbaric today and is, probably quite rightly, considered wrong. The most we are supposed to do to our children is put them on the naughty step for a few minutes. I say 'probably quite rightly' as I am in two minds about this. As I was born in a time of corporal punishment, I can actually see little wrong with it but I can also see that corporal punishment can so easily result in the punishment being given out of the frustration of the punisher, rather than for the misdemeanour perpetrated.

You may be asking what the above paragraph has to do with religion. My point in talking about this is harking back to my *Wonderment* chapter on superstition. In these modern times, we are so set against corporal punishment and yet, because of religion, we are still openly willing to have the foreskin of our male children cut off for absolutely no reason at all. Aren't religion and religious people being totally contradictory when we cannot smack a child's legs but can mutilate his penis?

We are told incest is wrong and yet that is how the Bible says we came about. In the story of Lot being seduced by his own daughters, it almost seems to glorify the act. To me, the writer seems to rejoice in it and get some kind of perverted kick out of his writings.

Homosexuality, it seems, is part of nature and those who are homosexual are as normal as anyone else, and yet religion seems to bring such a hatred towards them that they are discriminated against, despised and even killed for being what they are. I have said before that the thought of two men having sex together does not exactly fill me with wonder or make me, myself, rampant for sex, but that is my problem entirely. It certainly is not their problem at all. Why are religious people so ready to judge them when, if we were all created by their god, it was he who made them the way they are in the first place? When the US introduced same sex marriage I saw it as a great step forward for those involved and the world at large, but the anger it bred within the religious community was tangible. Why was it, on the whole, that it was the religious who were so angry and judgemental and yet it was the atheists who congratulated them? Shouldn't we all congratulate love in whatever form it takes?

They ask, what is next? Will it be brothers and sisters being allowed to be together? Or men and animals? Men and animals is out of the question because a sheep, for instance, cannot consent. Even a horse can only say 'neigh!' But what of a brother and sister, if their love is so great that they cannot bear to be apart? Like homosexuality, even I do admit it doesn't sit too comfortably on the mind but, in reality, why not? God cannot say it is wrong because if he is to be believed, we all came from one mother and one father, so without incest we would not be here anyway.

Brothers and sisters breeding together would cause problems, as there would be a high chance that interbreeding would cause birth defects that affect the child's life, but if these two people were so very much in love and they did not have children then would it be all too bad? Shouldn't true love be the biggest thing that is taken into consideration? My gut feeling on this subject is the same as it is for homosexuality but I am educated enough to realise that just because I have a gut feeling, it doesn't make my feelings correct. In no way can my mind be the creator or destroyer of anyone else's happiness. Yes, I do write, sometimes strongly, about my views but that is only putting my views forward. In no way am I trying to force anyone out there to live by them.

I have been told I only 'cherry-pick' the parts of the Bible I wish to write about and that there is much good within it. I am truly sorry but I fail to see it and I believe that for anyone to believe in it at all, they must 'cherry-pick' themselves.

Let me 'cherry-pick' a simple contradictory error. If we look at Genesis 1 25.27 it says that God made all the animals on a Friday and then made man (Adam) on a Saturday. If we look a little further ahead to Genesis 2 18.19 it says that out of the ground the Lord God formed every beast of the field, and every fowl of the air and brought them unto Adam to see what he would call every living creature; and whatsoever he called them, that was the name thereof.

It seems the order has changed and is almost like a theist asking an atheist which came first, the chicken or the egg? Having said this though, the piece could be read differently. It does say that God formed every beast of the field etc and brought them unto Adam to name. It doesn't say that Adam was around when God created them. Did he create Adam and then bring the animals to him that he had created the day before? As you can see, it is all, possibly, allegorical.

As with everyone else, I have made mistakes in my life but I have always tried to live it in a benevolent way. I cannot believe in the Bible but that does, in no way, mean that I am judgemental. I know people who do truly believe and that is fine with me as long as they do not force their views upon me and do not hurt anyone else with them. I do not think you can support God despite everything he is said to have done, and yet judge and discriminate against people who are what they are and do not harm anyone in being that way.

I was born into a beautiful 1950s world and was taught that to start with, it had all been planned and planted there by God but it wasn't long before I was questioning that statement. I would lie on a grassy bank in the sunshine and look up at a skylark and questions would flood into my mind, questions that demanded answers.

Why did God make that little bird? What was its purpose? If he came about by creation, then a purpose must have been there. If I was to make a bookcase it would have to have a purpose and that purpose would be plain to see. It would stop my wife tripping over books on the floor but what of Mr skylark? God made all the millions of animals in just one day, one 24-hour period? He was a busy man that day. Why would we have particularly made a skylark? The following day he was to make man to have dominion over the earth and you could understand God making a pheasant or chicken or rabbit as they would supply food, but why this gorgeous and yet somewhat insignificant little bird? Did he have time to think of a bird which would only be there to delight man with its soaring and chirruping? God later made Adam toil in his fields through thistles. It was back-breaking work and perhaps he thought the skylark would be a welcome distraction and diversion for him. You may say that the skylark was made before Adam's weeds but perhaps this was all part of his cunning plan.

If we look seriously at the skylark or any other bird, we see difficulties in its manufacture. Firstly, most birds fly as they need to escape predators and in order to fly, they must have a strong and yet very light skeleton. We can see how, over hundreds or even thousands of millions of years it is possible for such a creature to evolve, but here was God making a minimum of a hundred and eighty-five animals each second of this twenty-four-hour period and then he had to assemble each one with infinite precision. The bones have to be robust and yet thin and each one had to be fitted precisely in the right place and with the correct alignment and ligaments. Each bird had to have enough muscle to power it but not too much as to not let it lift itself off the ground and each wing had to be just the right size and shape aerodynamically to give it lift. Even each feather would have to be shaped differently and placed at different parts of the body, as each of them would be performing a different task. Body feathers are largely to keep the bird insulated while wing feathers are there to give it lift and flight. Tail feathers have to be long and are used like a rudder to give the bird stability and direction. Just a tiny mistake in a bird's wing size could very easily see it flying around in circles.

They say there are ten thousand different living species of bird and although the concept is roughly the same, they all have different bodies and characteristics. God is supposed to have made them all in one day, together with all the other animals, but even if we were to put all of the top scientists of today together in a laboratory for a month and with all the technology and resources we could muster, they could not possibly come up with a skylark in a year, let alone 185 birds in a second.

I wrote *The Tiger's Tale* and came up with the same problem, and that problem would persist for every single one of the millions of species we see on earth, whether they were birds, mammals, fish, reptiles or insects. With any logical thought and rationality, we have to see this as impossible and implausible and yet everyone is free to believe it if they wish. Religionists do still argue that evolution did not happen and they have to say this, as it flies totally and fiercely in the face of their beliefs, but it did happen. Our Mr Skylark soars into the sky because of millions upon millions of years of natural selection and not just because of a god's will.

I find it so absolutely amazing that we have the absolute privilege we have of living on this huge rock, which is revolving around the sun at an incredible sixty-seven thousand miles per hour. I find it amazing that the skylark and all its cousins fly in the sky above me. When I look up I do not see heaven, I see the huge wonder of the universe with its hundreds of billions of galaxies, each containing hundreds of billions of stars which can have their own solar systems of planets and, perhaps the biggest thrill and wonder of all, is the fact that on some of those planets there may well be creatures looking back at me. To my mind, the supposition that 'God did it all', is all too bland and spoils my wonder. Out there we know there are stars dying and exploding, and thus giving to the forming of new stars and possibly new planets and life. It is all happening all of the time. Nothing is constant, as the Bible would have us believe. A constance of life would, again, be bland and boring. I look and my mind almost explodes with the sheer scale and beauty of everything. Our home planet, Planet Earth, is but a tiny speck of dust sitting almost at the edge of a small spiral galaxy and that galaxy is only one of almost countless others. In no way are we the centre of the universe and in no way are we the reason for it. I'm sorry, but to believe this has to show no imagination at all. Isn't this view arrogant as well, as I have said before?

According to religionists and the Bible I am condemned to hell for all eternity and yet this is how I live:

I think long and hard about everything and everyone and I draw my conclusions through it all. I also think long and hard about myself and the only difference is that I do judge myself, but I do not judge others. Of course I form opinions about others and occasionally those opinions are wrong, but if they are wrong I simply change my opinions. I highly admire some people and I do feel sorry for others, but it is not my job to be judgemental.

I cannot possibly say a homosexual person or a Christian or a Muslim or Jew or black or Asian or tall or short person is any different from me and therefore I do not discriminate. Why should I be any better than any of them and why should I hold anything against them? In fact, I do love to see a mixed-race couple living happily together. It shows they are truly in love and are living their lives as they wish. They are not being dictated to by people who have no love or imagination at all, only judgemental natures.

I live my life with no anger or hatred inside me whatsoever. Sometimes I do become sad when I see people mistreating their fellow human beings and it does sadden me to see someone destroying their own lives with anger and stupidity, but anger does not come into mine. I debate and love to do so but I totally refuse to debate if that debate then turns into anger from the other side. If this happens (and it does) I calmly walk away.

People use many four-letter words in anger but, to me, the only four-letter word that really matters is the word, 'Love'. I try my hardest to love everyone and through this I have a wonderful wife and family and wonderful friends. I don't care if that love is between two men or two women or between a black person and a white one or even between a brother and sister. As long as those involved are of an age and understanding to consent, then what is the problem? I do feel, in our world today, more and more hatred is infiltrating our society and ruining it. Is it due to overpopulation and my 'Mr & Mrs X' theory, or is it due to the pressures we have wrongly inflicted upon life today? Whatever the reason is, we are at war with hatred and I sadly and deeply feel this will only proliferate to a state of hysteria and hurt in the near future. If we were to replace all this aggression with love, then we could live together in a wonderful world again. Just imagine what 7,000,000,000 people could do if we all worked together and loved each other.

I'm not saying here that we should all wear tie-dyed T-shirts and put flowers in our hair before smoking pot and giving free love as they did in the 1960s, but we should all think long, hard and deeply and try our damnedest at loving each other in a grown-up way. Our whole planet seems filled with stupidity and we all need to become educated and turn to love instead. Here again, when I say educated, I do not mean we should all go to Oxbridge and get a degree. (Am I starting to become allegorical?) Even the feeblest of minds can learn the difference between love and hate and even the weakest of people can choose the former. To hear someone sincerely utter the words,

'I love you', is about the best thing anyone can hear. We should all hear it from time to time as long as we deserve it being said to us.

Without boasting about it or being presumptuous or silly, I do feel I am the patriarch of my immediate family and that is only because I have earned their love and respect. I am always there for them whenever they need me. That is as long as when they ask a question, they are not afraid of the answer; but even if the answer is not what they want to hear, it is given in a constructive and loving way. At the time of writing this book one of my dear daughters has just announced she is expecting her third child and she was worried at my response. Bloody hell! I love her with all my heart and she is giving me my eighth grandchild. Why should she be worried about my response? Her decisions and actions are nothing to do with me as long as they do not hurt anyone else. As I said, jokingly, to her husband yesterday, it is my wife's job to buy Christmas presents for that side of the family anyway, so why does it affect me? (George was born 23rd April 2016.)

Love is the greatest thing in life and I really do feel sorry for those who only live with hatred in their hearts. My life is absolutely chocked full of love in every corner. I have a fantastic wife, fantastic family, fantastic friends and a fantastic world to live in. What more can a man ask for?

My life is free. Providing what I do does not harm anyone I am free to do what I like, eat what I like, wear what I like, drink what I like and think what I like. I ask or pray for nothing because I realise, in reality, the only thing in life that I can truly rely on is me. I support myself without relying upon God, any god, alcohol, nicotine or any other drug. Life does throw shit in your face occasionally but you just have to wipe it off and smile through it. Believe me, smiling is of far more benefit that praying. If we all laughed, loved and smiled at or with each other, the world would be a terrific place for us all to live. Isn't a good belly laugh about the best thing ever?

I am not bound by guilt over what I have done in the past or what I do today. Like everyone else, there are things in my past which should not have happened but providing we learn from our mistakes, these things should never blight today or our future lives. We cannot be miserable today because of something we did thirty years ago. Neither can we be miserable today for doing things that the Bible classes as sins. Being an atheist is a sin, masturbation is a sin, looking lustfully at a woman other than your wife is a sin and having sex outside marriage is a sin. Well, that's me done for. Believe me, I am way past worrying.

I always love to learn and I always listen. My ears are never turned off from either. If I think two and two is five and you can prove it to me that the answer is really four, then I am with you.

I have jabbered on here about me again, but I have not done it to say how great a person I am because, according to the Bible, I am not. I have written this piece simply to illustrate a point.

In my humble life, I try my hardest not to hurt anyone and always try to give a little more than I take. I live just as I have described in the above paragraphs, with love flooding out of both ears and yet, according to this god, I am condemned to hell to burn in fire and brimstone for all eternity because I am an atheist and I refuse to repent of my sins. What bloody sins! What the hell have I done to deserve it?

If I am condemned to hell for not worshipping this person or thing despite living a truly open, good, honest and passionate life, then so be it. What gets me though is, if the Bible is to be believed, then God made me the way I am, so isn't it his fault I am the way I am? If I was to bake a cake and burned it, could I blame the cake? If I neglected my wife and she found someone better, wouldn't that be my fault and not hers? And if I never ever serviced my car and it broke down, would it be the car's fault? Could I blame the machine for its demise?

If I must go to hell, then so be it. We all have to die in the end and when I do, I shall be carted off to hell to receive my punishment for just being a good person. They will burn me forever and in my burnings I shall probably scream at the top of my voice but, believe me, they will never be screams of pain, just screams of irony.

Thank you for reading.

Epilogue

I have been an atheist for some fifty-five years now and have thought long and hard about it and life in general. I live my life according to the law although, by being an atheist, this law has not always been God's law. Some will understand this and some will curse me for it but I do try to lead the life I have been given in as good and fulfilled a way as possible. My way of life sees me not being judgemental in any way and it also sees me bearing no grudge or malice whatsoever and although many of you will totally disagree with my thoughts and findings I will always wish you well in your lives whoever you are or whatever your beliefs and thoughts are.

If I have written this book and cannot see that it is me who is wrong, then please inform me. Show me proof and I'm with you. Show me a horse with a horn and I shall call him a unicorn.

If you do totally disagree with me and you feel you need to go on praying to and worshipping your particular god, then I sincerely hope you receive his love and all that you pray for and you have a good life. I sincerely do not think I am wrong but, as it says on the back cover, 'If I am wrong then you can stand back and watch me burn.'

Thanks very sincerely once again for reading my books.
All the best of everything to you,
Barry R Boughen.